To Katherine
Thank you

Upshot

Eric Hammer

Travis Street Press

This is a work of fiction. Names, characters, businesses, places, events, locales, and incidents are either the products of the author's imagination or used in a fictitious manner. Any resemblance to actual persons, living or dead, or actual events is purely coincidental.

Copyright © 2020 by Eric Hammer
All rights reserved. This book or any portion thereof may not be reproduced or used in any manner whatsoever without the express written permission of the publisher except for the use of brief quotations in a book review.

Printed in the United States of America

First Printing, 2020

Travis Street Press
Torrington, CT

ISBN 978-1-7356593-0-5

www.eric-hammer.com

Cover design by Madeline Stenson
www.madelinestenson.com

For Renee,
Your arms, my safety net; your words, my inspiration;
your boot my motivation.

CHAPTER 1—TUNED-UP

Confidence and reckless joy screamed almost as loud as Silver, my Kawasaki 125 dirt bike. Clutch popped, throttle full, fountains of dirt splayed behind me during my final practice run at Jack Gourley's track. In a few days I would know if I just felt good or *had* the goods when I went up against some of the area's best teen motocross riders in Marionville, Georgia. Years of practice and competitive racing made everything feel second nature. March's chill had chased the less obsessive riders and given me the run of the course.

After going full-out, I geared down to a more pedestrian speed, when my thoughts began to drift. Recent first place finishes got me thinking I could ride myself clear into the national championship. Maybe I was getting ahead of myself, but no one ever reached the top riding small dreams.

Jillian also came to mind. I pictured her, stretched out on the thick rug in her bedroom, cross legged with unmatched socks playfully swaying to tunes. She'd be editing some film or maybe researching our proposed summer trip. The soft plan, and my girl always had one, was for Jillian—a solid dirt-bike rider herself, to join me and my dad to ride the La Playa trail in Baja that coming summer. Lately, extra practices for the qualifying races had kept us apart more than I wanted. But this weekend she and her dad would be joining us for a trip to Marionville for the big motocross event. Just then, all fantasies regarding future stardom and love were chased by a sudden high-pitched whine that closed fast from behind. Probably Jack, the track owner, out to chase me off so he could close up shop. The quick glance back brought surprise and a wry smile. Not Jack. Instead, a hot blue bike and its rider I'd gone a few rounds with. Coming full throttle, Blue easily closed on me. As it passed, a friendly middle finger taunted, *Game on, Colby Weston. Catch me if you can!* So I did what I always do with the competition—chased it down.

Throttle returned to full, Silver soon closed to within the shadow of Blue and its bold rider. Near the base of a tall hill dubbed Devil's Back, we evened up. Just then I recalled the first attempt of that steep beast. Me, a struggling tadpole, age eight, halfway up the slope, thinking, *Oh boy, I'm taking on Mount Everest.* I lost all nerve, got tentative and went down hard. Through brave tears and my dad's insistence, I righted my bike, climbed on and gave it another try. That next attempt proved successful and countless ascents since have shrunk that hill to a mound sized bump on the track. But familiarity can also cause focus to soften, especially when the views and company around it become more interesting.

Silver devoured the slope, but not surprisingly, so did Blue, which tenaciously stuck to my side, clear to the top. Our bikes launched over the crest, within touching distance from each other. This part never got old. From the suspended vantage point, everything below us dwindled: sound, the track, glimpses of Darin's pathetic downtown and the sprawl of woods to our west reaching clear to the

Mississippi River. Beyond all that? Pro dreams and a rich life waited to get real.

Before gravity could have its way and yank us to the present, I briefly let go of my motorcycle grips and punched the sky a couple of times—showing off a little for my friend. But Silver's back wheel was angled too low in descent. I was no stranger to last-second subtleties needed to save my ass, no panic. I released the rear wheel brake that was causing drag and inched forward in my seat—maybe too far forward? The front wheel led at a sharp angle and the hard terra firma was coming fast. Bam! *Now I could panic.*

Silver slammed the ground and compressed me to the size of a peanut. Air shot out of me and those three able fingers clinging to the grips were the only reasons why I was still alive and seeing sweet Tennessee soil blur by. Meanwhile, Silver's knobby tires had wandered to the new ruts Jack had recently added to the course *to weed out the amateurs.* Involuntary grunts blew out of me atop Silver-turned-paint-shaker as all cockiness exited Silver's exhaust pipe. Had I hinted a moment ago that I might someday be a good fit for the pros? Right then, I more resembled an expendable cartoon character.

No way should I have survived this mechanical bull ride without being tossed clear off. Yet good fortune spared me when a hard jolt from the next rut vaulted me upright and back into my seat. *Thank you!* But that didn't make the view as sweet. Silver had now taken a dangerous liking for Blue and threatened to broadside it, and its rider, at termination speed. Seconds away from becoming a co-mangled track memorial of flesh and steel, Silver's screaming engine alerted my rival. A cocked leg, suddenly raised, was ready to knock me down should my machine encroach an inch closer. The deadly heel began to thrash wildly, inches from my middle. Luckily, I had dealt with a fair share of belligerent boot heels in my face over the years, so instincts kicked in faster than a passing gear. A shift of weight, a last second swerve, and we barely averted disaster.

Once control returned, we became a side-by-side, head forward, full-throttle, RPM rage to the finish line—like two storied foes battling for the American Motocross Association national crown! At least in my mind.

As fortune would have it, Silver inched out Blue at the track's finish line. With a champion's flourish I sent my machine into a tight, one-eighty spin. "Wooh!" I yelped and launched my brain bucket skyward, happy the two of us were alive. I leaped off Silver and spun into a funky war dance. But Blue's rider sat stoic with crossed arms; rage leaking from that shielded helmet. All this begged for diplomacy. This wasn't just any bitter rival who had showed up for revenge. The yellow leather jacket exploded off Blue with clenched fists: Public Enemy #1.

"Colby! What was that? You almost broadsided me after that hotdog stunt of yours!"

Helmet yanked off and tossed, it bowled past me down the bottom of the hill and rested a mere two inches from mine. I fought off a grin. Even in this uncorked state, she was something to behold. She pushed her thick brunette hair from her face to reveal those Caribbean azure eyes most mortal dudes would have long ago drowned in. Smudged black eyeliner running down her cheeks; this was the stuff pirates chased, but I was in no hurry to bury this treasure. So while her thick lips spouted sass and flecks of spit grazed me, I sucked it all up. When she paused for a breath, I jumped in.

"Sorry about all that, J-Girl."

J-Girl. Short for Jillian Carter—girlfriend, artist, a bit unpredictable at times, but never dull. Like me, she was a junior at Jefferson High and always kept one eye on the horizon—for her escape. She also could ride, and plenty, but her goal was to do something with film. Jillian's artsy photos had taken top prize at the county fair, appeared in the yearbook and were now plastered all over my walls. All great, but my immediate concern was to keep those shots coming and us, *us*. Babbled excuses flew from me.

"That wasn't me, today. Damn wind gusts, bad landing and Jack's new ruts brought my machine a little too close to you and Blue, but can you blame Silver?"

Even playful, snapped eyebrows couldn't save me this time.

"Colby Weston, I don't blame Silver, I blame *you* and that ill-timed stunt you tried to pull off so close to me. Charm will not save you this time."

Smile still intact, I said, "Well, having a boot in my face wasn't so charming either, J-Girl."

She bristled. "You're the one who taught me that Kung Fu kick a while back."

"Something I now regret." I braved the next question. "Now you and your dad are still planning to join us for the Marionville event, this weekend?"

After a long stare of disbelief, she snarled, "Yes, we're still planning to go. Happy?"

I shrugged."As happy gets."

Jillian's rage petered with every next exhale. "Sorry I blew, C-Boy, but my life flashed before my eyes back there."

"Mine too. I messed up. I suck."

She hugged me, lips now inches from my ear. "No crime, no foul I guess. Just watch yourself out there, you damn fool."

I kissed her forehead. "I will, but you know what *is* a crime, J-Girl?"

Her eyelids batted in slo-mo. "What?" she said.

"You not running Blue this weekend to qualify for the regional. No kidding."

"We're talking the Southeast Area Qualifier." Jillian shook her head. "Mean, badass girls. Also, I can't be filming and whooping on hills at the same time. That's your dream path to run, C-Boy. You and your dad. I aim to document this all the way to the national championship come August. And that could become my centerpiece when I apply to film school next year."

Suddenly I didn't like that picture. "Can you bring a boyfriend along? How's that work?"

"One per bag, I think."

"Hmm, what would I do?"

"Don't know. You could model naked in the art room."

"So many great options; so little desire."

Jillian said, "But this coming weekend you'll be modeling my Go Pro on your helmet, getting the up-close dirty action for me to edit in later. But get it straight, C-Boy: this director is looking for actual magic; trophies. Not your swerving drunk-ass shit you were showing me back there. That'll crush the whole story line, C-Boy."

"Mine too, J-Girl. You're always armed with a deadly plan."

"Gotta be if I ever want to direct the stars someday," Jillian said.

"Hell, I'm still seeing them." My arms found her waist. "So, do I win at the end of this film of yours?"

A playful finger jabbed my jacket. "Not one to give away endings, C-Boy, but expect thrills."

"Long as you're in the frame, I will." I drew her closer. "All forgiven?"

Her eyes penetrated mine. "Never do nothing that keeps me mad, Colby."

"Send me the list, in case," I said.

Our extended make up kiss got squashed by parental agenda that arrived in the form of a speeding pick-up truck armed with a raging horn. Mr. Carter hollered from a cracked window. "Jillian! Whatcha ya'll doin' with him here now? We're late!"

Jillian whispered, "Oh well, guess it's party time!" She threw up her hands and offered an exaggerated smile. "Grammas' big sixtieth. Whoo-hoo!"

Another honk.

Jillian's venom rang my ears. "Coming, Dad!"

"Do you have to go?" I said.

"No weasel'n out of this family fiasco." Jillian broke away. Honk!

"I'm outta here." Jillian started for her helmet.

"Hey, bring me back some of that home cookin'."

She retrieved her brain bucket then lowered it over her head. "You might just get a slice of something real nice . . . if you can behave."

Jillian swung a leg over Blue. With one powerful kick she brought her cycle back to life. I gazed upon her with boyish awe. *I'll marry that girl someday.*

A jut of a chin, some snaps of the throttle and two impressive donuts later, Jillian Carter exploded away through the canvas of her own dust. She zipped past her dad with only a mock salute, leaving Mr. C. and his truck to peel after his once devoted princess.

The sound of Blue faded, replaced with a voice from the announcer's booth. We had not been alone.

"That girl is booold," Jack said, head craning from the window. A smile spread his mustache wide as he fixed on the last of Jillian's settling dust.

I braved asking Jack how my ride looked. His face dropped to serious as he eyed me for a hard second or two. I braced for a verbal tirade after a debacle that had almost cost

Jillian and me both. Instead he released me with a single word—the one I most needed to hear from the ex-pro right then.

"Ready."

CHAPTER 2—THE RIVAL

"Time to rise, and I do mean shine." The hyper hand that jolted me into reality belonged to A.L., short for Arthur Lee. For as long as I can remember that's what everybody called my dad, and that's what I called him, too. From my toasty sleeping bag, one bleary eye watched A.L. perched in the open door of our claustrophobic camper. It lacked heat and a TV and the sprawl of the Carter's camper. He gazed outward as the morning light anointed his compact, athletic build. His hair was dark like mine, but curlier and always seemed to find its rightful place, unlike mine. Arms crossed, A.L. took in the campground and sprawl of RVs that bordered the Marionville track.

I had joined my dad at Marionville twice before, but only as a cheerleader. Both times I'd watched with pride as he nailed down a berth to the regional event. Now, the distant, sporadic gunning of engines and the occasional waft of exhaust from the dirt bikes around us put knots in my stomach. This time I was part of the show, trying to earn a chance to ride against the best in the Southeast Regional

Championship. What had once been a side hobby—a fun, father and son thing—had ratcheted up to become the driver of our lives. Though A.L. was getting up there in athletic years, he still clung tenaciously to the youthful dream of touring with the pros. We arrived in Georgia with a common goal: qualify here, advance to the regional competition, then dominate the national championship. Nothing too lofty, after you discount the odds. Despite my skills and recent winning streak, I wasn't so sure I even belonged on the same track as these guys. The plan was to go all out and let fate and talent do the rest. I'd have a clearer picture come late Sunday afternoon.

A.L. didn't need to worry. He had made the national finals the year before, so Marionville was closer to ducking into the Piggly Wiggly for a loaf of bread, about as close to money as it comes. Word was out: A.L. Weston's ride was A-game and he'd been claiming most of the lion's share of late. But his competitors hadn't been his only casualties. His recently failed marriage to Mom was another and that had to weigh on him like it weighed on me. But what was done was done. We both tried to put it in the rear view and move on. We kidded around and fed off each other, more like brothers. We never gave a thought to the long odds of a father and son duo making it all the way to the top. That might end the dream. Ride our best, and we'd write our own fairytale.

A.L. took a long, taunting sip from the speckled tin cup. "Man, that's good camp coffee."

It did smell good, just not quite enough to budge me.

He said, "You got back kind of late last night. Feeling a bit sluggish?"

"Was it late? Jillian and I met up, hung out with some dudes by a bonfire."

"Worth losing sleep before an important event? And look at you, head on your arms, no pillow. You gotta plan better, son."

"I'll have a good talk with my pillow about that when we get back. Until then, my vote's for advice-free mornings going forward."

He still talked towards the trees. "You'll get free advice is what—also, who said you were old enough to vote? Who were you all hanging with by the fire? Boy scouts or guys you'll be racing against?"

"Mayans, actually, A.L. Think *we're* challenged? Back then, they were impaled when they lost. Anyway, what's it matter to you?"

"I just don't like all this cavorting with the enemy," A.L. said.

"Enemy?" I asked. "Nobody was packing, far as I know."

"Look, we didn't trek this far for a social affair. You're too casual about stuff."

"It was that or hole up here and watch more super slow-mo shots of my past F-ups while you point and scream. You do the math."

"I don't *scream*."

"Where'd that permanent ring in my ears come from?"

"Why are you so oversensitive and . . . pathetic in the mornings?"

I rose to support myself on two arms. "I like to get the bad stuff out of the way? Also, not as oversensitive as tossing wrenches after your last race when Klaus Ketty edged you out at the finish."

"Sure, bring up my *occasional* weak moments if it amuses you; just don't mention that man's name, serious." A.L.'s open palm slapped the wall.

"He's already getting into your noodle, dude. Don't let it happen."

"The bastard's here, you know."

"That surprises you?" I said. "He was out spreading the word of Satan last night. Either way, cop me a front row seat for that showdown. You'll take him like you usually do. Just don't get on my case about buddying up a bit, okay? Come Sunday night, when dudes are packing up their gear, heads bent low, they'll know that friendly kid from Darin, Tennessee, fascinated with flaming marshmallows, can also char moto asses."

"Big talk don't pay nickels. Can't earn squat just lying there, boy. Get up!"

I surrendered my warm nest to brave the February a.m. chill, but an involuntary groan of pain still lingering from a recent spill triggered genuine concern from A.L.

"Hey, son, you good to go?" he asked.

I tried not to favor my left knee. "This won't stop me, tell you that."

"Better see that same cockiness pouring from you come Sunday night, hot shot," he said.

"Only if you're swaggering with me, A.L. Until then, pass the extra strength, pretty please, my drug lord." I snapped the Tylenol bottle out of the air. "Also, thanks for all you've done over the years, dude, and not just for all the pills."

A.L.'s view returned to the great outdoors as he mumbled to himself, "Think you hurt now? Wait until you're my age."

"Gotta be awful," I said.

"Hey, I feel spryer than your sorry ass that can't itself drag out of bed."

"How so?" I said, trying to align the safety cap just right, too early in the morning.

"Who was walking the whole track at dawn to visualize the layout while you were nestled in your bag like a toddler?"

"A freaking dinosaur is who. What teen would do that? Uh, not me. No dude, I visualize everything from my cozy sleeping bag as my laptop updates me with detailed satellite views of any track and their condition with a touch of a button. Technology, A.L. Keeps one *warm* and informed. But just in case, what'd you learn on your fog shrouded walk?"

"That it hasn't changed much from last year."

"So it's true. Damn it! Geology does run slow in these parts."

"But faster than your sorry ass can motivate, clown prince. Git! Breakfast will be served, with or without you. In fifteen."

I chucked down two pills, jumped in my jeans, hoodie and flip flops, grabbed my toiletry bag and bolted past A.L. into the morning chill. "Why do they have moto qualifiers in March?" I complained.

"Check your laptop. It'll say if you mess up here you can still try again at another area event. Me? I'd like to wrap up this weekend and use the rest of the season to sharpen our game for the next step up," A.L. said.

I shot him a thumbs-up and kept walking.

Towel flung over my shoulder, my flip flops prattled towards the restroom as I fired off a good morning text to Jillian. I honed in on some of the bikes and their mechanics busying themselves with last minute adjustments. The sights, the high-pitched revs, the sweet exhaust that wafted through the trees, all served to quicken this rider's step.

Morning business complete, I steered back to our campsite. Along the way, I found myself following a tall, lanky, blond kid in full riding gear. He stalked along in a bird-like, bobbing lurch on the side of an older, balding man in a Yamaha-emblazed leather jacket.

Could this be Tooley Cumberland? If so, geeky gait forgiven, I trailed behind the next ordained prince of motocross. Everybody was talking up this guy on moto forums. His three game win streak was impressive but no longer than mine. I just hadn't broadcasted it to the world. Maybe I should have—Tooley had nailed down a national sponsor. That meant free gear and even the latest hot bike to power his cause further. I imploded all jealousy for a friendly connection.

"Yo, Tooley? Tooley Cumberland?" Both turned with deadpan faces. Straight, cropped, blond hair; small, tight lips; strange, alien-looking, black eyes, he judged me like I was a single-celled amoeba.

Tooley fired back a cold response, "Sorry, do I know you?"

"Probably not." I extended a hand. "Colby Weston, Darin, Tennessee."

The cautious, lame grip said one of two things. He was dead or confused.

I added, "I didn't see you at the rider's mandatory fireside meeting last night."

Tooley shot his handler a panicked stare like some inbred monarch needing council.

When none came I helped him out.

"It was a party, bro. A bunch of us met there."

"Oh, I don't do that," he said.

"Hang out, you mean?" I asked.

"Oh no. Certainly not with the opposition before a big race."

"Truly, you're the son my dad always wanted." I mentioned I'd been following his progress online and had checked out snapshots of his new bike. *That* fired him up at least.

Tooley's eyes grew wider than Silver's knobby tires. "It's my third bike in three years." He beamed. "Did you check out my videos on Tooleyrocks.com? My new ride chews up courses like a freaking farm auger doing sixty. Not to brag, but I've snagged three straight wins to back it up."

Funny. Sounded like a brag. "I don't know which to be more impressed with, your wins or the three bikes you've had in as many years, bro. I'm still on my first and I got that one used." At least the Yamaha guy grinned at my self-deprecating chuckle.

It was like I'd just told him my dog had just died. "I'm really sorry about that," he said.

I waited for the other shoe that never dropped. "Guess all I can do is try to make you work harder for the fourth in a row." I shrugged.

Tooley recoiled. "Wait, you're racing in *my* group. Against *me*?"

"You and thirty-eight others, amigo. It's my first qualifier. I'm hoping to finish in the top seven or eight; nail down a spot at the Regional. Wouldn't that be great to pull off?"

"For you, maybe. Me? I'm not even thinking about *qualifying.*"

I fell deadpan. "Then why did you come?" The Yamaha rep covered his chuckle.

"What I meant was, anything short of an outright win and well . . . " Tooley offered a long farting sound.

The sideman pivoted back, ready to scold his protégé. Tooley never noticed. The elder collected himself. "Hi, Colby, I'm Sam Wright." He offered his hand and I gladly shook it.

Tooley dug his hole deeper when he interrupted the man's next words. "I've got this, Sam. You probably don't *know* this, Weston, but Sam Wright is an ex-pro previously known to his competitors as—"

Now *I* chopped Tooley short. "Dead Wright, I know. It's a privilege, Mr. Wright."

Again, Tooley cut his trainer's next words off. "How'd you like an ex-pro coaching you, Colby?"

My focus stayed on Wright. "I read your piece in *Moto Sports*, recently. Good tips, sir."

"Appreciate that, Colby," Dead Wright said.

Back at the campsite, smoke billowed as A.L. did his best impression of Chef de Partie at the Coleman stove. I said, "Now over there gentlemen, that man armed and dangerous with a spatula? That's A.L. Weston, last year's winner here; coach, mechanic, cook and my dad. How's that for getting your money's worth, huh, Tooley?"

Tooley rolled his eyes to Wright. A.L. spun and gave us a quick spatula wave.

Dead Wright asked, "Where you all from again?"

"Darin, Tennessee," I said with a hint of pride.

Tooley teased, "You must have heard of Darin, Tennessee, Sam. C'mon, man."

"Sorry, Colby," Mr. Wright said. "We're all from Tallahassee."

"Tallahassee. Darin, Tennessee. What's the difference, huh, Tooley?" I joked.

Tooley flicked his chin. "One is a lot easier to forget."

So Tooley wanted war? I took a step toward him and stared. "Maybe not after this weekend, huh?" I said.

"Uh oh, this guy means business, Sam," Tooley said in a mock scared voice as he eyed our machines. "So Colby from *Darin*, which bike am I going against? The green one, or the—"

"The uh, silver-splattered one. That's mine."

Tooley couldn't fathom. "Who did the paint job?"

"My girlfriend snuck in one night and painted it like that. She's an artist, of sorts."

"Seriously?" Tooley birthed his first smile.

I mustered a look of pride. I looked back at Silver. "Can't say I was thrilled at first but I went with it. Believe me, her magic and my tolerance has paid in spades, you know?"

"What l know is vandalism when I see it," Tooley huffed. "I would so *slap* that around if she did it to mine."

"Don't diss my girl or my bike," I warned.

A.L., stepped forward, ready to employ his spatula into his own slapathon if needed. Dead Wright deployed damage control. "Nice meeting you all! Have great rides and fun this weekend, huh?"

A.L. remained stoic. "We *had* planned on it, sir."

"Oh, look at the time! Morning rider's meeting in fifteen!" Wright said. "Let's give these two some space, Tooley." Hand on Tooley's back, Wright hustled his disciple ahead.

Tooley sneered, "I'll give him some space, alright. Enjoy the dust, Weston!"

"Mine or yours, Tools?" I shot back.

Still within earshot, Wright halted Tooley. "Trying to light a fire under the competition, Tooley? Not smart. Also from now on, you'll refer to me as Mr. Wright to your peers. Understood?"

After a reluctant nod, Tooley sulked behind his trainer's surge.

A.L., mouth partly agape, watched them leave. "Who *was* that kid?"

"Just a dude with a big mouth and bring-it skills."

"Like your bring-it skills? Don't let him or anyone else wrangle your melon. Focus on your own game," he said.

Bad vibes melted with the butter as we dove into A.L.'s killer French toast and bacon. I also welcomed the friendly faces traversing down the hill. Jillian, camera bag slung over her shoulder, looked like she'd just bagged an ESPN gig. Mr. C. found a curt smile but as usual said little beyond, "Morning, guys."

Jillian, on the other hand, boogied with her gear shaking. "Are we up, Weston boys? Time to join the party!"

After an extended, dopey smile, A.L. tossed his napkin aside. "You know, she's right, son. We should go."

"I'm going ahead, C-Boy," Jillian said. "Wanna stake the best spot for my tripod. Better shine out there, Weston boys. You all know the camera never lies."

"I'm going to nail down a spot for you, J-Girl," I said. "Love you."

"Hell yeah. Let's kick this thing!"

The Carters walked off. Beyond view, the gunned engines intensified. I was anxious to get Silver out there with them. We crammed in last bites and hastily cleaned up, barely a word said.

CHAPTER 3—MOTO ONE

The usual pre-jitters dogged me as I rolled Silver up and found my starting slot. Each rider pulled up to their individual drop gate. Unlike most races, where riders start at or near where they finish, in motocross they mostly start at the track's side. This keeps the action continuous for the fans; soon as the last rider crosses from the previous race, the gates drop and the next wave follows without pause.

Vivid colored bikes, suits and helmets shouted down the line. Some I knew from previous contests or from the campfire the night before when we laughed and swapped tales. Excitement, yes, but there was no laughter or loose talk now. It was all about finding one's calm and confidence before the true chaos began.

Forty pairs of anxious gloves gripped their throttles, waiting for the previous moto to finish. I clicked on Jillian's Go Pro to review the run later. Ahead of us, a start card turned sideways. Down the long line the bikers leaned forward and extended out their elbows, a method of warding off any contact once rolling. Determination and focus chased most of the early nerves. Clutches in, throttles to full, the high RPMs filled the venue like a swatted hive of pissed off bees. Sweet music to this boy's ears.

The gates dropped. I popped the Silver's clutch and sped off with the masses, not thrilled with either my start or the middle-of-the-pack position. A couple of early wipeouts raised eyebrows. In both cases the riders hopped right back on their machines without getting squashed.

After a couple of laps of being boxed out and trapped in the middle, I felt tight and didn't trust myself, well as I should. I told myself, *you belong here, Colby. Show it!* Competitive orneriness took over, and Silver began to pass other bikes at a good clip. In the final two laps, I rallied to overtake ten bikes to finish seventh out of forty. Not bad, but if I wanted to be compared to the elite riders, I would have to trim my time in the next moto.

With bowed head, I rolled Silver off the track, past my dad's cold stare and folded arms. He bore the look of a man that craved technical dissection—but I knew what needed fixing. I shot him a glance. *Not here or now with fellow riders around.* A.L. must have read my thoughts. He dismissed all public scolding with a nod and faint smile and said quietly, "Alright, ace, *you* tell me what needs fixing."

"I don't know . . . couple of things . . . slow off the line, pussyfooted up that second hill, thought I whooped up on it in the closing laps . . . too little, too late . . . cornering kinda sucked, no balls in general. Let's see, what else? I let myself get boxed in one too many times. Besides all that, I feel like I won." I held a deadpan face.

He spoke. "Son, just do those things you said, add on a little controlled aggression and you might just earn yourself a spot in the regional." A.L.'s chill approach eased my doubts.

Something stole his attention. "Well, lookie there," he grinned. "Recognize that guy with the AMA logo on his jacket?"

"Wow, dude. That's Mark Beck, right? Two-time national pro champion."

"Yep, now recently retired and doing some scouting for AMA," A.L. added. "Also, is that the same odd kid we met at breakfast, talking to him?"

"Tooley, the gangly geek with the perma-pout?" I said.

"Yeah, him. See how he's chasing those connections, Colby?"

"Well, he'll be chasing me in the next race."

A.L. sighed, "I've gotta get my bike. I'm up soon. See you after." He strolled away.

Jillian and Mr. Carter replaced A.L.

"Hi again," Jillian began. "Got some decent coverage of your practice run. It was, you know, ok."

I shrugged but seethed inside. "Show you something better next time."

"Wanna review it? Say in our special viewing room in our camper?"

Mr. Carter wore a face of uncertainty. "Guys just keep an eye on the time and . . . remember there's already too many people on the planet."

Her eyes blinked heavy with disgust then pivoted to charm. "Uh dad, can you take my video gear while we review Colby's run. I don't want to lug it back and forth."

Mr. Carter grumbled, "Fine, fine, just watch the clock guys."

"Thank you, sir, we will," I said.

Compared to our closet-sized box, the Carter's camper sprawled like Willy Nelson's tour bus. What was not to like? The long couch, or Jillian's shoulder brushing mine as she loaded my run onto her laptop and parked a hyper foot on my lap. The video soon became Hell relived. It pained me to have my girlfriend giggle and say things like *whoops!* as she pointed out the slew of weaknesses. But Jillian was also a rider and summoned mostly spot-on advice. Minus a few self-loathing obscenities hurled the ceiling's way, I think I accepted the torture well.

I begged Jillian to fast forward to the good part when my ride looked, at least okay, but she suddenly folded it down and said, "That's a wrap." In less time than an airborne stunt gone bad, she tucked the laptop away in a safe place and I found mine when Jillian pushed me on my back. She said, "You know what happens when you sway too close to a woman rider?"

"I get knocked down and like it?"

From the deep recesses of her throat came the most primordial tiger growl ever. Pudgy lips devoured mine. But everything concluded way too fast for this big cat. Her phone vibrated. "It's my dad. Showtime, C-Boy." She sat up. "A.L.'s group is about ready to go off."

A longing groan escaped me. "Okay, we should get going. Thanks J-Girl. This little session really helped straighten some things out." I winked.

"Listen wise-ass, miss the cut and I'll dump you for the winner, or at least use him in my next film."

"Now I'm motivated."

I left the Carter's camper more relaxed than when I entered—until I neared the track which reminded me I needed much more finesse if I was going to make anyone's highlight reels.

Gates dropped and unlike me, A.L. dominated from the start. He dictated a brutal pace—a not-so-quiet statement that he hadn't come for leisure. A.L. had declared himself the

Alpha. I heaped praise on him but hoped he had saved his best moves for when it counted.

Fast forward four hours. A.L. and I strolled about the place with stubborn grins. He'd duplicated his practice run and led his class to a convincing victory in his first moto. I had buttoned down and shook off the slop that was my practice run. It was a strong enough finish to put me in serious contention.

CHAPTER 4—ICARUS

The mood was subdued as A.L. and I let our thoughts pool over a plate of eggs and grits by the fire. The clink of our forks replaced the usual idle chatter. A.L. finally uttered, "Made some minor adjustments to Silver's carb while you snoozed. Should give you a little more punch up those hills for your deciding race today."

"Thanks man."

A.L. mused over his four-stroke Husqvarna which sat on its work stand, already looking like it was going fast. "Everything's good to go, man . . . just need to kick down the barn door today then it's off to the Southeast Regional. You joining me there or what?"

I gazed at Silver and nodded. Regional sounded good—now the getting there part.

I pushed Silver down the hill to the start, my legs, wet noodles. Stranded in our own thoughts, every rider's ambition soared. The race before us raged on. I picked out a random bike and could about picture every detail of the terrain she was seeing. I took note of the physical subtleties the lead riders were doing and why others, though good riders, were losing ground out there. Tension grew with every minute that ticked down. I pushed back all the analysis and nerves; focused on my slow breaths. Some old joke from my friend, Beach Moody, invaded and drew a smile. I also thought about my Mom and if she was at all thinking about me today. Not even a text to wish me good luck, but I hadn't exactly made an effort lately, either. If A.L and I both advanced, I'd let her know.

The white courtesy flag signaled the last lap of the race in progress. The intensity of their finish heightened my excitement. Nervous, snapped throttles intensified all down the line. Final reminders to self: *Controlled aggression, Colby. Don't overreach and please, don't let me go down.*

On the track, the leading clump of four women battled to the finish. The first wave of leaders crossed the line. Shrieks came from those who had claimed a spot and would advance to the next round in a few weeks time. Finally, the last of the stragglers finished.

A rumble of determination erupted down our line. We were penned bulls, and our repeated revs boasted a bust-out desire. All attention focused on pulling off a clean start. I brought the Go Pro to life. A glance towards Tooley, six spots down, never tempted me because there were another thirty-eight, hungry riders besides him.

All eyes glued to the one-card. When it turned sideways, we only had seconds. In unison our red line RPM screamed, "Chase this," as we filled the sixty-acre facility. Close by, as a rider hooted, I stared ahead, eyes glued to the lip of the gate. Throttle grip and a clean clutch release was the immediate goal.

All gates dropped and the once-straight line of dirt bikes turned into an uneven, all-out, chaotic charge as cycles fought for the front spot. I nailed early success with a hot start and solid position. I gunned Silver up the first hill, put a decent amount of air before me and landed without a hitch.

Just six colorful-clad backs bested me. Not bad, but I desired an even more unobstructed view. Little changed for the next couple of laps. Occasionally a new rider would threaten from behind before a well-negotiated hairpin turn held him at bay. The rhythm I had hoped for locked in. With each successful lap, confidence burned brighter.

But early success invites greed which can in turn cause slips. I eyed the leaders, Tooley especially, and tried not to overextend in the opening laps. *Stay steady, boy. Stay on them and take what's given.* The stubbornness of this elite clump would last a good while.

With two laps to go, Tooley still led, but I had weaved to the top five. His back taunted me like a bull's-eye, one that begged me to go bold and catch him. But Tooley not only *had* the machine, he *was* a machine. Good fortune came when I maneuvered my way into the top four then picked off the next two. Now the only thing in my way was the gangly blond from Tallahassee. I got some love from the crowd after I scaled over the next hill and hooked them with a stunt.

The finish beckoned, but so did the desire to kick this run over the top; maybe get some pros or sponsors locked on my game. After a slick pivot at the base of a hill, Tooley, who had led the whole way, now found himself in my shadow. Because Tooley's machine was a tad hotter, my chances of winning outright would be sorely tested in the final straightaway.

Then I was dealt a high card. Ahead of us was a slow rider to be lapped. Tooley tried to avoid him but his move only put him on a collision course with a hay bale. I knew my rival had no choice but to drop back and swerve in behind me.

But somehow Tooley narrowly split the bale and the slow rider—about the same time I figured Satan had to be riding on the back of his cycle. Tooley found his rightful place—on my side *again*. This close, our engines screamed as one with the finish in sight. He pulled almost even. He lashed out a warning kick, not unlike the one Jillian had unleashed just days before at Jack's.

I didn't budge. I stayed put, a hair's distance from reach. I scrunched low. *Love me now, hotshot?* Maybe A.L.'s last-minute adjustment to my carb might just save the day yet. The crowd rose and their cheers celebrated our exciting finish. This was as good as it got. I had never felt more exhilarated or more alive!

"C'mon, Silver," I shouted above the din, throttle full. The Kentucky Derby without the crop. Tooley's close proximity taunted me. His next leg kick baited me to swerve away, loose a second of my gain. Ahead, the man with the checkered flag leaned in, titillated by the hard-fought showdown. I had lost ground, but the lead? I screamed up the hill and snapped a last, quick look. Only the sight of people cheering! Stunt time. I caught myself some air, pumped both arms skyward and punched the sky. "Thank you!" The landing, smooth as a homeward bound interstate. In a bang-bang finish, I figured I nipped Tooley but spun one-eighty, anxious to get official word.

C'mon, c'mon, I thought.

"And . . . it's . . . number 58, Colby Weston at the finish!"

Who could resist spewing a little dirt in a tight circle? I pushed Silver off the track, dropped to my knees and rolled on the ground, confident that I was moving on to the Southeast Regional. Who knows? Maybe A.L. and I would ride in the National Championship; Weston boys on parade!

My two biggest fans broke through a seam of spectators. Arms waving wildly, Jillian led the charge as I braced for the full body blow of her love. A.L. also hooted but seemed content to resume his primordial flailing by himself until Jillian had her fill. Mr. Carter hung back with a tight smile and curt thumbs-up. Tooley dusted himself off, *my dust,* as he rolled his bike past, head hung low; ignoring the praise I tossed his way.

There was little time to bask. Team Weston had unfinished business. Now I became the motivator. "It's all you, now, A.L. We go to those playoffs together. C'mon!" I pounded his chest hard, thankful that his protective breastplate was already in place. He told me he loved me, his custom before any race. A.L. walked off to collect Gremlin and position himself at the staging area. That was it.

Jillian took my side as I began to wheel Silver through the crowd. Some pats and "Nice rides" lauded me from a few strangers and fellow riders. I was still mostly numb with disbelief.

I ran into a small cluster of riders we had shared fire time with. Assuming they were up to their necks with envy, I shrugged off all mumbled congrats and humored them with past riding tales that ended funny. Soon we were all laughing and talking louder than everybody else around.

Laughter turned to awe when my eyes spotted Mark Beck—and he was heading our way. My mouth went to sand.

"Hey, guys. Anybody having any fun?" Mark Beck asked.

A jubilant volley of agreement arose from the gang.

Mark's friendly, quick gaze passed over the faces but grew more serious when it settled on mine. "Colby Weston, is it?" He extended his hand.

"That's me." *Firm shake, look him in the eye, stay cool.* "An honor, sir."

Beck was chill, but there was that star-power presence about him. My eyes zeroed in on a tablet he clutched to his side. It could contain observations on a thousand hopefuls—

notes that could punch somebody's lucky ticket all the way to the pros. Mine for instance.

"Glad I caught your race, Colby."

"You saw it, huh?" I wondered if my face looked as apple-red as it felt. "Well thanks, sir." I felt exhilarated and tried not to say anything totally messed up. "Everything kind of fell together. Luck was in my corner today."

"And solid skill, young man," Beck said.

"Wasn't easy," I said. "Lots of strong talent out there."

"True, but your ride kind of hogged most of my attention."

Jillian, who had been clutching my sweaty palm, squeezed it.

Mark added, "Also liked the flashy stunts at the end. Nice exclamation point."

"Didn't want to bore the crowd, I guess." I grinned at shuffling feet.

"The crowd loved it. Just don't get yourself hurt."

"Yes, sir. I mean no, I won't, sir. Get hurt that is." My tongue was a tangled mess.

I rewarded the couple of muffled wise cracks that leaked from behind me with a friendly middle finger.

Mark opened his tablet, asked some questions, and punched in the data. I was wowed but it almost left me feeling apologetic. All the guys wanted this.

I pulled in closer to Beck. "Yes sir, I'm sixteen, going on twenty-one… Uh huh, next year would be my senior year . . . Why hell yeah, I'd travel the world with motocross, excuse me, sir . . . No, no, Mr. Beck, no trouble with the law . . . No, I don't do web sites; that's more for spiders . . . Contact number? You bet. You can reach me at . . ."

Freaking Fairy Tale Time! I was now on Mark Beck's watch list and imagined touring MX world, getting free gear and being hand fed bonbons in Japanese spas. Beck produced a business card squeezed between two fingers. "Let's keep in touch, Colby."

I pawed it like the golden ticket. "Sure will, Mr. Beck."

"Call my dad that," he said. "You can call me Mark. Glad we hooked up." He nodded to the other riders and moved on.

Jillian and I stood star struck, ogling at a business card from an AMA scout! But a sudden boldness took me. There was another rider I wanted Mark to consider.

I released Jillian's hand and jogged to Mark's side. "Mr. Beck, I mean Mark, there's one more thing, if you can."

He gave me that *what, you again?* look, before the grin returned.

I blurted, "You also might want to fix your eyes on the man in the lime green suit by the pole."

Beck combed the line of racers readying at the start. A five-pound smile finally crossed his lips. "You mean number fifty-seven? That wouldn't be your dad by chance?"

"Why you read minds sir. Many people consider A.L. Weston among the best amateur MX riders in Tennessee."

Beck nodded. "Good ole A.L. Not our first meeting. Saw his run at the Loretta Lynn Championship last year."

"You remember?"

"Don't often forget a face and never a superior ride. If he hadn't gone down at the end, who knows how far he might have gone? Funny. When I saw him today, all he seemed to want to talk about was you."

"We're each other's biggest fan. You know, Mark, maybe the MX fans might get into a father-son duo on the tour. Think of all the famous father-son combinations and what they've done for other sports: the Unsers, the Earnharts, the Mannings—"

"Okay, ease up on the throttle there a little, kid. I appreciate the loyalty to your dad, but he's getting up there in jock years, isn't he?" Beck's tone framed his doubts.

"All due respect sir, after you see his ride, I think all age issues will take a back seat."

Mark Beck chuckled through rolled eyes. "Alright, young man, if he steals the show out there, today, I'll add his name alongside yours." He tapped his tablet. "Fair?"

I beamed. "Fairer than fair." I extended my hand and thanked him again.

A.L. now carried the ball. All he had to do was show off his plus game and drop some pro scouts' jaws in the process. One foot parked in bliss, once fantasy, now real.

Beck meandered off and Jillian pulled to my side. "I don't even know what's happening, C-Boy," Jillian said. "Tuck that card somewhere safe."

Nerves that dogged me before my run returned, this time for A.L. Too nervous to sit, I paced near Jillian, who repositioned her tripod closer by. There was one nice bonus in A.L.'s upcoming race, which mine had lacked. Known as a holeshot or mad dash for cash, it was awarded to the first rider to reach a designated point, usually at or near the first left bend on the main track. That dude could smile knowing there was a nice wad of extra green waiting for him at the end, no matter where he finished.

I surveyed the line of bikes at the start. Besides Klaus Ketty, A.L.'s long-time rival, I recognized a few others in the mix from our parts—solid vets like Clay Benton, Neil Price, and Doc Morrison—all with tools and youthful dreams but still knowing A.L. was the man to catch.

Many of the men crouched down and fussed with last minute details before being led to the gate. Not A.L. He sat perfectly still on the bike he called Gremlin. With crossed arms and a straight-ahead stare, A.L. looked more like a bored video ace waiting for his shooter to load. He had shined in his first moto, and now appeared ready to cause havoc and leave no doubts here.

Mr. Carter joined my side. He grumbled he had enjoyed the weekend but didn't look forward to Monday. "Who does?" I asked.

The next three-dozen souls throttled up. It was time. The crowd's noise rose with the engines. When the gates dropped everything became a thunderous, streaked blur of colorful ambition. When A.L. sank between two hills, I weaved my way to higher ground for a better view.

"C'mon, A.L.! Kick up some dirt and paint all those wannabees baby-shit brown!" I shrugged off a mother's glare.

Another rider stayed on A.L. around the holeshot point. Good news once again exploded over the PA. "It's . . . Weston! A.L. Weston has taken the holeshot trophy, ladies and gentlemen!"

My arched hoot topped the polite applause. A tidy sum for the Westons. "Hey baby," I yelled toward Jillian, "Four-star steakhouse on the ride home tonight!" But her head stayed glued to the viewfinder, capturing the live action, totally dialed in.

The one thing I can say for sure: A.L. had already put that holeshot win behind him, quick as he claimed it. He wanted to qualify with an exclamation point. You could see it in his ride. In no time he widened the gap, easy as he had done before, with dancer-like deft moves. It was as smooth and confident as I'd ever seen. Maybe too confident. I'd watched him enough to know when *The Bliss* had taken him. The body language, the way Gremlin melded with its rider, a flawless, airborne dance with man and machine.

Pride for my dad turned to awe as he ripped off jumps and sky-bound maneuvers that only pro elite riders would attempt. Merely qualifying was no longer enough for A.L.

The crowd poured into his corner and cheered him to greater and greater heights. To sweeten the occasion, Mark Beck reappeared, this time a converted fan. "Hey there, Colby. What'd you do? Sprinkle a few PEDs on your dad's pancakes this morning? You were saying something about a father/son team?" He laughed. "Why not?"

Wait. Was he serious? Beck's endorsement kicked all doubts aside. From now on, everything was going to change for the better, for both of us. Maybe stars would align and we'd enter the pros together!

A.L. continued his dominant run. With over a lap to go, not Ketty, not Morrison, nobody could catch him. Everyone else was playing for second, to quote the great Larry Bird. With every jump, every explosive cheer, A.L. indulged the fans more and more while the rest of the field battled in a separate race. His final jump left all, including me, in disbelief. He kicked off his seat so the only thing touching his cycle were the mere fingertips of his gloved hands. A.L.'s reminder crept in my head: *Don't get too cocky out there, like Icarus, too close to the sun.*

A.L. flew parallel to the ground, a master at his apex, Superman, minus the cape. Of course there are no supermen. Only those who dodge kryptonite for a while before gravity or the odds sprawl them like discarded junk, back to earth.

When I replay it in my mind, it seems drawn out, slower. But it happened in a horrifying few seconds. I had turned to say something to Beck when the cheering turned to a collective "Oh!" from the grandstand. Usually the reaction of a rider going down, *but who?* I cranked my head back to the track. I could barely see some bike on its side, but my view was blocked by a crowd that drew closer to the pit. I no longer saw A.L.

Jillian's cry sailed over the engines "Oh God. Colby!" Jillian had apparently abandoned her camera, while it was still running.

Much of the grandstand crowd remained standing, hands to mouths. The flagman, late to raise the medical flag, finally signaled *wheels down*. Sober confirmation came over the PA. "57, A.L. Weston is down. Weston is down."

It had hit my stomach before my ears. *No. Please, not now.* I bulled my way through the crowd for a closer look. A shallow gorge separated us, but I saw him. A.L. lay face down, still as a root. Falls were common, and I stubbornly clung to the hope that he'd gotten the wind knocked out of him, would snap back up and maybe even salvage a qualifying spot.

I nudged a few steps closer and bellowed, "Get up, poo-pot!" Forever our silly, running chide that dated back to my earliest days when I first learned to ride. When one went down, the other yelled it. Always. In dirt biking, because it was soft dirt, most of the time you found your breath, kicked yourself, and in a few seconds vaulted right back up and rode banshee for the finish. This time A.L. didn't.

Most within earshot scowled at my irreverence. But they didn't know us or the toughness of A.L Weston. Here's a man who would begin each fishing trip with a sip from the very waters he was about to cast into without a hiccup. I yelled. "C'mon, A.L.! Get yourself up now, don't give it away now!" But all my teasing, all my coaxing, couldn't budge a pinky on the man. Not this time.

Everything dropped away—the crowd, the riders, Jillian's pleas. Reality stiffened. No one did anything, just stood and ogled at his lifeless body. I took a step closer to the pit's edge. "A.L.? C'mon now!" My toes inched closer until they lipped over the side. A force I couldn't control possessed me. I spied a clear break in the field of cycles and calculated my next move, a desperate one. Only seconds to beat the next wave of cycles, not enough to think twice. Mark Beck must have switched glances from A.L. to me and read my intent, fast as I flashed it. He swapped out all hesitation and lunged to grab me.

"Colby, no!" he yelled before Jillian's scream.

It made no difference. I was airborne and landed barely ahead of the next wave of riders. A bolt of pain shot from my knee, the result of hitting a rough patch on the ground. I fought through it to press on. Such action could disqualify my win, but I wasn't thinking about consequences, not then. Through pain I scurried to A.L. while trying to avoid becoming a victim myself. Everything turned to noisy warfare as bikes, late to oblige the warning flag, bore down and narrowly missed us. I screamed at those expressionless helmets that scaled over and around us like bombers. But it had no more effect than the wind they sliced through. Of course, I got their competitive reasoning. This was a qualifying race. Sympathy for any rider would only follow after the finish line.

A.L. stayed facedown and unresponsive, one gloved hand extending towards the finish. I touched him gently, but he remained lifeless. Desperation almost overtook me until my head was turned by a hard thud behind me. Boots.

A strict voice barked, "Don't touch him, son!"

I snapped my hand away.

The first of two EMTs placed a hand on my shoulder, a voiceless reminder for me to make room. The pair methodically worked to stabilize A.L. to the point where they could fit a neck brace on him and lift him onto a portable stretcher. All trust had to be turned over to these guys. A.L. was lifted to the lip above the pit where supportive fans stood by to rally him. Pockets of comments rose from a huddled crowd.

"C'mon, A.L."

"We love you, A.L."

"See you at the next race, buddy."

And so on.

Some in the quiet crowd peered in blank fascination, while others sought the refuge of a nearby shoulder. Silence hung thick, interrupted only by the movements and occasional commands of the EMTs. A helpless urgency stormed me. I turned back towards the stands. Through a tear stained gaze, Jillian extended a desperate arm. She made a sudden, mad lunge. "Colby!" She was literally plucked out of the air by Mr. Carter. I caught sight of Beck, too, staring, stunned as all the rest.

A.L. was carefully lifted into the back of the awaiting ambulance to a smattering of weak applause. His fans never got the thumbs-up from him they hoped for. The back doors slammed and the truck began to ease away. I hobbled after it in futile desperation, then screamed, "STOP!"

Red taillights. The doors swung open and the lady EMT popped her head out. "What are you waiting for? You can't do any good for your dad standing there. Climb in!"

CHAPTER 5—WILD RIDE AND HOSPITAL

Ambulance. Worst ride for hire I can recall. Medical stuff clanged and got tossed around as the truck lurched over the uneven field. Even I knew none of this was good for A.L.

Barely seated, a hard bump slammed me to the floor. The jolt relit my wounded knee, but I shoved the pain aside. All concerns were on A.L. A stare from the EMT with "O'Conner" on her ID badge chased me back to my seat. The pounding continued as I tried to figure out the seat belt. The driver barked, "Hang on, back there. We'll reach the road soon."

A.L. had been fitted with a white neck brace up to his chin, but every violent bump that shook him fueled my frustration. None of the jarring, however, knocked O'Conner off her game. She successfully hooked him to an IV and coupled him to monitors that spat out vital signs.

Though out cold, his slightly parted lips almost appeared desperate to speak. I sat there, a useless spectator, hoping for things to turn out right. His green and white riding suit was covered in dust and revealed tears and scratches from the fall. But it was the ugly angle of one boot and arm that temporarily spun my eyes away. A quick swipe with my sleeve wiped away the tears but not the desperation.

"Hang in there, darling," said O'Connor, "we're going to get him there. What's your name?"

"Colby, ma'am. Colby Weston."

Her eyes narrowed after noticing my leg. "You're leaking." She reached behind her.

"Just a scratch. Tend to my dad, please."

"Call me squeamish, I have this thing about blood all over the place." She frisbeed a large bandage and an alcohol prep pad into my chest. "Clean it and slap that big one on."

The rocking ceased after we hit smooth tar. *Come on, driver, kick this thing!* He did. Siren now blaring, the driver went to his radio. "Marion General, I have a trauma alert for an adult male; motorcycle race crash victim. Male; thirties; unconscious at this time, over."

"Roger that," a crackled voice acknowledged.

The engine rose. More speed offered hope. But the high-pitched alarm from one of the monitors launched a new round of panic.

"What's that?" left my lips.

O'Conner's quick, wordless actions said everything. Something was going very wrong. She reached back and produced two paddles mounted to the side. *Oh my god*, I thought, A.L. was dying.

"Clear!" she shouted as the shock arched his lifeless body. Her hands still clutched the paddles above him as her eyes fixed on the machine.

"No response, Freddie!"

"Again!" the driver barked back.

"Clear!" Once again the current shot through A.L. but this time the calm, spaced beeps returned. O'Conner's cheeks puffed relief and I could breathe again. For now.

I broke the rules, unclipped my belt and dropped to A.L.'s side. A judgmental stare came from O'Conner as the next round of pain shot from my scraped knee. I pulled within whisper's distance of my father's face.

"That's smooth black top whistling back at you, A.L. You hang in there a little while longer, hear?"

He didn't. I squeezed his beefy hand but got nothing in return. A wordless jut of O'Conner's chin returned me to my seat.

Arrival. The driver killed the siren's deafening scream. The back doors opened, and A.L. and his stretcher's wheels smacked the ground. At least he had made it here and was still breathing. A.L. was pushed through the auto doors and soon had four medical personnel huddled over him. Two hospital staff peppered the EMTs with questions while I attempted to follow. O'Conner spun and stopped me, dead in my tracks. "Listen now, Colby. Y'all park yourself in the waiting room. We'll be out with word, shortly."

The auto doors opened, and just as fast, slammed in my face after A.L. got wheeled through. I was left alone, thinking his failed ride would have a greater impact than my winning one. I found a seat in the waiting room and tried to even my troubled breaths. A few seats down a child fussed on its mother's lap and I thought of Mom. She was now shacked up in Ohio, with a couple of little kids that came with the new guy. I thought about calling her but didn't.

The phone pulsed, I checked. "Hey Jillian… Yeah, rough ride over… Not good, no… Don't know. Alright." Time stalled. They don't call them *waiting rooms* for nothing.

The return of the familiar EMTs alerted me. O'Conner said, in short, A.L. was in intensive care, in the hands of a quality surgeon. *Great, but what was actually happening?* She didn't elaborate, because she couldn't. Medicine was as much art and the will of the patient, I recall her saying. I hoped

A.L. could still hold up the back end of that equation. O'Conner added that the surgeon would visit me with a clearer picture soon.

Great, but I already had a picture: a dark one. A.L. had had his share of spills, but nothing that left him this wrecked—never mind flat-lined in a meat wagon. All I could do was turn everything over to The Man and hope the doctors were having their best of days.

O'Conner asked if anyone would be joining me and I said, yes, soon. Her hand touched my shoulder but my eyes stayed glued to my racing shoes. The two EMTs then walked away, hopefully still within earshot of my muttered, "Thanks guys."

"Colby? Colby?"

I startled. The citrusy scent and the long hair that tickled my face was Jillian's. She labored to smile through watery eyes as Mr. Carter towered behind.

"What's going on with A.L., Colby?" he asked.

A shook head and a lurching recap of what had been shared was all I could muster.

Mr. Carter plastered on a take-charge look and sought the admissions desk. He soon returned with a woman in tow. "Colby, hi, I'm Janice Libre from social services."

I rose from my seat. "Social services?"

"I need to get some info from you. Can we talk for a minute?"

She didn't wait for my permission and extracted a pad and pen. "Now, you and your father were racing this weekend at the Marionville track?" she asked.

"I guess, yeah." I felt almost defensive for some reason.

"And your dad's injury occurred during the race?"

"Uh huh. Have any update by chance?"

"He's in intensive care. Dr. Kendall is performing a procedure to release the stress—"

"Stress? Where?"

"His neck and back, Colby. Dr. Kendall will visit you, soon as he's done."

Her sweet tone stiffened with the rise of her clipboard. That's when the questions began to pour: Where we lived, nearest relatives, contact info? So, it was really raw data she chased.

It was complicated, I divulged. Mom was in Cincinnati and the nearest next of kin was her sister, Demi Ross, who might as well be dwelling on Pluto.

"Answer the lady, straight, Colby," Mr. Carter said looking away.

"Back home, miss, it's just me, A.L. and the animals."

"So you'd be alone, if your dad had to remain here for a while."

"I don't know yet. Maybe. I'm good," I said.

Mr. Carter repeated his request, more insistent this time. "Will you *please* just answer the lady's questions, Colby?"

Jillian arched up. "He's trying to, Dad."

The woman stayed calm. "Tell you what, Colby, give that some thought." She asked for A.L.'s wallet for insurance info.

I said, "Wallet? That's probably back in the camper. Crap."

Mr. Carter nonchalantly produced it. "I got you, son."

Mr. C. must have grabbed it from the Boler. She took down the info then requested a private moment with Mr. Carter. She abandoned me easily as a paper cup.

"What's up, Mr. Carter?" I asked after he returned alone.

"I worked it out. They're going to let me take you home."

"Thanks, but I don't plan on returning to Darin, not without A.L., anyway."

Jillian squeezed my hand and looked to her dad, "Can I stay, too?"

"What, Jillian? No, neither of you can." He turned back to me. They think A.L. might have to lay up here for a while."

"I don't care if it's a month, Mr. Carter. I'm staying."

"You're upset Colby, I get it," he said.

My mind wasn't changed, but I let it go.

Mr. Carter said, "I think I'll find us something to eat."

He returned with food and coffee that went down easier than expected.

Jillian spoke through a bite, "Probably not a good time to bring this up."

"But?"

"There was some talk of having you eliminated because you jumped in the pit and crossed the track to help A.L. Can believe that? That weird blond kid bitched to the officials."

"Tooley of course." I hadn't thought back to the race. "Will I have to forfeit?"

"You're moving on, Colby."

She hugged me but all elation had crashed with A.L.

Mr. Carter shrugged. "Colby, they gave me an envelope with your plaque. Did you win money, as well?" Mr. Carter asked.

"I don't think so . . . Oh yeah. This must be A.L.'s holeshot money."

Mr. Carter's puzzled look was justified.

"Even if he didn't finish, he had already won it," I explained.

"Or maybe it was out of the mercy of their hearts?" Jillian got two pairs of rolled eyes.

Check removed, it birthed a whistle from her. "A *thousand* bucks? Wow."

I tucked it in my wallet.

"A timely gift, I'd say. Don't lose it," Mr. Carter said.

"Oh I won't, sir. Thanks for grabbing this and his wallet, sir," I said. "Who won A.L.'s class, anyway?"

"You're thinking about that?" Jillian said.

"No, but it will be the first thing A.L. asks, you watch."

"Klaus Ketty," she said.

"Figures." I dropped my head and sighed. "A.L. had it sewed up."

Jillian combed the back of my head with her fingers. "I know, baby, but I'll tell you A.L.'s pain will be less knowing you're going home with a ticket to the Regional."

"Hmmm."

A haggard-looking doctor in green scrubs calling for the Weston family was the best thing I'd heard in hours.

I sprung to my feet. "I'm Colby Weston, doctor. This is my girlfriend, Jillian, and her dad."

"Doctor Kendall." He took my extended hand then Mr. Carter's. "We've been working on your dad. He's tough, a fighter."

Pride found me. "Yes sir. The man's no stranger to falls. So where are things at?" Jillian's squeeze intensified around my sweaty palm.

The doctor hardly minced words as he painted a picture: an ugly one. There was evidence of neck and spinal contusions in addition to lesser, non-life-threatening injuries, including a broken arm *(again?)* and foot *(damn)*. More tests were needed to evaluate the full extent of A.L.'s injuries. His evaluation and stay in intensive care might take days, probably longer. They had induced him into a coma state, so there'd be no talking to the man.

My world spun; my throat went thick. "Coma state? Doctor, I realize he's all checked out, but I'd like to stay here with him, at least a night or two if I can."

"I'm sorry, son, that won't be possible unless you have an adult family member present."

"Okay, but—"

"The best thing you can do is go home and be with your family."

I nodded, but never divulged I was A.L.'s only real family, and as far as I was concerned, he was mine.

No four-star steakhouse post-celebration as planned. Sunday's traffic soon thinned to a six-hour, numbing ride back to Darin. Jillian nestled close as I drove our truck with bikes and Boler in tow. Talk was mostly stunted as we followed her trailer's taillights. The worst had been abandoning A.L. at the hospital like some science experiment. A dark pessimism settled in as robbed champion became more robbed life. *Why did he have to showboat on that final jump?* I didn't know all the facts yet, but expected that somehow he'd rebound and ride again this season. This was my highest hope anyway.

Hey, son, I'm still alive. I swore I heard his voice fill the cab as Jillian, fast asleep, clung to my side.

CHAPTER 6—HOME

Monday. Still on the dark side of predawn, we had driven through the night. Jillian was passed out balled up against my side. Mr. Carter flashed his blinkers. Beyond our exit, the Southside Liquor sign loomed. This usually acted as a beacon welcoming our return to town. This time my stomach plunged with dread.

We drove through the shuttered, dark streets of Darin until we reached the Carter's house. Their mammoth RV eased into its usual spot beside their garage. I gently shook Jillian's shoulder.

Her head popped up and she rubbed her face. "I don't even know what's happening, C-Boy."

"Either do I, J-Girl, but we're home."

"Do you want to stay here? Are you going to be cool alone?"

"I'll be alright. The animals need me."

She hugged me. "See you at school?"

Jillian's dad interrupted, "Jillian, I've got to be up in like three hours. So do you guys."

"I know, Dad. Go ahead. I'll be right in."

Mr. Carter took my side. "Good luck with everything, Colby. We're here to help."

"Thanks for everything, Mr. C.," I said.

Jillian and I held each other. Reality blurred with uninvited tears. This time saying good-bye meant I'd be alone. The championship confidence had abandoned me.

Fifteen minutes later, my headlights revealed the red reflector on our mailbox. I was home, but too exhausted to pull the bikes from the truck.

I entered El Relaxo via the garage and into the kitchen. I wasn't concerned with the stack of undone dishes or the mail our neighbor had put on the kitchen table. No, all my senses honed on the mound of reeking dog shit in the middle of the floor. This told me a couple of things: Mr. Stevens had probably fulfilled his promise to feed the animals and Bubbles, our Dalmatian, still needed some sort of canine counseling.

There were no immediate greetings from the pets, only the cold, thick, country silence. I switched on a light and dropped my keys into the tray by the door. The fact that Bubbles didn't bark or even greet me didn't necessarily mean she'd run off or worse. She was a natural born coward, prone to taking refuge in the basement at the sound of any stranger; sometimes even us. Shortly after, the Dalmatian braved to surface from the dark basement stairs. She donned a guilty face and we both understood why. Despite being exhausted and annoyed with my gift of feces, open arms embraced her. Bubbles returned my affection with a generous tongue bath before pawing at the front door. I released her into the cold dawn where she began sniffing and combing the immediate area as if something was missing because there was. Bubbles eventually broke a rule and from her back legs, peered into the blue-flecked Ford truck.

"Get your paws off that door, Bubbly. You know better."

Bubbles obeyed but I sensed her desperation. Something, specifically someone, was missing and we'd both have to deal and probably for a good while. She romped off to explore the property, past silhouetted moto practice hills that stood hushed as foreboding monuments now. Out there A.L. and I had honed our games and planted the seeds of our future. Like some horrible flash flood, all optimism had been swept away—at least for the time being. I left Bubbles to roam, returned inside and jacked the heat. The living room was how we left it—a chaotic bombshell with multiple projects in progress. Fly-fishing lures and engine parts lay splayed on the brown terrazzo floor in front of the TV.

A slight stir from our sun porch alerted me. Had it been daylight, Commander Whitehead, our African Grey parrot, which A.L. had won in a poker game years before, would have greeted my return with a piercing yelp, maybe my name. But it was still slightly early for my friend. Hunger steered me back to the kitchen but my first assault of reality still reeked and demanded immediate extraction.

Yet I still delayed, and instead grabbed one of A.L.'s beers and cracked it open for a bit of courage. After a yank of the tab I took a long pull. I collapsed on a kitchen table chair beside unopened mail that didn't interest me. All motivation was long toppled but the beer relaxed me. I eventually summoned the will and tore off a wad of paper towels, cupped the fresh, repulsive clump in one hand and exited through the garage door with a slight case of the dry heaves.

The sound of Bubbles' trot broke the night, and she was more than happy to join me with her carefree *What up, Colby?* prance. "Hey, thanks for the welcome home gift, crazy mutt. Next time, use the damn newspaper I put down for you in the sunroom." But because my sarcasm came in a lovable high pitch, the dog's happy tail interpreted my critical rant to mean, "I love you."

I walked to woods edge and hurled the entire package into the dark abyss. Bubbles' sudden pointed alertness towards the woods framed her lunacy. But she soon remembered, *Oh yeah, that's my dog poo!* and relaxed. I stroked her head and she followed me inside where Billy the Kid, aka B.K., now presented himself, yet another defective chromosome prize. Everything was rare about B.K., even him being a him. Barely one in 3,000 calicos are male. But more to the point, only one in ten thousand calicos were as messed up. B.K. was Bubbles' BFF and they prided themselves by getting into some pretty macabre mischief. His typical straight-from-the-bowels-of-hell meow greeted me with more demands than love. I poured some kibble, into their respective bowls and they dove in immediately.

The two brought temporary diversion, but the new reality was already setting in and it wasn't a comfortable one. A strong feeling of helplessness and confusion consumed me. Tired but restless, I putzed around a little before hitting the couch. I aimed the remote at the TV to chase the quiet, set my alarm and pulled the blanket up to my chin, hoping to score a couple of Z's before school. B.K. jumped up expecting his ritual nightly rub. I obliged my friend but he got the short version before everything fell dark.

Monday morning greeted me again but this time with daylight. I tried to shuck the exhaustion as I scrambled upstairs for a fresh tee and my book bag. My wounded knee rebelled with every step up the stairs. I felt sick-tired. *What am I doing?* I relaxed the stiff hand that held the strap, and the backpack struck the floor with a thud. I tumbled onto my bed where I could debate the options a bit longer, but sleep again robbed me of all second-guessing.

I woke about one. Bleary eyes searched the dusty trophies and old family photos that shouted optimism and happier times. Close to Mark Beck's AMX poster—yeah, I actually had one of those—hung a framed newspaper article from the local paper, a piece on A.L. and me. The color photo showed the two of us atop one of our hills, clad in our racing gear, arms crossed, back to back; beaming. The reporter had titled the piece, *Up Shot*. Life would literally become one blissful sandbox after another. We so believed.

What should I do, who should I call? A.L.'s parents had died in their own tragic accident, and he had fallen out of touch with a mostly transient, younger brother. Except for my Aunt Demi, the key accomplice to my mother's escape to Ohio, I had no family in these parts. I alone would have to take the handlebars of El Relaxo Rancho and steer things for how long, no one yet knew. Downstairs, I tended to the animals' needs. Bubbles and B.K. were fed, then released to roam outside. Commander screamed my name and frantically circled the bars of his cage. I opened the cage door and the African Grey scooted his way up my extended arm and took root on my shoulder. How could a bird detect the situation or my low state? But that seemed the case as he nestled in and rubbed his beak repeatedly against my face in a way he had not done before.

I walked Commander into the kitchen, cleared one sink then ran a tepid stream of water. Once lowered in, he joyously pranced through his morning shower while I freshened up his cage and added fresh food and water. I returned the parrot to his sunroom day perch where he liked to gaze through the glass and mock the free birds—and especially the ever-scheming Billy the Kid.

As I numbly contemplated the gurgling coffee drips into the pot, I punched in to damage control. I phoned A.L.'s boss at Drake's Lumber Yard. A.L. did the company books and helped plot the drivers' routes for Mr. Drake and they were definitely looking for answers regarding why he had never showed. He promised A.L.'s desk chair would always be waiting, once healed. With Mom and her income gone, it seemed scraping by on one salary would barely keep enough food in the fridge, never mind support our motocross habit. Yet A.L. always seemed to pay the bills and still find enough extra to purchase things like mods to our bikes.

Next, I phoned Jack—the same Jack who'd watched Jillian and I almost end ourselves on his track—in what seemed like so long ago.

"Colby, what's going on?" he started in. "Got a call from a rider who said A.L. had crashed and was hospitalized in Georgia? That true?"

"Afraid so, Jack. They got him in some induced coma."

"Coma?" A deep sigh left him. "Oh my . . . For how long, any idea?"

"They're doing tests. Could be down there for a while. Damn, I don't know, Jack, could cost him the season, maybe more." My voice cracked.

Jack, as much as anyone, knew how committed we were. "Really sorry, Colby. He was riding as good as anyone of late . . . damn . . . Who's with you now?"

"The animals."

"Don't like you out there, alone. You pack up your stuff and stay with me and the Mrs. You can take Robbie's old room until A.L. returns."

"Appreciate the offer, sir, but with the pets here and all."

"I suppose . . . alright, just be safe and keep me in the loop, hear?"

"Sure will. Thanks, Jack."

"Godspeed. Hey, almost forgot, how'd *your* ride go?"

"Good, I tucked away things Sunday with a win . . . so I guess I'm moving on."

"You won it outright? Wow, Colby!"

"Wish I could feel more excited."

"Well it's not A.L.'s first mishap, right? He's tougher than a cockroach and he's bounced back from some pretty mean looking tumbles, boy."

"I know. You're right. Thanks."

Coffee in hand I gently nudged myself along on our porch swing. I contemplated our yard and man-made hills out there. A text came in, Jillian wondering how things were going. She promised to drop by later. I needed to move, do something. A walk in our woods cleared some of the cobwebs. On my return through the open garage I paused before the poster-sized print Jillian had taken of us. The striking, black and white photo froze A.L. and I, airborne and displaying two insane stunts. I turned towards his bike. Except for a few new scratches, Gremlin had fared far better than its rider.

An incoming call interrupted all reminiscing. No name, just a number. "Hello?" I tightened as Doctor Naylor from Darin Hospital introduced himself. He requested I swing by his office that afternoon. He said he had news from Marionville.

"I'll be right over, but is he, is he—?"

CHAPTER 7—TWO PALS VISIT

"Your dad is stable and resting, Colby." Dr. Naylor's quick strides and white ballooning coat felt like a minor workout as we headed for his office.

The meeting turned out to be more of a recap of knowns. A.L. was still sprawled and in a coma—damaged goods, yeah, but how bad? The doctors at Marionville General were still running tests, Naylor explained. What spoke louder was his prediction for a possible long recovery time. What I wanted to hear was that A.L. would return, regardless of the shape he was in—and soon as possible. Dr. Naylor promised me updates when they arrived

The sight of Jillian's truck in my driveway pumped me with instant life. She was lounging on the outside porch and she'd brought company. Beach Moody enveloped me with massive, sympathetic arms, while Jillian locked on my eyes, trying to assess me.

"Come in guys . . . Excuse the mess," I said.

Beach looked around." Mess? I don't see a mess."

Jillian wasn't as merciful. "Uh C-Boy, you all need a maid, dude."

"You're offering? I pay ten compliments an hour."

Jillian smirked. "Make it twenty, I'll still pass."

"Sucks about A.L., man," Beach said.

"Yeah, I'm still trying to deal."

"But I heard my boy rode really well and is moving on. What up with that?"

"Haven't given it much thought since," I said.

Beach was always my wingman, someone who kept me safe on the football field and in laughter off it. He also had pro sports dreams, but not from a dirt bike's seat. As an all-county offensive lineman, Beach was all about football and creating gaping holes for scatbacks like me to run through. His ultimate dream was to make it to Mississippi State where his father had once starred as a tight end. Based on the stream of college scouts that had visited our games, Beach had a pretty good chance. Now all he had to do was connive his way to scoring a high school diploma.

He soft tossed a bag that landed with a thud on the coffee table. "Here," he said. Based on the delicious scent pouring out of that greasy brown bag, something delicious had fallen. "Never be depressed on an empty stomach, C," he said.

"Oh, man!" I peeked. "I could smell it, soon as you arrived. Tell me I'm staring at a bag full of Mama Moody's finest fried chicken."

"That'll shake off the blues some, C-Boy," Jillian added.

Beach tossed the bag with chicken on coffee table. "It's all there, man, down to the mashed potatoes and the collards."

"Sweetness, thanks man." I rolled the bag's top to save it for later and chucked it on the coffee table. "I miss anything interesting at school?"

Jillian replied, "It was a Monday at JHS. What did you think you missed?"

"I *wasn't* thinking, J-Girl."

"I brought you something else." A wry smile came from Jillian. "Sorry, it's not dessert. I visited all your teachers; collected your stuff like it was trick or treat." She unearthed a pile from her bag.

I looked at it. "Awe J-Girl, you shouldn't have." It was energy sucking.

Jillian and Beach leaned forward and almost said together, "Anything from the doctor?"

I told them what I heard; they were continuing with medical tests. Restless, I stood and cued some tunes.

Beach held up the bag. "You gonna have a piece?"

"Nah, later. You guys want some, go ahead," I said.

An offer like that should never have been made. Seconds later, Beach ripped into the bag. His face turned cartoonish after his teeth sank into that first bite. "Heroin."

Jillian's eyes rolled towards the bag as she begged in a little girl's voice. "Can I try just a little piece, too?"

I tossed her the bag.

"Pepper me up, C-Boy!" She took a bite. "Beach, this is killer."

I surrendered to everything and poured them some half-flat Mountain Dew. I watched appalled, as growls and grunts accompanied their feast. I was in the company of piranha.

Jillian collapsed onto the couch after reaching hypoglycemic bliss. She licked her fingers. "Phew," she began, "That last piece took it out of me, Beach. Compliments to Mama Moody."

"I'll pass it along—after I pass out. Nap time!" Beach announced.

I grabbed the much lighter bag. "Guys, I was hoping this would last me a week!"

"I owe you C-Boy." Blood sugar restored, Jillian sat up and asked about A.L. again. "So, back to A.L. What's the actual plan?"

"There is none. A.L.'s still powered down, trapped in Coma Land."

"I don't get it," Beach said, hands folded on his huge frame, eyes to the ceiling. "Why don't they just pop him out of it?"

Jillian said, "Beach, it's not like a siesta."

I said, "Doctors sometimes drop dudes into super chill so everything is less stressed and the body can fix the mess."

"Why didn't you just say that before?" Beach said.

I turned to Jillian. "One thing I did find out; sometimes they'll transport dudes home in a coma. Who knows? Soon, maybe?"

"Wherever, whenever he comes to, A.L.'s going to storm back," Jillian said.

Beach agreed. "True that."

Jillian turned to me. "And what about you, Mr. Truant? You gonna home school yourself now?"

I shrugged.

Jillian told Beach, "Can't let Einstein tumble off the honor role."

"How do you even do that honor role thing, C?" Beach said. "Especially in English. That's where *I* slip into a coma."

"Beach!" Jillian shrieked.

"Now how did that just slip out?" Beach looked perplexed.

"I don't usually divulge secrets with dudes who just ate my dinner but . . ." I leaned towards Beach, "Study a little."

"What?" He screwed up his face.

Quarter sized splats outside began to assault the windows.

"Rain is good luck, C-Boy," Jillian said.

"Not when it might break windows," I said.

I checked in and out of the conversation between Beach and Jillian; let it roll over me as the drops ran down. At some point Beach's face tensed and he claimed something needed doing somewhere. He rose, practically swatted the ceiling with a stretch and started for the door.

"Walking home, Beach?" Jillian smiled with an unhurried leg flung over the chair arm, jiggling her keys.

Beach feigned confusion. "For a minute there, I forgot how I got here."

Jillian straightened, patted my knee and rose. "I should be heading back, too."

She kissed then hugged me. "Call me?" I walked as far as the porch and hugged the post as the two shrieked and scampered through the downpour for her truck.

The rain wouldn't let up. I built a fire in the kitchen's wood stove to chase the chill. The last piece of Mama Moody's chicken relieved my hunger but not the blues.

Wrapped in a blanket, TV on, I tackled the schoolwork Jillian brought me. As I did, Commander peered down from my shoulder like a doting professor. But after a large plop of guano soiled the math page, I summarily sentenced the bird to hard time behind bars.

Later, I opted for the upstairs and my warm bed but soon kneeled for a view out the window. Our mounds flashed blue with each dramatic lightning bolt. After one, I counted four seconds before the next crack. That launched a memory, getting stuck outside, riding in the start of heavy drops; A.L. counting *Mississippi four* after a flash then subsequent loud crack that signaled the strike was a mile away.

I retrieved Commander and placed his cage on my desk upstairs so he wouldn't panic down there alone. B.K. studied him a bit, but never abandoned the soft refuge of my bed.

Restless, I picked up a new issue of *Motocross* and flipped through it. It didn't launch me to far places like it usually did. I tossed the magazine and batted out the lights. Explosive lightning flashes triggered my count: *Mississippi one, Mississippi two,* BANG! Rain assaulted El Relaxo. Photos of A.L. and me would light up; then go black. The next bolt would flash; I'd count and brace for the next crash.

CHAPTER 8—HOME INVASION

A bright red Cadillac sat in our driveway. Instant alarm bells. Deep breath, I paused before braving the front door. I had left it locked, I thought, before I went to the grocery store. *Hmmm?* A cautious turn of my key ignited Commander Whitehead, but not with his typical greeting.

"Helllllllllp, Colby!" Obviously what Bubbles lacked as a watchdog Commander made up for in translation.

"Shhh!" I said with a finger to my lips before being shushed back. A swirl of monotone singing, running water and clanging pans poured from the kitchen. Armed with only panic and two bags of frozen food and cookies, I darted my head around the corner for a glimpse. *Please no.*

Imagine walking into the worst kind of home invasion. Now double it. I knew that portly backside. No wonder the parrot had cried for help. *I* wanted to cry for help. Aunt Demi stood at the sink, earbuds in, singing along in a grating monotone, "Take me in a little closer! Put me where I don't belong . . ." Her furious pace caused water to scatter everywhere before dripping from the counter to form a puddle beneath her feet. She cleaned and stacked every neglected dirty dish and pan we owned with yellow, Playtex *Living* Gloves! The mere name launched dormant childhood phobias. Since Mom's flight for Mr. Moneybags, they had sat buried under the sink. Now they had come alive again and all this teen could do was clutch my grocery bags in horror and watch. After all, this was the same aunt who had gleefully commandeered my mother away from El Relaxo when Mom made a run for it.

Demi paused from her scrubbing, still oblivious of all other life forms and waved her arms above her and attempted a spastic dance. To me? Those two waving, yellow caution signs warned me to backstroke the hell out of there while the gettin' was good. This for sure: once this queen of gossip realized just who was staring six feet behind her, the demands would fly, voluminous as the sink water.

Though my mother's sister lived just a fifteen minute ride away, I hadn't seen auntie since Mom's great escape. A.L. and Demi had never seen eye to eye on much, so her presence here reeked of agenda and trouble. At some point I knew contact with this specimen would become inevitable; then again, scaring her might precipitate cardiac arrest, then what?

A couple of loud clearings of my throat were no match for the buds or her swollen feet pounding the floor. I flicked the light switch a few times. Blame the blinding afternoon sun, Demi's mind remained scattered on Pluto. Perhaps a friendly hello or knock on the wall as if I had entered *her* place? Nothing. My patience was melting faster than the weeks' worth of frozen dinners in my bag. I eased closer and tried a gentle tap on her shoulder. My mistake was not using a yardstick. She spun around and doused my groceries and front with a tsunami of hot, soapy water!

"Fuck, Aunt Demi!"

Her shriek easily out-blasted mine. "Sweet Mother of God, Colby! Do you always sneak up on people like that? And tone down the language."

Steamy water from the faucet continued cascading off the bottom of an over-turned spaghetti pot and flew everywhere but down the drain. Panicked, she slapped the faucet hard. But as fast as the anger from surprise boiled, it collected and cooled, replaced by a forgiving smile and wet, blubbery, sprawling arms. "Come to me, nephewww!" I became pinned in a death-hold against her enormous breasts. "You probably caught my sing-along. How embarrassing."

Soaked and suffocating in her clutch, with a final breath, I flat-lined, "Oh no, don't feel embarrassed at all, Aunt Demi."

Her head lifted for examination as squeaky strokes from those Living Gloves assaulted my face. But the wet, clammy, rubbery reunion lasted only seconds.

She shoved me back and grimaced. "Eww. You're all wet!"

"Well yeah, Aunt Demi. Feels like I just got run through a freaking car wash!" I used my excuse of melting frozen dinners to pull away and stock the freezer. While I did, Demi's words predictably shifted to a Gatling gun of criticism.

"Frozen dinners? Is that what A.L.'s feeding you now? Not healthy."

Minus my response, she hopped to the next gripe. "And Colby, this floor?" She pointed. "Disgusting! Much like the rest of this place."

"Wasn't my idea to turn the kitchen into Lake Erie."

I hunted down a mop and gave it a couple of swirls before giving up. I looked at her deadpan. "Better?"

"Worse."

Demi recoiled as I aimed the dripping mop head past her nose and over to the sink where the muddy filth twirled down the drain.

"My bet is it's been a while since Mr. Mop had a decent work out," she said.

"Busy with Mrs. Mop, I guess. No worries. I'll get this all buffed up nice after you go."

"Go?"

"As in leave, you know. Also, how'd you all get in?"

"The front door was locked and the garage was closed." A proud smile found her. "But not the porch window."

"*You squeezed through a window?* Sorry I missed that."

Like a cat burglar she detailed her unlawful entry, but her boastful smile was short-lived. "The only snafu? Landing heel deep in dog doo compliments of Miss Bubble Trouble." Right on cue, Bubbles braved an entrance. "Awful dog," Demi said to Bubbles. "Guilt's tattooed all over your face." The dog retreated down the cellar stairs. "What kind of dog defecates inside anyway?"

"Only a covert, strategic one, Aunt Demi." I walked over to a bowl on our small kitchen table, lifted out the last apple and bit into it really hard. Through stuffed cheeks I said, "It's a kind of tactical defense. She carefully positions her piles like land mines. Don't I know it. Anyway, what brings you by?"

Demi's beady, dark eyes narrowed even more. "Oh, *you* know, Colby."

Bells went off. "Mom call you about A.L.?"

Without a shred of compassion, she asked, "What happened to the daredevil this time?"

"Long and short, he went down and suffered injuries during Sunday's race."

"Damn, rotten dirt bikes. Still in the hospital?"

"In Marionville, yeah," I crunched my next bite.

She shook her head. "Your mother called from Cincy. She was concerned about A.L., but also you, obviously."

"With me? She didn't seem too concerned when she ran off."

"Oh, she was concerned. Concerned about losing her mind from the constant drone of motorbikes as you all tore up her once beautiful wild flower field."

"She didn't plant them and we always stopped by eight . . . usually," I said.

"Don't get snide, Colby. She was also informed you skipped the last two days of school."

"How did she find that out?" I emptied the dishpan of dirty water too forcefully and water sloshed onto the counter and dish rack.

"Be careful, I just cleaned those! Anyway, the school probably tried her number after A.L. never picked up."

I said to myself. "Maybe I shouldn't have left his phone with him . . . Look, Aunt Demi, I needed a couple of days off to chill and for A.L. biz. That a crime? My girlfriend's been bringing me my schoolwork. I'm keeping up. I'll get back in the game."

"Make it soon. Mom's orders."

"She could call if she's so concerned. Surprised she even cares, with that bougie house, her new man and his two rugrats. Figured I'd be easier to forget."

"Awe . . . that almost sounds . . . pathetic. Once a son, always a son. She asks about you all the time."

"Uh huh. Mr. Moneybags treating her okay?"

"It's *Millybaugh*, get it right."

"My Milly bad."

"You should all pay a visit and meet the family." She drew close. "The place is big; decked out like Disney."

"I'll hold out for the real Mouse House, thanks. But yeah, I might ride up there on Silver someday; maybe carve some circles in their lawn."

"At least you're not bitter. Family's important."

"I've got all I need right here. A.L.'ll be home soon, back to aces."

"You hope. You been in touch with his doctor?" She asked.

"Yeah, the one in town. Dr. Naylor said—"

"Wait! Dr. Naylor, Naylor. Let me write that down." She went to her purse and retrieved a small notebook. "How do you spell that?"

"However you want."

"What about A.L.'s folks? Anything from them?"

"That would take a Ouija board, since they died in a car wreck a while back."

Demi's forked tongue spared no one mercy. "Oh, that's right . . . kind of an accident-prone family, don't you think?"

I winged my apple core into the trash.

"Wait. Doesn't A.L. have a brother? I met him once. Kind of a vague; moved out west. What's his name?"

"Uncle Ben? He grows medical marijuana now. Downright lucrative. Makes a teen think."

"Say no more, Colby. Standards these days are muddier than this godforsaken kitchen floor."

"Anyway, I haven't been able to reach Uncle Ben. He might be off hiking or busy cultivating his product."

"Blasted out of his gourd, more like it! Either way, doesn't sound like the cavalry's coming anytime soon." She sighed. "Looks like I'm your best option now."

"Option? Does it look like I need options? I'm fine."

"Listen. Your mother asked me to camp here until A.L.'s home and back on his feet, keep an eye on things."

Camp, as in stay? Panic! "Demi, that could be days, maybe weeks."

Once the snatch of confused panic abated, she recalled, "All I know is when I was sixteen I needed supervision around the clock."

"Don't feel obliged, Aunt Demi. You're too busy and . . . what about Uncle Pete?"

"He's away at his law office most of the time."

"And your kids?"

"Peter and I have had this discussion. He'll have to father-up a bit more. None of this would even be an issue if the Weston boys didn't spend all their free time zipping around on crotch rockets."

I entered the living room and sank into the couch and hid behind a moto magazine. "Man's got to follow his passions," I mumbled to the rifled pages.

"Straight to an emergency room? You all should find safer options."

"Tell that to the pro scout who slipped me his business card."

"Someone should slip him poison, the exploitive bastard! How long did you say A.L. will be laid up?"

"Could be shelved for a long while, Demi, yup." I continued paging through. "I'll see to his needs just fine after he returns."

"What *I need* is to get in touch with A.L.'s doctor for real answers. Until then, guess I'll pitch my tent here."

"Yeah, yeah."

"Now grab my stuff from the car, will you?" she said.

With a too loud groan, I tossed the magazine down and rose from the couch. I fetched her half-ton suitcase—not a good sign—and a lighter, red gym bag. "Anything else?" I panted.

With hands on hips, Demi gazed at the apocalypse that was the living room. "The next thing we do is address this rat's nest before I go stark raving mad."

"Aunt Demi, do you know how hard A.L. and I worked to get everything just so?" I said.

Demi scoffed. "Pass on the sass or I'll kick your . . ." Her eyes flitted. "I should probably just call an exterminator. "Colby, start by ridding this, this . . . man cave of beer bottles and . . . Wait, did you drink all these beers?"

"No, they're A.L.'s."

"Such a fine role model he is. And what's that stuff sprawled over the floor by the TV?"

"You mean the engine parts? It got cold before the trip, so we dragged the bikes in from the garage to tune them up before the event. No biggie."

"From now on, this room will not serve as a Midas Muffler shop, you hear?"

"I *used* to hear just fine," I grumbled.

Whoever Demi was talking to after that, wasn't me. She paced circles. "I'm telling you, I'm stuck in some hoarder's nightmare. I'm sick to my stomach, sick! I need air." She turned back to me. "Colby, get to the task!" Back to circling. "I think I'll visit a friend's place for a while."

I broke her spell. "Great, go. Catch up on the town gossip. No rush back."

A controlling smile possessed her. "Take my bags upstairs; A.L.'s bedroom will do fine."

"You're going to sleep in *A.L.'s* bed?"

"I'm sure as hell not sleeping on the porch with dog shit and a squawking bird. Are there any clean sheets?"

"What?"

"Like in the linen closet?"

"Don't know if we have one of those, seriously," I said.

"Colby, I want fresh sheets before I crawl into A.L.'s bed. Most of all, I sure don't want to tuck in and find myself rubbing against somebody's hard crankshaft or something. Strip the old man's bed and do a load of sheets while I'm out. You *might* want to throw yours in, too. Probably been a while."

"So . . . engine parts, dog poo, crankshaft, laundry . . . that everything?"

"Oh, that's just the warm up act, nephew. Plan on a total makeover before I'm done." She stormed out of the front door, her hands in an upward flourish. "Clean this dump up, or else!"

Did I look like somebody's cheap Cinderella? With Commander rooted on my shoulder, making tsking sounds with his beak, I paced tight, angry circles. I didn't even know where to start, so I called a trusted ally for moral support. Besides the laugh medicine, Beach offered no actual advice of help. That might be found from Jillian, so I gave her a call. In seconds my wonder girl calmly came up with a plan to seize back control of El Relaxo. She cautioned me to keep my cool, buff up the place, do all as demanded, then whip up a nice dinner for Aunt Demi.

"Like nuke frozen burritos or boil hot dogs?"

"No, dude," Jillian insisted. "Take *command* of that stove top. It'll create an image of maturity. Women love an accomplished, manly cook."

"Wish you had told me before. Dunno if I'm any of those things."

Jillian said, "Well dig deep. You still have any of that frozen river bass you and A.L. caught a while back? It was delicious."

"Because *he* breaded that shit and cooked it."

"Cooking is simple science, C-Boy. With the right guide, you, too, can become the master."

"But—"

"No buts. Do you want to impress the aunt? Show her you're worthy and can be trusted alone. Make the place shine then stuff her like a hog. I'll meet you at the market in an hour."

I whined like I was five. "J-Girl, I was just there."

"You like freedom?"

"Maybe."

"Freedom's gonna cost you, C-Boy."

A.L.'s holeshot reward was in an envelope, yet to be cashed, but I discovered a jar with a few twenties stuffed in it. Jillian greeted me at the grocery store with a reassuring smile. When she pointed, I didn't ask or complain about the expense of things. I simply cowered like Bubbles and dropped the stuff into the cart. Jillian assured me all this crap was essential if I was to win Demi over. I listened intently as I covered my head with a produce bag and flailed my arms. Jillian ignored me and pushed the cart on.

Outside, I clutched two bags with expensive groceries, slapped on a brave face and kissed her.

"Hey, I have a better idea. Why don't *you* come over and cook while I get Auntie loaded?"

"No, this has to be all you, C-Boy."

I shook a fist. "I will do this, damn it!"

"Yes! Stuff her with fine food and booze and act grown up. Make her believe, C-Boy."

"You mean make her believe that I'm something I'm not?"

"Exactly, C-Boy, exactly."

CHAPTER 9—PET TRICKS

Jillian convinced me to play along. Powered by rage, I tossed, stashed, vacuumed and scrubbed while the sheets tumbled in the dryer. The more I impressed, the sooner she might find reason to leave. I could only hope.

Soon her Cadillac roared up, the car door slammed and she burst in like a vice raid. I was upstairs madly tucking in fresh sheets after scraping off petrified toothpaste from the bathroom sink. This sucked! Sweat wiped from my brow; it wasn't Motel Six, but maybe a Four. I floated downstairs with debonair charm.

"You're back. How was your afternoon, Demi?" A smile never hurt so much.

"Good . . . Well-well, lookie here. We made some progress, yes we did."

"Yes. We. Did. But my best is yet to come. I'm going to browse the kitchen stock and see what I can dig up for din-din for us."

"Like one of your little frozen surprises? No thank you. I'll get pizza delivered."

Man, that sounded good. A bubble appeared above my head. Inside it stood Jillian, cross-armed and all business.

I said, "Frozen dinners? Ha! I feed those to the dog . . . How about a specially prepared fish dinner."

"Fish?" Demi perked up.

"Yes!" I said.

"I mean, I do love fish, but—"

"Great. Cooking's a bit of a side hobby of mine, actually. I do most of it for A.L. He always appreciates a well-prepared feast waiting for him when he gets home from work."

"I see." Demi's stare was clearly skeptical. "Honestly? You can do this?"

"Sure."

"*Without* burning the shack down?"

"I am Chef Colossus." I drummed my chest.

"Colossal disaster maybe . . . Something's changed in you since I've been gone," she said.

"Changed? Not really. I'm just trying to make your visit chill. I mean, if you don't trust me, play it safe and dial up the pizza guy."

"Who trusts any teen boy? But if you want to cook, knock yourself out."

"Let the Gourmet Games begin. Now, how 'bout a little drink to sedate, I mean, relax you." I went to the cupboard. "Let's see. We have whiskey, a little gin . . . A.L. must have inherited all this from his dad. He's more of a beer guy."

"Yes, I've been introduced to his brewery."

"But not anymore," I said.

"Alright, Colby. Pour me a little whiskey and Coke, if you're up to bartending."

"Sure thing." I poured her a two-finger shot with a couple of rocks and a soda splash. "Here you go, Demi, cheers. Enjoy the view from the porch while I prepare your feast.

Sometimes you can catch a deer or two moseying by this time of day."

"How lovely, thank you. My husband never spoils me like this."

"Dump his ass." It escaped a little too loud. Her head snapped back to me. I tossed up opened palms. "Just kidding."

Her face eased after a sip. "Ah. I may never leave!"

What?!

To cook is to relax. My mother's words, not mine. Two bass fillets stared back at me, ready for my magic, wherever I put that. Everything became instant overload as culinary attempts turned into anxiety central. This was stupid. I was never going to budge this woman out of here until A.L. got back. And what if she liked it? I might have to do this every night!

Needing a life line and directions, I called the head chef.

Jillian answered, "That was fast. I said bake the shit not microwave it."

"I haven't begun, C-Girl, can you walk me through it again? Also, Demi's loving my bartending skills."

"Better hope she's not a mean drunk. There's serious work yet to be done at El Relaxo, C-Boy. Me, I'm painting stars on my ceiling with glow paint, dreaming about the future."

"Future? What's that?" I said. "I wish A.L was back."

"Me too, baby." Her voice went silky. "Listen, after dinner, come on over and you can check out my nebulae."

"Pepper me up. Meanwhile, I'm surrounded by sharp knives, hanging pans and burners that hiss explosive gas. What next?"

"First rule, the iron chef never snaps under pressure, no matter the occasion. Stay with me now." She geared down her playful voice to business. "Alright, the fish, is it thawed?"

"Kinda."

"Nuke it for 30 seconds."

Ding!

"Done."

Jillian's in-control voice chased away the hopelessness, and soon, I found my skillet groove. "So, I've got the pan buttered, which has started to smoke."

"Time to sauté the baby spinach leaves before the head of Oz leers up again. Also, what's that high-pitched noise, I'm hearing? Is that the—"

"Smoke detector? Uh, yeah. Hold on."

I held the phone with one hand, doused the flame and waved wildly at the smoke.

"You're hopeless, C-Boy. Silence the shrill beast! I'll be here painting. Painting stars and waiting." She began to hum.

I parked Jillian in my pocket but she wasn't the only one concerned. A slightly slurred inquiry snapped from the sunroom. "Colby, I recall telling you *not* to burn the house down!"

"No worries, Aunt Demi. I'm pre-smoking the fish." I continued to wave. "Everything. Is. Going. To. Plan!" I ripped the heart out of the smoke detector and opened a window. Nine-volt pocketed, peace returned.

Demi nosed in. "Colby, I thought you knew what you were doing."

"I did. I do. Just an over sensitive smoke detector is all. How's your drink?"

"Slid down fast," Demi said.

"Slide 'er my way. Another round?"

Demi held up two gapped fingers "A tiny bit more."

The once moody tigress was tranquilized, almost too compliant now. She raised her restocked glass. "You're alright, you know that? I don't care what they say."

"Who says what?" I asked.

"No one says shit." Drink in hand, she floated back to the porch.

A sort of calm took over me as I caught a culinary wave. *Was this actually working?* But high hopes came crashing down when a zen-killing scream erupted from the sunroom. *What the?* I hurried to Demi. "What's wrong?"

She didn't say anything, only pointed toward the field as she gulped air. I got her horror. Bubbles pranced by the louvered windows happy as always. But from the Dalmatian's mouth dangled the body of Billy the Kid! My cat flopped about in a pathetic, dead limp.

Demi's moans and slow words accelerated to shrill. "Colby, find me a gun or shovel to kill that dog. Now!"

My indifferent sigh must have baffled her. "Relax, Aunt Demi, I got this."

Outside, I eased toward Bubbles with B.K. still hanging lifeless in her jaws.

Through the open louvers, Commander Whitehead weighed in with his two cents, "Naughty dog! Awwwk!"

I crept closer. "Eaaasy, girl. You heard Aunt Demi. Be a good girl and drop the cat."

After a teasing delay, Bubbles complied. She coughed up BK who fell to the ground slick with dog saliva, but on all fours and unharmed as always. Bubbles wisely bounded off into the woods.

Billy the Kid offered no thanks for my rescue. He turned his back and began a furious post-trauma tongue bath. B.K. then pranced off in the very direction of the jaws that had just clenched around his paper-thin skull. "Another life down, fool," I shouted his way. Since B.K. was a cat, safe to say if he had a middle finger it would have been raised at me for breaking up the fun.

Problem resolved, auntie willed reality away with her next swig as she stared out. "Great! When's dinner?"

I resumed my place at the stove and unleashed Jillian's muffled babble from my pocket. "Sorry, J-Girl, I had to break up the cat head circus act that's always such a hit with visitors."

"Refocus C-Boy, the plane is tilting down."

"And whose idea was this? Boiled hotdogs would have worked just fine."

Jillian pushed on. "Ready? Okay. Spinach leaves in pan, add jar of salsa, let it all stew."

Finally, I got on a roll. As the sauce cooked, I applied honey and breadcrumbs to the fish, smothered everything with the sauce and slid it into the preheated oven. I added potatoes to an already boiling pot of water, set the timer to twenty minutes then, prayed for deliverance. My forearm swept the sweat off my brow. Operation Impress was back on.

The timer chirped. "Okay, J-Girl, the fish mess is bubbling furiously . . . Potatoes feel soft. I just sprinkled on the feta and poured a mess of whiskey over everything as requested."

"Whiskey? I said white wine. Also, next time, the shit goes in *before* you cook stuff."

"There is no next time," I said.

"Whatever, C-Boy. Sprinkle on more feta. Cheese covers all sins," Jillian said. "Then, warm the bread and set the table."

"Done. Show time. I'm sending you a picture."

"Believe me, I already have one. Bon appetite," she said.

"You're the best, J-Girl."

"No, you are. Now serve this experiment and wow that woman. Then tell her to git. I have my own plans for El Relaxo." She growled like a lioness.

The moment of truth arrived. Demi wobbled to the table, swishing around the little whiskey that remained in her glass.

"What *is* this?" she said.

"It doesn't have a name."

"Then name it, damn it." She giggled to herself.

"Alright. Great White a la Florentine Zing, topped with sprinkles of feta."

"Life couldn't be betta," Demi murmured and spanked her glass down. "Whoa, I forgot this kitchen spins. Some water will you please, love?"

I did.

"Smells good, anyway. Does A.L. get this same treatment?"

"Oh yeah. This is one of his favorites after a long day at work."

With baited breath, I watched her cheeks balloon and blow on the first, dripping forkful. She committed, then jerked back. "Colby, what is this?"

The way she said it, I thought I was screwed.

"This is fantastic!"

Praise J-Girl and the chef gods! I tried a bite. Wow, this was some smoking bass.

"I expected nothing but total disaster from you, Colby. Only a while ago, I pictured us holed up in some Burger King booth lamenting about charred fish, or worse, charred house. But this? You deserve your own reality cooking show."

"Let's call it, *How I Burned My Way to the Top,* okay, Aunt Demi?"

The schmooze flowed. She was impressed with the house upgrades and now this. I hit the things she wanted to hear, sometimes making it up as I went. I strategically avoided all mention of anything motocross. Maybe my efforts had softened her: the clean place, the salsa bass and the rounds of drinks. Demi relaxed and shared family stories, some I hadn't heard.

She finished her last bite with a deep sigh. "Your mother should call more often, I guess. She still worries about you. I'll touch base with her tonight; see what we can work out. Either way, when the sun comes up, it's back to the salt mines with you. Understand?"

Back in my room, nose in chemistry book, my focus was short as a mayfly's so my phone's ring was a welcome diversion—especially discovering the voice belonged to Mark Beck. Apparently Mark was a decent guy, too. He had called to check on A.L.'s progress. His recall about A.L.'s race touched me the most. He called A.L.'s last ride, "One for the ages," one he'd never forget, at least the part before the crash. He told me to keep in touch. I thanked him and promised I would.

Sleep came a little better that night.

CHAPTER 10--SCHOOL AND NEWS

At the Jefferson High entrance, the human flood of hump-backed students scurried madly to beat the bell. Usually, I'd be there, too, another blowhole in the pod, but I still hadn't shaken off A.L. concerns. Only Demi's insistence had forced my hand. So there I sat, slumped in the front seat of my truck, waiting for conviction to budge me.

The sight of Jillian slugging against the flow to comb the parking lot doused the urge to slam the truck in reverse. A half-grin found me. The crowd thinned and Jillian gave up and slowly turned to bring up the rear. I unclipped my seatbelt, grabbed my pack and from a dead run yelped, "Where do you think you're going?" She spun and her face burst to life.

"You dragged your ass out of bed."

The tardy bell couldn't kill our embrace and kiss. We might still be there if Matulis, Jefferson High's designated goat herder, hadn't appeared and doused our fire. We scooped up our late passes and headed our separate ways.

Homeroom. Morning announcements from the TV blared while the early hour left most students looking shell-shocked. I dropped my late pass on the teacher's desk, but he was far too absorbed in his pre-calculus master plan to even notice me. Still, I respected Mr. Benson's dry nuances. While many teachers had pictures of their beaming spouses and kids on their desks, Benson had an antique photograph of a confederate general that glared back at you. If Mr. Benson's goatee, slicked back hair, and intense stare made him look like a dead ringer for the man in the photo, that's because he spent his summers taking part in Civil War reenactments, and for one role only: that of General George Pickett.

Sometimes if we worked hard, Benson would break from his mad math pace and slip into his Pickett character. The red, scrawled math symbols on the whiteboard would serve as the battlefield backdrop. Dramatic tales would follow, stories of glory and hardship that often concluded with Pickett's most famous quote, ominous words relayed to General Lee after the infamous butt kicking at Gettysburg. *General Lee, I have no division,* Benson would sadly conclude. A few excruciating seconds of silence would follow, during which you'd best not laugh, never mind whimper some dumb quip like, *General Benson, I can't DO math division.* The wise ass who mouthed that is rumored to be buried under the flagpole. After a time, the real Benson would pop back as if some puppeteer had yanked his strings. Boom, we'd be returned to our regularly scheduled math program and everybody could exhale once more.

I slinked to my seat and unpacked my stuff for pre-calc. I was in no mood for socializing. Despite this, a few whispered inquiries about A.L. popped up around me. Obviously, word had gotten out. All I could manage was a shrug to questions or a tight-lipped nod of thanks to well-wishers.

I fell into the final seconds of J-High's mostly drone-bomb Morning Show that blared from the board. Dana Raleigh, destined to become the next morning show time talking head, was winding up her usual peppy spiel.

My only physical contact with her had been of a violent nature. A horrible collision in the hall between classes the previous year had left both of us splayed and nearly concussed. I remember, Dana sat stunned for a second, long, tight-jeaned legs practically spanning half the width of the hall. Once revived, a scolding stare bored into me from the mussed blond head. What was her problem? I wasn't the mad fool who had careened down the hall at the speed of an ICBM—something she always did and still does between classes. After rendezvous by collision, I helped her up but she jerked away and ran off fast as she had struck me.

Now from my pre-calc seat I thought Raleigh was not unlike A.L.'s beautiful, handcrafted fly-fishing lures that seduced river bass. I was fascinated at the way she leaned in like she held a secret only for my ears. But no, I'd never trade my Jillian for some smooth-talking, blond rocket. Still, every morning at this time, her black magic leaped from the box on the wall. At some past occasion I had doodled *Untouchable* in my notebook. Maybe that's because some things in life were best left appreciated from the other side of the glass.

Untouchable wrapped up with, "And don't forget, guys, audition scripts for our upcoming drama production are now available from Mrs. Dejon. Tryouts are soon." She leaned in with Marylyn Monroe allure and her words slowed to a seductive drip. "I know *I'll* be there. Join me."

A kid from behind me whispered, "Almost drives a dude to take up acting lessons, huh Weston?"

Once concluded, Raleigh said, "Until tomorrow, guys. Work hard and—"

Untouchable's beaming face imploded with Benson's blasphemous touch of the off button. His voice rang loud. "As she says, we must work hard!" Benson's segue coupled with a raised pen foretold that math-battle was imminent. "It is Wednesday and your week can yet be saved, people. Weigh into your work, class. I implore you!"

His voice dipped to its typical math-instructional drone as he moved to the whiteboard. His red tip began to spill formulae like cavalry blood for us to copy. For some, pre-calc *was* like war. I was a bit of a misfit in that class. If you saw all the scrubbed faces you'd understand, but for some reason algorithms flowed easy as small talk from me. Though he didn't slip into his Pickett this day, I could count on Benson's usual blistering tempo and occasional dry joke to make the time fly by. He finished and tested us with a problem to try. Hands locked behind him, Benson began stalking the classroom. He paused by my desk.

"I sent some work home with your . . . friend. Did you get it?"

"Oh yeah, thanks." I took out the finished homework and laid it on my desk. He leaned in for a check. Traces of cigar wafted off him, as always.

"Let's. Just. See. All aces, Weston, very nice." Benson moved on.

The bell chimed and scattered us different ways into the usual hallway scramble.

The *Oh my god's*, loud voices, and the rattle of metal lockers snapping open and slamming shut grated on me worse than usual. After three periods, it was time for lunch. Jillian and Beach were at our table laughing about something with the rest of the gang. My appearance snuffed out the happy faces.

"Hey, don't stop smiling on my shitty behalf. What up, guys?"

With a tilt of Beach's head, the dude in the spot next to Jillian made room for me. She pulled me in with a one-armed hug. "There's my boy. Welcome back to the nightmare. How goes the home stand?" I had missed her sweet scent and the feeling of her mane brushing against me.

"The home stand is looking a bit more promising with Auntie strapped to a Jack Daniels intravenous drip."

"What's up with A.L.?" Beach said.

"Not a clue yet, dude."

Beach beamed above his lowered burger. "Any day now, A.L.'ll be back, and chowin' down ice cream and telling tales to the nurses."

"No doubt." While I appreciated the concern, I was anxious to ditch the subject. "So what's up with you guys?"

After drifting off to the usual JHS gossip, Jillian brought up motocross.

"So C-Boy, getting any riding in?"

"Riding? What's that? No, I haven't, really. It's been mad crazy."

"It's cool, just wondered." But her smirk admonished me. "How about I drag my hot wheels over there and tune your ass up?" Jillian's eyes squinted as her frisky lips colored her once clear straw, chocolate.

Beach moped. "How come I never get threats like that from the girls?"

"Careful what you ask for, Beach," I said. "Alright J-Girl. That's a go, soon as Auntie clears out."

As always, the bell chopped our talk and forced us separate ways.

I floated in a bubble the rest of the day, never quite plugged in. Last period finally arrived. English. Mrs. Dejon, old enough to have owned a pet triceratops, had also taught my dad! On a day I would have preferred silent reading she assigned read aloud parts for Shakespeare's, *As You Like It*.

Well, I didn't, and nothing felt funny. I mindlessly followed along in the thick anthology, praying I wouldn't get picked on. Spared at first, Mrs. Dejon eventually convinced me to read the part of Touchstone. I clowned enough to actually get a few laughs, though I didn't feel any funnier. The dismissal bell launched me from my seat. I was anxious to check in with the hospital but I wasn't quick enough to the classroom door.

"Oh, Colby. A word please," Dejon said.

What did she want? Except with her drama club minions, Dejon wasn't usually the social type. Figured something owed must be overdue.

"Yes, Mrs. Dejon?" My smile hurt.

"First of all, I heard about your dad and wanted to tell you how sorry I am. I remember him as a student. Not a great writer but always polite in class."

"Thanks, Mrs. Dejon. He'd love hearing that, I'm sure."

"I'm praying he returns back healthy and soon."

"Appreciate that, Mrs. Dejon." I began backstroking to the door. She reeled me back.

"Colby? This may be bad timing, but I wanted to say how very impressed I was with your reading of Touchstone today."

My eyes darted side to side. *Why was she telling me this?* "Oh, that. I was just clowning around, Mrs. Dejon."

"Touchstone *is* a clown, Colby. A jester."

"I know. I was kidding."

Mrs. Dejon nudged me. "You got me there, young man—but you played him well."

"Blind pig finds an acorn now and then, huh, Mrs. Dejon?"

"Never sell yourself short, Colby. Listen, there are some great male parts in our upcoming play."

"You must be thrilled. Sorry, what?"

Dejon closed the space and whispered like she held government secrets. "In fact, I think I have just the character in mind. Not a big role, mind you, but perfect for you."

Run! "I, uh, don't know what to say, ma'am."

"I need men, Colby. I always need men."

"Well, I did play a rabbit in fourth grade. Turned out I should've stayed in the hole."

She chuckled. "Oh, it couldn't have been *that* bad."

"Very bad. My mother sobbed at the end. Not at the ending, but me."

She waddled over to her desk like she hadn't heard a word I had said and returned with a small book. She forced it into my palm. "Well I know different. Here, take a script. You don't have to commit right now, but auditions are coming up. Read it. The Marty character will be perfect for you. Nothing too involved. Just consider it," she said. I stayed polite, just as I was raised, and promised I would read it and think it over.

The next two days of school sort of rolled over me like fog. Last period Friday was finally over. The quick trot down to ground level still echoed in the stairwell as I smacked the door bar to freedom. It was a sunny, warm spring day. Lime green leaves fluttered and my feet grew hyper. Before I could slap the truck into drive, my phone lit up. A quick glance, then I put it to my ear. "Hi, Doctor Naylor. What's up?"

"Hi, Colby. Do you have a second?"

"Uh, sure."

"I have news," he said.

A pit found my stomach.

CHAPTER 11—DEMI'S RETREAT

"Yes!" I punched the truck's roof with a balled fist a little too hard. The pain didn't come close to stealing my joy. A.L. was still in a coma but he was stabilized and the Marionville doctors had agreed to my request. I drummed the steering wheel as tunes blessed the spring air through the open window. Questions still hung, but I knew this: A.L. was coming home. I pulled in our driveway, grabbed my book bag and slapped the trunk of Demi's Caddy as I strolled by. *See ya!*

"Colby!" *Hello, Commander.* I dropped my keys in the tray. "Hellooo, Aunt Demi!"

Demi was bent over a legal pad on the kitchen table, writing furiously. "You steal that yellow pad from Uncle Peter's office?"

No response.

"Hope that isn't my to-do list." I chuckled.

My attention was quickly steered to a stapled brown bag that smelled an awful lot like Chinese. Instead of immediately begging, I opened the fridge and in long, thirsty gulps, began guzzling milk.

Demi went on, writing. "You better not be drinking milk straight from the carton."

I paused. "No, ma'am. That would be uncivilized." I looked over her shoulder. "So, what are you writing?"

"Reminders for you. You seem awfully chipper. Nothing spells red flag faster than a boisterous teen. Are you high?" She spun around. "Let me see those eyes."

I made a droopy face. "Need a urine sample, too? I'm not high. I just got off the phone with Dr. Naylor."

"Really?" she spoke to the pad. "Good news?"

"Well, yeah. A.L.'s on his way back to Darin."

She turned and peered over her candy cane colored reading frames. "What?" She found a smile. "That's great news. When?"

"Soon, maybe tomorrow, if all goes to plan. He'll still be in a coma when he shows, but they'll pop him out of that soon. After that, we should be good to motor."

Her magnified blue eyes rolled to one side. "Pop him out? Good to Motor? I've got to check with the doctors about all this." Demi released a heavy sigh. "Doctor say how long he'll be laid up there?"

"Don't know, but my money says not long."

"Your money don't pay the bills. Let's pray for the man but not get too optimistic."

"God forbid I swish an ankle in a puddle of hope. This is about as good I've felt in a decade."

"Well, good. Listen. I've also had something come up."

"Huh?"

"Mandy's come down with some bug." Mandy, twelve, was her youngest daughter.

"Bug? Call the Orkin Man."

"*Listen* for once. She should be good in a couple of days, but Peter can't take any time off from the firm. It's watch over Mandy or watch over my sister's kid."

"Go, Aunt Demi, go, no doubt. You have to take care of your own and I'm fine here until the old man swings home."

"But I did promise your mother I'd stay," she said.

I whispered, "Aunt Demi, c'mon, I won't tattle, if you don't."

"Stop batting those mischievous eyes. They give you away," she said. Her eyes bored into me. "Best not turn this place into some party zone with your friends. You made the place look nice. Try keeping it like that for a change."

"Your word is my command."

"Better be. Break the rules and it's game over. I *will* check in, now and then."

"Fine. I just hope Mandy's feeling better soon."

"Me, too. Now sit. We have business, you and I." She amassed a two-page, *Things to Do* list!

"Whoa! That's a lot to cover. Oops, you left out cleaning the gutters."

"I'll add it. Now listen." She held up three envelopes from the growing stack of mail. "These have that overdue bill look." She ripped one open. "Yep. Do you use electricity?"

"Now and then," I said.

She breathed a heavy sigh. "Got a checkbook floating around here by chance?"

"Somewhere, but I think A.L. pays most of his stuff online."

I led Demi to my dad's disheveled office and brought his desktop to life.

"Don't like digging through his stuff without his permission," I said.

"No way around it, Colby. The world keeps spinning even when one's dead to it."

"Blunt, Aunt Demi."

"Your dad would understand. Besides, time's not long off when you'll be paying your own electric bills."

"Another reason to get off the grid." Passwords were needed and I found them in minutes in a small notebook within arm's reach. We cued up A.L.'s bank's site and I typed in the code.

"Demi, we're in!"

"Hey, your father and I share the same bank . . . and what's this? Wow, your daddy's got more money in his savings than I do. Not bad for a lumber guy. Think he's dealing on the side?"

"That and he mentioned something about investments, I think. Maybe his folks left him something."

"However it sprouted, a long layup will eat into it."

"Appreciate the positive spin. Don't be talking this up, okay, Aunt Demi?"

"I'd never do that, Colby," she said.

Right.

A push of a button and in less time than it took to mimic a sucking sound, three bills were paid. Knowing we had some financial cushion eased one's worries. Business concluded, soon we were slurping pork lo mien, and devouring sweet General Tso. Afterwards, Demi felt compelled to repeat her rules. I went with it. Everything was good: Demi was packing and A.L. was coming back to Darin.

Bag in one hand, the other on the door handle, she spouted reminders from her To-Do list a final time. I was all head nods, smiles and yeah, yeah, yeahs, until, "Let's see, no visitors, never mind full-blown parties."

"But Aunt Demi, I'm marooned with a bunch of pyscho pets out here. What's wrong with having a friend or two over?"

"Maybe nothing, maybe a lot. When A.L. returns, let him monitor the hell raising. Until that time, N. O. Like I said, plan on a couple of surprise swing-by's. Good-bye."

I pumped a fist as I watched the Cadillac rocket in reverse. I had regained rule of El Relaxo and some rules were meant to be broke.

CHAPTER 12—BACK IN THE SADDLE

Demi gone, I wandered to the porch and collapsed on the swing. I stared out. With little to do I picked up my phone. Who did I call? Not Jillian, but Mom.

We yakked for a record hour. I gave her an update on A.L. and did my best to catch her up on other stuff. When she asked how things were going with Demi, I said great, but I didn't mention she had split. It was good to hear Mom's unrestrained laughter as she recapped some movie she'd seen. It harkened back to lighter times at Spanks Diner after a game, or something. Mom finished the call with a plea for a visit. I'd think about it.

Bubbles craved attention and I ran my nails through her spotted coat. "Bubbly, I should be hooting at the ceiling with all this newfound freedom, but I'm a lonely fool, not knowing what to do. Guess I should get some laps in." My mind turned to the upcoming motocross event at Jack's in a week. For the first time ever, I felt indifferent to it.

I lifted off the rocker and headed for the garage with B.K. and Bubbles in tow. I snapped the chinstrap of my helmet snug and flung a leg over Silver. I kind of broke the rules by not putting on my full protective racing gear. My foot came down hard on the starter. Silver puttered and died, a telltale sign too much time had passed. On the third try she came to life. Still in neutral, I gunned the throttle and the engine responded in kind. Noise and a plume of blue gray smoke scattered Bubbles and B.K. I looked out to our hill, popped the clutch and launched into the sunshine towards the first hill on our course. As I neared, it felt like the hill had grown since the last time I scaled it. Seconds into the climb panic set in, sudden and unexpected. I blamed the layoff and urged myself to push through this clinging doubt, hoping it would lift. I survived a scaled-down jump and continued through the motions but everything felt tight and out of synch.

Doubt is a killer. To be competitive, you need the perfect trifecta of speed, skill and confidence. Without the last, the first two suffer. Pissed, I stopped babying myself and pushed Silver harder, all caution to the wind. But not all problems are cured by slapping on a brave face. I lost control of Silver and struck the earth like a sack of bolts. Stars. I lay splayed out and prone, staring into the deep blue. Short labored breaths were reactions to the sharp pain of skinned arms and legs, now bleeding. Why had I rode with nothing more than a freaking helmet, alone on the property, no phone, miles from town; the nearest person a reclusive neighbor?

The only relief came in the form of Bubbles, if a dog's rough tongue can be a substitute for first aid. The good news, I was conscious and could move my extremities even through twinges of pain. I shooed Bubbles away and managed to sit up. I knew I had gotten off cheap from this one. I hobbled to the still-idling cycle and managed to right it with one good arm. I killed the engine and slowly pushed the bike to the garage.

Inside the house, I pulled out one of the many ice packs we kept in the freezer, gulped a couple of Tylenol and flopped on the couch. A sudden text lifted me north of my disgust. It was Beach inviting me over. I thought about it.

\>Laying low for a bit. Back 2 u soon.

The headache and nausea that followed sprung paranoia. Was it the fall or anxiety? I reviewed concussion protocol on my phone and decided that if I began to see hordes of iguanas or gremlins crawling up the wall, I'd call for the cavalry. This boy wasn't ready to swap out calc for basket weaving. I put a flex ice pack on my head.

Now I hungered for Jillian's reassuring voice. Two minutes into the call she sniffed a rat. She sensed something was up, maybe it was my uncommitted delivery. Told her it was nothing, just tired. She said she was editing a film with a friend, but she promised to swing by soon as she was finished. Her promise alone was therapy.

After the call, I drifted off until Bubbles roused me. Feeding time. I felt disoriented. Darkness had stolen the day and I snapped on some lights and fed Bubbles and B.K. I was still sore and not particularly hungry, but the nausea was gone and my head no longer complained as much. Two good signs, at least.

Schoolwork begged but the script Dejon gave me tumbled from the backpack first. I picked up *Lost Gifts* and found my part in the beginning of Act II. Marty, a character from the Middle Ages came off like a babbling village idiot, and I couldn't help thinking if this was how Dejon regarded me. With no one around to judge, I ran a few lines aloud. Stiff at first, I eased and began to get playful with it. When done, I tapped the script on my palm and thought maybe. But as quickly, I talked myself out of it. I didn't know anyone who was doing the play, and I had no idea what A.L. would say or even what life would be like when he returned. Better pass this time.

It was Friday night. El Relaxo stood dead quiet and everyone I knew had other plans—even Jillian ran long and opted out. Feeling like King Geek, I pulled out my pre-calc homework. It was about the only thing that came easy these days. The problems kept my mind off A.L. for a while at least.

CHAPTER 13—DREAM COME TRUE

Silent, dark stadium slowly fills with light. Packed seats. An explosion of cheers and hard rock. From an absurdly powerful machine, larger than anything I've ever straddled, I let the love soak in. Beyond the short straightaway lies a ramp with an extreme skyward arch. The ascent, ludicrous, this side of vertical, but there's no backing out. Spotlights bathe me. The full throat of a large crowd erupts after my name is announced. Ahead, black and white images highlight my best rides as they scroll up the ramp. Cheers evolve to unison chants of "Col-by, Col-by!" Behind me a regimental line of cyclists gun their throttles as they await their turn.

The sky explodes with fireworks. A siren blasts. Chaos, but my focus is locked in. Throttle forward; clutch released, I roar off on my back wheel at incomprehensible speed. I roll over the projected clips of people and races going faster and faster until I equal their speed. The slope becomes steeper. The RPM needle lowers; images race ahead, abandon me. But A.L. appears and lingers with some kind of advice until that's swapped for a look of distress. What, A.L.? He shouts something, but I can't make it out. He dissolves in a blur, as do the cheers from the crowd. Except for a droning, whistling wind, all sound drops away. The arch of the track bends upward at a greater angle until even the bike's immense engine can't propel me. I tumble back towards the cold stares of cyclists waiting for their shot. Blackness. A faint sound pulses repeatedly; the next rider ready to prove himself and propelled by the crowd, oblivious his destiny can only fail.

Shit! I snapped upright from the couch and looked around. I thought I could still hear the idling as if I was stuck in the dream. My phone pulsed a slow dance on the glass table. I swiftly silenced the TV and grabbed the text. Jillian at her cryptic best.

>Good A.M. C-Boy. Come out, come out, wherever you are.

>?

Nothing followed. *A tease for me to solve?* Still half stuck in a messed-up dream, I ran my fingers through my morning mop. I flipped away the blanket and snapped to my feet. My *Good Morning* came in the form of a sharp pain from my ankle, a holdover from yesterday's spill. I limped to the front door and cranked it open. Through shielded, decaffeinated eyes, I spotted Jillian in full racing attire, seated on Blue at the end of our driveway, gunning the engine with our newspaper tucked underneath one arm. After my two-finger whistle, Jillian shattered all country serenity, exploding into donuts, then a sixty-foot wheelie straight for me! Just when I considered leaping for survival, Jillian's knobby tires skidded within inches of the family jewels. *Damn, she was good.*

She removed her helmet. Braided hair, full protective racing suit, the serious mouth—all business.

"Special delivery," she said and spanked my hand with the morning paper. Seeing as I wasn't ready for anything, she rolled her eyes, killed the engine and swung a leg over.

"Someone just fell out of the sack," she snickered.

"Some people do their best stuff late at night."

"Here, all along, I thought your best stuff was on a track."

"Don't judge me, J-Girl. I'm still half-parked in the worst nightmare ever."

"Hate those. Any need for speed?"

Between the nightmare and my newly acquired limp, I was hardly up for a ride. But I once heard boyfriends that bored Cleopatra soon lay on cold slabs. I agreed to a couple of loops in back, probably the best way to shake off my nightmare.

I went to the bathroom, madly splashed water on my face and took the guest's toothbrush to a foul morning-mouth. Jillian bombarded me upon my exit. "Ready? I'm antsy," she said.

"Can I have a couple of minutes to reenter life, J-Girl?" I started the coffee pot.

She shrugged. "Fine, but I don't have all day. The 'rents don't even know I'm here."

A thought triggered. "Speaking of which, J-Girl, wheel Blue inside the garage and out of sight, will you? Always the slim chance Auntie might barge by in for a check."

"This girl's convinced. Be right back."

In a few seconds, Jillian reentered through the garage into the kitchen and gazed with an impressed nod. "Place looks great, man. Obviously you were threatened?"

"Obviously." Coffee machine prepped, I turned it on. "Forced labor. Actually, I kind of like it this way, not that I'd ever admit it to semi-Demi."

The coffee gurgled and dripped. Playful hands surprised me from behind. I turned and was rewarded with a kiss. *Why didn't every day start like this?* Her eyes eventually glided over the legal pad lying on the kitchen table.

"Ah! Demi's famous Declaration of Demands?" Jillian gave it a peek. "You poor, domesticated animal . . . wait, toilets, dude? You think she does this shit?"

"Hell no. Her maid from Uzbekistan covers all that."

Jillian opened her hands and let the pad hit the floor. "Have the maid find the right place for this, will you, darling?" But the uppity New England version of Jillian didn't last long. She got all moto. "Of course you know the *real* reason I swung by, C-Boy."

I shrugged.

"We've got a race coming up at the home track. Don't want to look bad there." Suddenly Jillian's eyes dipped to my wounded elbow. "Ouch. You take a spill out there?"

"Yesterday . . . Comes with the territory."

"I thought you looked a bit gimpy. Didn't wear your full gear, did you?"

"Save it. I already beat myself up."

"Yeah, I can see that, literally, silly boy. You good to go or what?"

"Couple a nicks, scratches, that's all."

As we walked out, her arm grabbed me around the neck and pulled me in. "Take it easy out there. I need you in one piece."

"Got it, Mom."

Jillian launched out of the garage like she was gunning for a holeshot prize. I followed, but the damn jitters still dogged me and were hard to shake. Everything felt as stilted as the day before, only this time I had motivation: my girlfriend easily caught up and passed my punchless ride. Her playful yelp lightened my mood, enough for me toss the caution behind and open up Silver some.

I roared up our tallest hill, grabbed good air and landed perfectly. The playfulness and moves rebounded, short of top form, but enough to find the fun again. Content with small gains, after a few rounds I called practice and motioned towards the garage. Jillian followed.

Once she quieted Blue, the country stillness returned. She lifted her helmet off. "Everything alright?"

"Totally," I said."

"Was that charity you were giving me in the beginning, or what?"

"Trying to be a gentlemen, you know."

Jillian smirked. "Wonder what A.L. would say to that answer?"

Felt like a shot over my bow.

"You also kinda kept things a little short, C-Boy. Yesterday's scrape still bugging you?"

"Not quite feeling it, that's all, whatever." I shelved my helmet.

With both our bottoms on the cool cement floor, we stripped off our riding gear. Jillian emerged in an orange blouse and frayed denim cut-offs. It was not long into spring, but already her sinewy legs were the color of midsummer toast. Wish I could say the same. She parked her helmet on her seat and draped her suit over her bike. Then she walked up to the large photo print of the flying dad and son duo. My arms found her middle and she accepted them with her hands and exhaled approval.

"My world makes a lot more sense when you're in it, Jillian Carter."

"Aw, C-Boy." Her gaze returned to the print. "I get why you're feeling cold out there. You just need time. You'll be ready when you need it."

"Plan on it."

Hand in hand we went inside. I poured two glasses of iced tea.

After a sip she cut the silence. "The mint really makes it," she said.

"Got a bush of the stuff growing outside. Did you know when it blossoms the flowers are a natural bug repellant?"

"Shut up," she said.

"Serious. I wipe it all over me when I go into the woods."

"Recently? I don't feel repelled."

"Doesn't work with big creatures like you, I guess. Let's get comfy."

Jillian followed me to the living room where I powered up A.L.'s stereo. "You might like this little mix I made just for you," I said.

"Nice." Jillian began to dance. A glance invited me to join in, so I did. "The place looks so clean, C-Boy. Come clean my room."

I danced along. "I'll clean your clock."

"Ooooo," she turned and danced off to check things out.

She floated away to the mantle and took down a magazine photo I had clipped and framed: two dirt bikes, riders unknown, clearing a dune in Baja.

"Don't suppose there's any chance the three of us can still head west and ride after school's out."

"Depends on A.L. and his recovery time, baby. It would be great if we could, but—"

"Sorry, not a good time to bring up vacation plans."

"It's cool." I walked up behind her and my hands glided down the arms. "He talked about it all the time," I said. "Someday we'll go. Promise."

The tunes helped fill the silent hole where a travel fantasy had been. Jillian returned the photo to its spot and faced me. She no longer flitted from thing to thing. Her eyes settled on mine, part caring, part determined. Something else unfulfilled lingered, and now there was no one around to stop it. My gut was ripe with anticipation as she tilted her head and took out her braids. She combed out her thick hair with her hands. "Better?"

"Beautiful."

I had forgotten the one intruder around that could nose in. Bubbles padded in. "She wants in on the fun," Jillian said.

"Yeah, well, I have a better idea." I lazily glided an open palm over the dog, but my eyes never left hers.

"Time for jealous doggie to take a long walk, you think?" Jillian said.

"Yeah, Bubbly, go blow off some steam with B.K."

Jillian let both out then boogied over to her iced tea and took another sip. Did that one-sided teasing grin to the floor suggest something?

I assumed the best and tossed all the couch cushions and pillows onto the floor. No protest came. Instead, "Wow. Look at this, C-Boy. You even vacuumed underneath the cushions? I was hoping to find some *popcorn,* at least."

"I can pop you up some," I said.

"It'll wait."

Excited, everything had to be right. One index finger held high, I hurried away from her mystified, semi-amused look. From the closet I extracted and lit a scented candle. A second need followed. I made a move towards the stairs.

"Now where are you going?" she said with a laugh.

"Right back!" I covered the entire stairs in like four strides. I unearthed the condom variety pack A.L. had tucked in my stocking last Christmas. It still bore the To/From label. *For a lucky day, Love Santa.* Great Santa, but which? I settled for *Ribbed Confidence.*

Back downstairs, as we made out, the room filled with music and a fitting scent of Pacific Breeze. Jillian, head in one hand, doing circles on my abs with the other, asked, "You think this is what the west really smells like?"

"That, and scorched earth. Gotta find out for ourselves."

"Until then, I've got another destination in mind." She whispered in my ear, "Roll on your belly."

Jillian had amazingly strong hands that ran down my back. She kissed my neck and all life's worries swapped out for high expectations. She closed her eyes and allowed me to undo her blouse, one slow button at a time. Once removed my hand explored every bit of her airbrushed skin. She responded with kisses and sighs of pleasure.

With anticipation, I attempted to unhook her bra. I pinched its clasp and prayed for one outcome: Jillian wouldn't resist. That happened, but I should have prayed for a second outcome—that her bra would actually open. Something was horribly wrong with it or me. It looked simple but was like entering Fort Knox after hours. Did it come with keys? It seemed jammed or something. Whichever way I tugged, wiggled, or bunched those latches, nothing gave!

Jillian remained still, either amazingly patient or silently amused. And she offered no suggestions or help. This was my marlin to bring in, alone. Thoughts turned to a couple hot shots on the football team, self-proclaimed bra masters who boasted they could strip a date with one hand as they diverted them with grapes in the other. I was tempted to dial one up for a quick how-to.

I kept at it and kept at it, until . . . POP! Miracle! The gates of resistance burst open! But the miracle being I tugged her bra so hard I shredded the latch! I dreaded the idea of having to draw from A.L.'s holeshot wad to pay Victoria's Secret a visit. But right now, I was in, and the whole snafu had gone unnoticed by Jillian. I stayed cool and tossed the thing aside without killing the mood. She flipped over, topless, totally cool facing me.

My inner factory turned to extreme production mode. She didn't mind that I drank in the locks of curly hair that tumbled over her full breasts or the fact I struggled as I shed my tight jeans in record time. Things heated up. Lips and tongues danced while hands pioneered into delicious places, once only dreamed. Finally, with little fear of interruption, Jillian found her boldness as we covered new ground in record time. I wanted to slow down, make it last but this ride came with no brakes. I loved her as much as I longed for her body. We cruised through R-rated territory like seasoned vets . . . until Commander's shriek sounded an alarm.

Jillian broke through a fog of ecstasy, "What's up with the bird?"

"No worries, baby." I kissed her again. "Commander's probably teasing his own love bird out there."

Jillian sat up. "Sure? That sounded more like a panic attack than love call."

"Too funny, J-Girl." I joked but I also knew Commander's early warning system was mostly dead accurate. "Okay, to put you at ease, I'll take a little look-see outside, juuust in case."

Clothed in nothing more than boxers, I scuttled on all fours towards the window.

"Naughty boy, naughty boy," the African Gray scolded.

"Commander! You best be fooling!" I hissed at the bird before giving Jillian a reassuring nod back. This I did know: whatever, whoever was out there, I wanted to kill right then.

Propped up on palms, Jillian weighed in, "Better not be my daddy looking for me, C-Boy."

"Let's. Just. See." One eye, an inch above the windowsill, launched terror. "Incoming red Cadillac! Hide, Jillian!"

No need to utter Demi's name, Jillian knew and flew into a spastic scramble. "Shit!"

The motor stopped and a door opened. We gathered our stuff, mad quick. I barked at Jillian to disappear, but she froze instead. At the edge of teary, she said, "I don't see my bra, Colby!"

"Don't worry about your damn bra. It's busted anyway," I said.

Clutching her clothes, her face turned inquisitive. "What happened to my bra?"

"Just take the rest of you and your stuff upstairs and hide," I whisper-shouted.

Jillian ran in place like a toddler in a tantrum, which got neither of us anywhere.

The urgent three raps at the door scattered her and annihilated any last lingering traces of our love mood.

CHAPTER 14—DUSTY BUNNIES

The next three raps were even more aggressive than before. Any lesser man would have broken down right then, but I slapped on a neutral face to mask my RAGE!

"Aunt Demi! What a surprise, and so quick!" I smiled.

Phone to ear, she surveyed me up and down with a pudgy frown. Demi looked off, turned and giggled. "Oh, I shouldn't be too long, Sandy. I decided to swing by my nephew's place for something. He's standing before me, right now . . . with only his boxers on . . . Say again? You naughty girl." A cackle. "See you soon."

All gaiety dropped with Demi's call.

"Hey, Demi. What's up?"

"Why are you blocking the door? Let me in, Colby."

I stalled her. "When you say *in*, do you mean—"

"I'm in a rush, damn it!" Her elbow plowed me aside.

"Oh, that kind of in," I said.

After a couple of steps and a quick perusal her hands found her hips and she glared back at me. Panic! That bit of mangled bra sticking out from the cushion was felony evidence. My throat grew so thick I thought I had swallowed my tongue. *Had she seen it?* Before Demi could muster her next complaint, she was nearly knocked down by Bubble's hard charge through the front door. Worse, Bubbles did not dive for her usual basement refuge, but galloped straight upstairs!

Demi pointed at her and cried out, "Colby, I'm going to kill that dog!"

Dog? I was more worried about her spotting the strewn bra without a woman attached. I tried to keep the mood light. "Oh, Aunt Demi, you love Bubbles. So what's up? You were away, for what, almost a whole day? Did Uncle Pete throw you out?"

"I told you before; I don't have the time for your playful nonsense, Colby. Also, why are you walking around in your boxers?"

"I would have rented a tux had I known you were coming. Chill. Dudes walk around their pads like this. But alright, I'll slip on my jeans for you." I retrieved my jeans and hopped into them as I endured her stare. "There. So, what *does* bring you back?"

She ignored that. "Look at this place. Was there a fight? This after one day, Colby?"

I tried to block her sightline while staying cool. "At least there're no engine parts. Look, I was just chilling on a Saturday morning, Aunt Demi. Made some coffee, threw around some cushions, put on some tunes and was studying a little."

"On a Saturday? Without books?"

"Okay, so I hadn't quite got to the book part."

"What were you going to study?" Demi said.

I stroked my chin. "I was studying some anatomy."

"Anatomy?" She stiffened.

"I meant biology."

"How could you study anything with that seductive, pounding music? Also, it seems kind of . . . dreamy? Rather odd for a teen boy, isn't it?"

"Guess I woke up in an odd place," I shrugged.

"You can say that again. Turn that shit down, pretty please," she said.

As I moved to lower the volume, a quick sideswipe of the cushion with my foot covered the incriminating evidence.

"Colby, did I leave a red bag?"

"Red bag?"

"My *gym* bag. I'm supposed to work out with a friend. It wasn't in the car. I think I left it here," Demi said.

A sudden, loud thud from upstairs swung both our chins toward the stairs. A bark followed.

Demi, the inquisitor, said, "What was that?" Distrusting eyes returned to me.

"Did you invite a little friend over . . . huh?"

"None that bark. Bubbles probably knocked something down and thought it began following her. Do you know any animal therapists?"

"Therapist? If it were me, I'd donate the useless hound to science."

"Yeah, well, back to your little problem." I pointed toward the porch. "I thought I saw your bag in there."

As soon as Demi headed off to search, I zipped around, threw the cushions on the couch, and crammed Jillian's wrecked bra underneath one. Not a second passed before Demi emerged from the porch, empty handed of course.

"No luck," she announced.

"Huh. Tell you what. I'll keep looking. If I find it, I'll call and run it straight out to you. Also, I'm expecting to hear more about A.L. any minute and was just getting ready to head over to—"

She didn't even acknowledge A.L. "Teen boys. You all couldn't find something if you tripped over it. Listen, I need that bag, now." Her tone lifted closer to pleasant when she noticed the cushions back in place. "My, you straightened up awfully fast in here. My influence, no doubt." Demi ripped off a short-lived cackle before she turned serious again and sniffed the air. "What's that smell? Like a scented candle or something?"

"Yeah. Pacific Mist."

"Are you trying to mask something? Colby, were you smoking a jay?"

"I wasn't smoking anything. I fried up another fish last night and wanted to kill the smell," I said.

"Something's fishy alright and I'm going to find out what, but right now I just want my bag." Suddenly she slapped her forehead. "What's wrong with me?"

"Well . . ." I began.

"I know *exactly* where it is."

My stomach flipped again. *Just don't let it be—*

"Upstairs, in A.L.'s room." Demi chuckled and began a heavy clopped ascent.

Upstairs was the last place I wanted Auntie. Who knows what lame spot Jillian may have chosen to hide in a rush? I pictured her facing the wall behind the door or something ridiculously transparent.

I rushed up to squeeze past Demi. "Relax, Aunt Demi, I'll get it."

But her beefy arm dropped like a gate and ground me to a halt. "Hmm," she said, "unusually eager to help. Do I detect a hint of panic from the young lion?"

I snipped, "Fine. Enjoy the hunt. I'll be down here, straightening and studying."

"Now you're getting the hang of this game, baby doll. I know *just* where it is."

I will always treasure Jillian's retelling of the next horrifying minutes as I rooted at the base of the stairs with pricked ears and an urge to vomit. Turns out Demi was not only headed for the same room, but the exact spot where Jillian had chosen to hide. She was under A.L.'s brass bed, topless, amid dust bunnies and ancient *Playboys*. But Jillian was most intrigued by the red sports bag that emitted a strong perfumed odor. Not at all what she would have suspected from A.L. Smug with a smile, she mused whether she should share this dubious discovery with me or not.

Things grew less cute when Bubbles showed up. The dog's curious, wet schnoz began exploring under the bed. Bubbles grew excited at the mere sight of Jillian and mistook this as a fun game of hide and seek. Bubbles barked, *You're it!* The same bark that had alerted Auntie Demi, downstairs.

Jillian whisper-shouted, "Quiet, Bubbles!"

It was too late for that. If the heavy clops from those heels told Jillian anything, it was that Super Storm Demi was on its way.

Dog, Demi, red bag. This wasn't A.L.'s, bag, it was Demi's! My dusty, half-nude girl thought, then had to think faster. Her only hope was to push the bag out just far enough so Demi wouldn't have to rummage under the bed. Jillian did this, but it was Bubbles who snatched the bag thinking it was a playful offering. Soon, the victorious dog joyfully swung it from side to side.

Demi's voice now painted the room the color of doom, "Drop that bag right now, stupid dog!" Breath held, Jillian listened through growls and panting as she witnessed six shuffling feet fighting for dominance and the prize! Demi hollered, "Give me the bag, now, damn animal! It's mine!"

A tussle ensued. Bubbles growled back. *No, it's mine. I found it. Let go!* At some point Demi must have tagged the dog with the pointed toe of her high heel or something. Bubbles yelped, spun fiercely, and nipped the leg of her assailant.

From the base of the stairs, I assumed Demi's deathly scream meant she had found my girlfriend and life as I once knew it would end over a stupid jock bag. Bubbles tore down the stairs and blurred out the front door.

Then I heard, "Colby! The damn dog bit me!"

I didn't answer because my breath was still held.

Demi emerged at the top of the stairs, furious and shaking her red bag at me. Then it occurred to me. She hadn't mentioned Jillian.

"All clear! It's gone, J-Girl," I yelled upstairs as Demi's Caddy peeled away in reverse.

A ragged, traumatized Jillian cautiously braved the descent downstairs and took my side, though now she wasn't even something I wanted to touch. Dust bunnies clung all over her hair and blouse, which she had buttoned up so hastily, one half-exposed boob popped out.

"I can't believe that woman or her timing, C-Boy," she said.

"*You* can't? Try living with it for three days."

Jillian sighed. "Another attempt at passion gone the way of the desert bandicoot."

"What? We'd have better luck robbing banks, J-Girl. Your dad, then this? Someday . . ."

"Oh, C-Boy," she blubbered to our antique mirror. "Look at me, I'm all dusty."

"Any interest in this?" I held up her mutilated bra.

She stared at the clasp. "Uh, not anymore. What happened to it?"

"I was rushed, and . . ."

"That will cost you a day of bra shopping at the mall, C-Boy."

"Uh, plan on us shopping for that online," I said.

"All I want now is a tub of hot water to soak in for seven hours."

I held up her bra like a dead animal pelt. "Want this?"

Rolled eyes. "Keep it as our memento of our failure," she said.

"I will, in a special place, like inside the box with my old Hot Wheel cars and other cool stuff," I grinned.

"I'm so freaking honored." Her smirk relaxed enough to kiss me. "Suppose I should start heading home to detox myself." She plucked off a huge clump of dust and let it drift to the floor.

"J-Girl," I said, "You can't ride home all covered in dust bunnies with a boob hanging out. Probably wouldn't be a big hit with the folks."

"Good call, C-Boy." Jillian retreated for the bathroom and emerged looking far less like a stricken refuge. She kissed me. "I'm off, C-Boy. Get your game back to razor sharp, and don't kill yourself trying."

Once suited up, Jillian swung a leg over Blue and kicked her machine to life. Something came to her before she popped the clutch. "Hey, I never told you. The other night, I had a dream. A.L. came home. He was happy and—"

I cut in, "Was he walking?"

A colored shield stared back for a while before her muffled voice said, "I believe he was, C-Boy. Yeah, he was."

After a few guns of the throttle she screamed off. An uneasy quiet replaced her.

The next Saturday I met up with Jillian at Jack's for an event. My practices had lagged but I went into the competition hoping I'd find the juice. Not so. From the start, both motos turned into a debacle of miscues and poor judgment from me. I finished the opening race in the middle of the pack but my morale took an even worse hit. This is how someone who had just qualified for the Southeast Regional shows off his stuff?

Hangdog, I walked past Jack, tuning out all inquiry about A.L. and peppy advice to boost my moral which was in the shitter. Jillian had taped it, stayed the cheerleader and offered to replay the footage at her place. "Erase it," I said. Head down, I pushed Silver to the truck, strapped it in and drove off, solo and embarrassed.

CHAPTER 15--ARRIVAL

Last bell. I bolted to the truck. The night before I had gotten the big news, A.L. had arrived back to Daren! His Marionville holeshot trophy lay next to me in the passenger seat. The ride over to the hospital wasn't long, but long enough for my brain to agonize over all the what-ifs, good and bad. His absence had felt much longer than the time he'd been gone. Would I find A.L. sitting up all pissy, raring to bolt like after his last accident, or still hooked up and trapped in Limbo Land?

My fingers, my knees, my feet, everything bounced while I waited outside Dr. Naylor's office. A nurse finally showed up only to inform me something had detained the doctor. She led me into a clunky elevator that felt like someone was hand operating it with ropes from the basement.

As it creaked along, I asked," My dad still in a coma?"

"Afraid so, Colby. Doctor Naylor should be freed up soon to answer your questions." She looked down at the plaque I held. "What's that?"

"My dad won it in the same race he went down in. That probably sounds funny."

"Yeah, but any award is a good award, I guess."

The doors painfully screeched apart and she led me down a long hallway at a brisk pace. My attention never fixed on any one thing for long: her blue scrubs, the stainless steel gurneys, the sound of medical machines, medicinal odors and snatches of talk from open doors. Finally, she stopped and turned to me. "Here we are. Ready?"

I wasn't, but I was excited to have him back. I tiptoed quietly behind her until a voice of reason said, *He's comatose, man. The Jefferson High marching band couldn't wake him.*

A curtain surrounded A.L. She screeched it back without ceremony and offered me a seat in an orange chair next to A.L.'s bed. There he was, down for the count in the worst imaginable circumstances, but at least he was back in Darin.

They had him hooked up to a barrage of tubes. A clear plastic mask covering his mouth kept him flush in oxygen. A ventilator whooshed slowly and rhythmically, cold and mechanical. Raised bags that dripped fluids into him marked the heavy seconds. He was totally dependent on beeping monitors, blipping life support machines and nourishing IVs. Each had their own quiet, mournful part to play in keeping him alive. His pulse was recorded by another small box in the form of spiking green lines. Was it the room's lights or was he really that pale? All of his legendary toughness seemed to have shrunken to something frail; vulnerable.

Again the nurse offered the seat, but I declined and stood close to A.L.'s side. To me he seemed no better off than the last time I saw him. He blurred through misty eyes.

I cleared a gluey throat and placed his holeshot trophy on the nearby side table. I wanted it to be the first thing he saw when he came to. I tried to chase the thought that this trophy might be his last. *Maybe I shouldn't leave it here. Would it bum him out? Why can't I think straight?*

I wasn't long perusing A.L.'s bruised arms and raised leg before a male's hushed voice came from behind. "How are we doing, Colby?" the man in the long, white coat asked.

I greeted Dr. Naylor with a shrugged nod.

"His vitals have stabilized," Dr. Naylor said.

"That's good, right?"

"Better than not. He's fought well."

"Has he come to yet . . . Said anything . . . Asked for anybody?"

"No, not yet, but that will change soon."

"Like how soon?" I said.

"Perhaps as soon as tomorrow," the doctor said. "We'll contact you, first thing when that happens."

"Then what, Doctor?"

"We'll do a few more tests. Then we'll have a clearer picture."

I paused. "But what about . . . ?"

"His mobility, you mean? Again, let's see what the tests confirm. Fair enough?"

"Yes, sir." I sighed heavy. At least everything seemed to be recording, beeping and dripping as it should be.

Dr. Naylor moved over to check A.L.'s monitors. "Let's just see . . ." Naylor finished the last of his observations, tweaked a couple of tubes, and signed off. "See you soon, Colby." He shot me a quick courtesy nod and left.

I studied A.L. and imagined tumultuous white blood cell battles raging in him, fighting to regain control of their empire. I dragged the orange chair closer and sat for a while. Occasionally my phone's quiet buzz announced a text. All but Jillian's went ignored.

I leaned in to my dad. "Listen to me, sky master. You and me, we're going to scale this hill, like the rest, hear me?"

Whoosh, swoosh. Whoosh, swoosh.

Let's see. What else might motivate him? It came to me. I leaned within an inch of his right ear and whispered in an ominous tone, "Demi, A.L. Aunt Demi? Your old friend's come and moved into El Relaxo to keep an eye on me. That's right. In fact, she was sleeping in *your bed*. Ordering around *your dog*, and *your son*, dude. I chased her off but she might come back, so I need you to rise up and rebel dude! Your castle awaits."

Out of the corner of my eye, I saw something. I was sure of it. A flinch of his arm, something. With little thought I slapped the red button on the wall faster than you could shout, PANIC BUTTON! From down the hall came a quick patter of feet. The same nurse who had led me here showed up with owl eyes.

"Nurse, get Dr. Naylor!" She never asked why, just shouted the request to someone in the hall. Doctor Naylor's return was fast.

"What's going on, Colby?" he said as his stethoscope met his ears mid-stride. He leaned over A.L. Quick, deliberate actions followed.

I felt intimidated and hoped this was justified.

"I . . . I thought I saw A.L. twitch or something," I said. Of course A.L was no help and showed zero signs of any life. Certainty tumbled to doubt.

"Twitch, you say?" Dr. Naylor asked. "What *actually* happened, Colby?"

"Nothing much. I was, you know, talking to him, when out of the corner of my eye I saw him flinch . . . pretty sure."

The nurse's eyes rolled to the doctor, then back to me.

Dr. Naylor stayed with me. "Okay, what part of his body twitched?"

"Upper body, maybe?" I said.

Naylor felt A.L.'s chest.

Flinch or do something, A.L.! The three of us stood frozen over him waiting for something to happen. Anything. Nothing did.

Dr. Naylor sighed. "I don't see any major change, but you keep vigilant." He left.

"Nurse? What's that other word for stupid mule?"

She giggled. "Don't be hard on yourself. The lighting in this room constantly plays tricks." She left.

"Okay, A.L. I'm in a little fix here, old man. Can you help me out a bit?" I leaned in. "I think you heard me before. We need to do something about . . ." I leaned in and repeated Demi's name, three times, each time louder.

My phone buzzed again. I took a quick peek and gasped. Witchcraft! Demi! She probably knew I was mocking here from way downtown. "Hello, hello," I said with as much charm as I could muster given the woman or timing.

She sounded frazzled, as always. "Colby, it's Aunt Demi. Where are you?"

"The hospital, with A.L."

"So he finally made it back, huh? How's he look?"

"Like a dude that hit the ground at fifty."

"God. Is his doctor there?"

"No, Dr. Naylor's on his rounds, Demi. I just talked to him. I can give you the low down."

"No," she snipped. "I prefer to hear it with my own two ears—*from a professional.*"

Back at El Relaxo the air still hung heavy. I didn't want to ride but I didn't want to be inside, either. So I gathered Bubbles and we ran and ran through the woods, far as my legs could take me.

CHAPTER 16—NAYLOR'S NEWS

Next day, Jillian fed my frustration at lunch. "Any word from the doc?"

Her timing couldn't have been better. My phone buzzed before I could answer. I read the text and looked off.

Beach asked, "What up, man?"

"Doc wants to meet at 4:30." Long exhale. "Day of reckoning, I guess."

"Need back up, C-Boy?" Jillian said.

"Appreciate it, guys. But I have to fly solo on this one."

Naylor appeared in the waiting room, ten minutes tardy. "Sorry, running late again Colby." I studied him for any signs that might tip his hand, but he stayed neutral. "Let's head for my office where it's quieter."

I followed the doctor's quick strides to a stuffy, tight, cluttered space. Between the heavy air and the worry, even breathing was no longer easy.

I was offered a low, beat-up folding chair across from his desk. *Seriously, dude?* I crunched down like it was fourth grade all over again when I had to square with the principal after accidentally hitting Gale Sebeka with a rock at recess.

Naylor sifted through the piles on his desk, trying to locate some missing data or x-ray. *Just spill the beans, man.*

"Here it is, sorry, Colby." Flat palms gently slapped the desk. "It's terribly hot in here. Something's up with the A.C. Can I get you some water or anything before I start?"

"Not now, thanks. Feel free to deal the cards right out, sir. What's up with my dad?"

"The positive news is your dad's out of his coma—"

Like some deprived mouse crawling up a wall for a crumb of protein, I leapt upon the good news. "Oh man, that's great! So he's awake, huh?" I pumped a fist. "Decent."

But the sober face across from me hinted there was more to the story.

"I wish it was all good news, Colby."

The folding seat creaked as I imploded back. Now I didn't want his words. I wanted to run. Run anywhere as he systematically explained A.L.'s life was wrecked. He fired out bits and pieces of medical speak that swirled and cut into me like twister debris.

"If it's any consolation, your dad's fate could actually have been worst if . . . We found some minor breaks beyond the major area of concern, right here . . . We also ran a battery of tests . . . double-checked . . . Colby? This caused the cataclysmic fracture on the number four vertebrae spinal region, right here . . . His deep contusions will need time . . . Understand? Very unfortunate . . . Rehab for some weeks . . . I'm sorry to say . . . Social services will contact you . . . be some time before . . . With extensive rehabilitation and accessories your dad might attain a decent degree of mobility allowing in time, his return to a productive . . . Do you understand everything I've said, Colby?"

My attention diverted to the doctor's side table, where among the cluttered and stacked folders sat a small trophy, a bronzed golfer in a proud pose of confidence after his ball strike. The brass plate revealed the doctor had once sunk a hole-in-one, probably a week after he'd graduated cum laude from medical school. Everything had broken this man's way. All I had come to seek was a little break for my dad, one time, when it really mattered.

Finally able to speak, I asked, "Doctor, do you think there's a chance my dad could, uh, race again?"

His eyes darted around in search mode. "Race? On a motorcycle? Your father is a paraplegic now, Colby. We can't reverse that, not at this point." He leaned in like Dr. Feelgood peddling Plan B options. "But here's the deal, son. He'll still be able to drive, work, most things. Sure, he'll have to learn new ways and habits, but my money says he will, what with his past determination."

"I get all that, but motocross was everything to him. His sights were set on the pros. What about that?"

"Life and bad luck test many a good soul at times, but he's a scrapper. With his competitive spirit and your encouragement, he'll fight through this like a race to be won."

I rubbed my chin for a couple of beats. "I got all that, but is there any chance he might compete again?"

"All your questions will be answered in time, after the rehab process."

I didn't raise my voice at the man as much at our rotten fate. "Well if you were a *bettin' man*, sir, what would you say? Honestly, right now, Doctor?"

I asked for straight and got it. "Alright. Long odds against him racing again, for sure. With the help of aids and medical breakthroughs, as I said before, he'll be able to do most things. But riding, especially motocross, would be very risky. I realize all this is tough to swallow," Naylor said.

The long wait of clinging to hope and denial were over. I fought off tears that begged to spill with every thick breath. Sick and a woozy, I stood up on wobbly legs. Dr. Naylor rose with me and gave me a minute to float randomly toward his window. Afternoon light from a scattered sky swept over the woods and the distant tributary river A.L. and I had fly-fished countless times. We might have been there now. I'd be watching him with a broad smirk as he kneeled at water's edge to sip the river water before his first cast.

The memory drifted off. Still staring out the window, I asked in a weak voice, "You told him all this?"

"Most of it. He was pretty bleary. I can't be sure what, if anything, he understood."

"Best I talk to him," I said.

"He'd like that. Everything will work out for the both of you. Your dad's going to get the best of care. He'll adjust, you hear?" Naylor's arm curled around my shoulder in some big brother gesture. But I'd survived my whole life without siblings and I didn't care to be touched now. After a hard glance, he removed his hand. I began my exit but paused at the door to offer a weak thanks. I told him I'd take things from there, but I was nervous even talking to A.L.

I inched the curtain back. His bed had been adjusted to the upright position though his eyes remained closed. I placed a hand on his arm and patted it. I almost startled when his eyes fluttered, then found me. Though the news was bad, I still clung to this reunion, a rebirth of sorts. At least I still had a dad. I knew a few who didn't for one reason or another.

A.L. reentered a world that would regard him differently now. He'd have to reinvent himself into something new, but what? *Where do I begin?* My fist nervously parked between my teeth as I tried to keep my emotions in check.

His first words came out mumbled, incoherent, but it was a start at least. I greeted him with all the pep I could muster. "Welcome back, old boy," I said. "Can you hear me?"

In a weak voice, he said, "Colby?" The smallest mention of my name nudged my confidence.

"Yeah, man, I'm right here. The same guy who's been holding down El Relaxo while you've been chillin'."

Good to see he could still find that famous glib smirk. A weak thumbs up from him followed. *Hope.* "So, A.L., I just talked to the doctor. He came down before and talked to you. Remember?"

He struggled. "Did he? Oh yeah. Um . . . Doctor, uh—"

"Naylor, that's right."

"Everything's a bit dusty, you know."

"I get the dusty part. You've been doing a Rip Van Winkle for a couple of weeks, dude. Hell, I feel grateful just to be talking to you. Anyway, do you recall what Dr. Naylor said, I mean about your injuries?"

"A little, maybe. I . . . I had an accident. I'm here. What else did he say? Tell me, son."

I cleared my throat. "Once you're a little stronger, they're going to move you to a special rehab place, alright? You'll be there for a spell, but I'll be swinging by often."

"I see." He gnawed the corner of his lip the way he would do when he got fidgety.

"After that you'll come home and we'll take things from there—"

"Maybe do some riding together when I'm stronger, eh?"

Had he not gotten the doctor's memo? This sudden, misguided optimism from my dad impaled me. When he took my hand, I tried not to crumble. Short breaths barely fueled my words.

"Not sure about the riding, A.L. But if you work really work hard there at rehab . . . shit, A.L. The news ain't all that great."

I choked up, rendered useless. He looked at me. After a pause, he said, "I figured so." He patted my hand and withdrew it. His head turned towards the empty bed beside him. "Could be worse, I guess."

I went to his table where the holeshot sat beside a pitcher of water. I poured him a cup and held it for him. While he sipped, his eyes stayed locked on mine, more determination than defeat.

"Don't you worry, A.L., I've got your back. Everything's going to be fine, old boy, hear? Bubbles sure misses you. And Commander must holler your name eight times a day."

"Appreciate that. Don't worry about me. It'll work out," he said. "You're going to have to take the mantle for a bit."

"Yes sir. You just keep fighting, get your health back and we'll take it from there, huh?"

His tongue searched his lips. He swallowed hard, maybe in panic.

"Another sip?" I said. He nodded and drew from the cup.

His eyes fluttered and his voice sputtered weakly. From left field came, "Colby? Colby? Where's Mom?"

Hard to say which he was asking for, the one who had died or the one who had left him, but neither was around. "What are you asking, A.L.?"

His hands labored to animate, but just as fast dropped. "Bad bounce, bad bounce."

He drifted off. The moment he checked out, I bee-lined it for the lobby doors. I couldn't get enough air. I barely made it outside to the first convenient hedge and threw up. An approaching elderly couple groaned and turned away in disgust. Weak legs reached the truck.

Friday afternoon but there was nothing T.G.I.F about it. I couldn't decide where to head. I ignored the phone's nagging pulse. Not even Jillian's words or her promise of sympathetic arms motivated me. She deserved to hear how things had gone but I was no better than a sack of futility. It could wait. My mouth was foul. I craved water and a long drive into the country.

CHAPTER 17—UNEXPECTED VISITORS

Outside a convenience store, I squeezed cold water into my mouth to rinse the puke that still clung. But no amount of it could chase the finality of A.L.'s news. I finished the bottle and winged it towards the trash. It missed the mark and caromed off to freedom. The bottle drum-rolled merrily down the parking lot until an oblivious tire squashed it flat.

Feeling lost, panicked, and numb, I left Darin for long, nameless, rural roads. I drove on and on, not for cheap answers, but to speed away from life. If I had to pick one day when my boyhood ended and manhood begun, that day might be as good as any. Whatever was coming was change; no one ever escaped that. A.L. would have to rely on me to run things for a while; hard for a man accustomed to ruling the roost. I drove far as the Mississippi, found a secluded spot to stare at its continuous flow. I felt ripped off for both of us; only low cards in hand. Pity would have to yield to conviction and eventual acceptance of new routines. I was determined to adjust, but could he?

"Colby!" *Hey Commander.*

Started the wood stove and I tugged open the fridge door to survey the stock. No food tempted me so I just grabbed a Coke. Bubbles padded in, head seeming a little low. "It's going to be soon, Bubbly. Now A.L. ain't going to be chasing after you, throwing Frisbees and all, but least he'll be home soon enough."

Logistics punished me with the subtlety of meteorites. Was I the new designated grocery fetcher? God help me. Who did we know who could mod-up his van? The way he looked, all zoned out, how long would it be before he could even return to work, never mind the riding? From my perch on the couch, I finished the Coke and rifled the can into the wall. I moved to the porch where my shoulder became Commander's perch as we stared at the field. At least Jillian called and said she was on her way. I was down for getting held like I was eight again.

What I didn't expect was for Jillian to tote along a band of boys with her. The quartet pasted on hangdog masks so it felt more like a funeral. I offered soft greetings as they trudged past me in silence. I didn't mean to park a hard stare on Jillian but that's what came. She fired one back: *I was only trying to help.*

Beach thrust a greasy small brown bag in my face. "Here, man. This time it's all for you."

"Right, Beach. I should probably store it in the safe." I blinked heavy. "Thanks bro."

Sid, a motohead, followed me into the kitchen. "Bummer about A.L."

"Thanks Sid." Sid showed some skills on the track but his arrogant tendencies sometimes betrayed him. In perfect times I liked him.

Sid said, "This has gotta be messing with you, man. Shit, I knew when I beat you on the track last event, especially after Marionville and all, something had to be up."

I stared at him. "Take 'em when you can get 'em, I guess, Sid."

Tunes helped to drown the funereal vibe and the boys ventured around to check out the place and Commander.

If Terry Blain lacked athletic ability, he could be counted on for pure entertainment. This time, with A.L.'s audio set up. "Rocking system, dude," he said.

"Huh? Oh thanks, Terry," I said. "A.L. copped this 7-1 system from a moto buddy,"

Terry nodded. "It cranks, man." He bent over and checked out each speaker that punished his ears. "Wow!" Terry responded to everything with naïve wonderment like he'd just been dropped on Earth, everything always amazing and new. Maybe his voracious pot intake helped.

On the porch, Beach tried to teach the bird to curse. Sid, meanwhile, pasted himself on Jillian and sucked her in with charm and bullshit tales. Jillian's laughed response to something he shared launched my next jealousy rocket. I needed any excuse to clear myself from the scene.

"Anyone up for some popcorn?" No one heard or responded but I escaped to the kitchen anyway.

Not long in the kitchen, Jillian's arm soon cradled my shoulder. Her droopy mouth said everything as we both stared into the cast iron pot, waiting for five test-kernels to blow. The first explosion nearly blinded my inquisitive wonder followed by the next that whizzed by. The third, a pop-up, got snatched out of the air by Jillian, smooth as a trained dolphin. I dumped in the mother lode and stared at it blankly as it simmered.

Terry's odd dance migrated into the kitchen. I marveled at the way his limbs worked so independently, like the twenty-foot balloon guy outside Southside Liquors. Pulsed hips leading, Terry swayed in closer. "Hey, Colby, this mix is GREAT!"

"You really like it that much, Terry? Take it when you leave."

WRONG!

Jillian said, "I made you that CD!"

I backstroked. "Oh, that's right, sorry. Terry, copy it, whatever."

Her answer? A pout. I turned my back to kernel watch.

"Hey." Jillian's grip yanked me from my thoughts. "Sorry. You okay?"

"Sure." A touching moment except for the popcorn that started to launch all around us. "You might want to cover that pot, C-Boy," she said.

"Or let everything just fly." I covered the pot. The heavy lid contained the white missiles. She looked puzzled. "What's wrong, J-Girl?"

"Why are you making popcorn like it's a party or something?"

With pot holders and mad vigor, I shook the pan over the burner. "What the fuck, right? Just thought the *unexpected guests* might enjoy some while they mingle and dance and what not."

Her voice lowered to a hush. "You're upset I brought the guys. Sorry. I thought it would soften the blow, is all."

"I get it. It's not them, just the timing and . . . Look, I'm still trying to sort all this crap out, okay?"

The tinks from inside the covered pan grew furious and attracted more interest. Beach appeared in the doorway, then Sid and the kitchen was now stuffed as a rush hour subway. "That's some old school, shit, man. . . So what up with A.L., exactly?" Beach said.

The popping tailed off. I gave the kettle a final shake and slapped my oven mitts down. "News aint so good, Beach," I said.

"What's not good, dudes?" Sid floated in and rooted close to Jillian. Again.

"A.L., Sid." I didn't mean to raise my voice at him.

"But he'll ride again, right?"

I mumbled, "No, not likely."

"What?" Sid turned towards Terry, "Lower that shit down man, I can't hear myself."

I raised my voice. "I said, Sid, he probably won't ride again!" The music came down; hardly a sound, not even from the popcorn, which began to burn instead. I mindlessly lurched for handles—now piping hot. My bare hands rebelled. "Ahh!" I threw the iron lid down and the last of the popcorn flew everywhere. Waving my hands in pain," I yelled, "A.L.'s paralyzed, okay? Bound to a wheelchair!"

Silence detonated the place. Group remorse followed initial bewilderment. Jillian took my arm. "C'mon, Colby." She led me and my burned fingers to the sink and began to run cold water over them.

"I'm fine," I said staring at the stream that spilled from the faucet.

"Keep your hands in the water," Jillian ordered.

"I'm okay."

"Do it!" Her voice peaked, but quickly softened. "It'll blister if you don't."

I complied for a while then shut the water off.

"Wow. This is one rude mood." Beach yanked me into his mass of flesh. Meanwhile, Jillian's sniffles escalated. Trapped, I could only watch half-smushed as the grand lizard, Sid, wrapped himself all over my girl.

Jillian accepted his embrace and I totally overreacted. I broke loose from Beach and informed Sid that cuddle time was freaking over. His cocky smirk caused my fists to clench, and that triggered the next volley of pain from the burns. I yelled, "That's enough, man!"

Sid back-stroked away from Jillian. "Dude," he said, "I'm cool. Really sorry about your dad. Not seeing him do his thing at the track? That's going to be freaking insane. He's like an idol, bro."

"Appreciate it," I said. "You know what, guys? Cool of you all to drop by and all, but I'm just not feeling the party vibe. I need space. Take the popcorn with you if you want. Sorry."

A voice gently prodded the thick air, Terry asking if I could get him a copy of the mix that was playing. With a shake of the head, I quick-stepped into the living room, withdrew the disk, found its sleeve and handed it to him. "There you go, man." Terry's pulled out his wallet. "No, man, you don't have to pay me. Jillian can make me another."

"Sure I can," she said an octave too high, before returning to civil. "That's fine."

Terry's compensation came in the form of a joint. "Here, man. Medicine for your burned digits."

"Thanks, bro, but I don't—"

But Terry dropped the joint into the key bowl. "All yours, man."

Jillian held back while the rest exited.

From outside I caught Sid's whisper, "Colby's freaking out, man."

"Fuck yeah," Beach snapped back. "What with his dad, and you, draping yourself like a Dracula costume all over his girl." The bickering muffled with the slam of the doors from Jillian's truck.

She shrugged and embraced my middle. "Sorry, C-Boy."

I wanted her to stay but she was their only way back. Jillian found conviction, swung around me and steered for the utility closet. She began rummaging.

"Uh, lose something, J-Girl?" I asked.

She produced a tube of first-aid ointment. "This will help." She dabbed it on my hands while I stared at her. "Better?" I nodded. "Reapply and keep it iced," she said.

"I don't deserve you," I said.

"You don't deserve this day is what." She held me until a tear-stained face lifted with an idea. "You shouldn't be out here alone, not tonight."

"You're right, but—"

"Come home with me. Sleep in the basement next to Squeeze. The folks will understand."

"*Squeeze?* Your five-foot-long python that stares at me through his purple light like I'm a Whopper with fries? Thanks anyway, J-Girl."

"Have it your way, C-Boy. Meet you at the duck pond around 4:00 tomorrow? I want to hear everything the doctor said."

"No you don't, but okay."

A beat passed. "We'll get him back, C-Boy."

A rap, then a voice barked from behind the door. "C'mon freakin, love birds!" Sid, of course.

"Better go," I said. "Keep Sid Luscious at an arm's length, will you?"

"Sid?" Jillian rolled her eyes. "Just like out on the dirt hills, C-Boy, you ain't got no competition."

Fingers medicated, the pain subsided some. I slipped on a jacket and headed for our patio with my fingers wrapped in an ice pack. Coast clear of visitors, Bubbles joined my side, then B.K. We all camped out there for a good while until first stars appeared.

I added wood and some kindling and contemplated the fire. From fragile beginnings, the timber soon roared and released the sun's long dormant energy. I sat in wallow before I looked back toward the patio door and thought, what the hell.

I rose and grabbed the joint. It was small and I figured it to be some fake basil thing Terry had been conned into buying. I lit it, took a small hit then soon realized this was no basil. *Wow.* A bit terrifying at first, broad space above me suddenly got more intense. "Bubbles, I think I understand the universe, girl." Red cinders danced up in attempt to meet the stars until they inevitably burned out. I removed my prodding stick from the coals and spun orange circles in the air. B.K's eyes watched with intrigue. Sometimes the hoot of an owl or the scuffle of brush alerted Bubbles. "What's that?" I'd fuel her. Once the embers faded, the late evening's chill drove me inside.

CHAPTER 18—VISIT TO REHAB

"Good afternoon."

"Hi, I'm A.L. Weston's son."

"Colby, right? Your dad's been talking you up. He's still in his rehab session but I'm sure they won't mind if you look on."

I was led to the physical therapy room. Someone about my age struggled to master his steel crutches. Each attempt was a nail to my heart. But the receptionist maintained her cheer. "That's Mr. Clark over there working with your dad."

I'll never forget it, the cold reality of seeing A.L. in a wheelchair for the first time. Those wheels were his legs now. The PT admonished him to stay with his task of pulling tension ropes. The receptionist whispered, "Mr. Clark is doing a lot of upper body strengthening exercises with your dad. His sessions will soon bump up from three to up to five hours daily."

I looked on blankly. "He'll love that."

"All the hard work will speed up his recovery." The quick nods and flash of big teeth resembled a bobble head souvenir.

She continued. "Each day begins with listening sessions before the start of the physical therapy session."

I lightened. "Listening sessions? He'll never leave here. He likes blues guitar, sometimes a little metal, if that helps."

She quickly bounced back from confusion. "No. This is probably a little different than the stuff he's been boogying to."

"He doesn't really *boogie* to it—"

She ignored me."It's called N.M.T," she said.

"Haven't heard of them, ma'am," I said.

"It's not a band, Colby; it's a type of therapy that helps ease post-traumatic depression."

I'd seen A.L. pissy, but depressed? "Does everyone here listen to these, uh, N.M.P. tunes? I mean, is my dad having problems with—"

"Post-traumatic depression?" she cut in. "A little; not uncommon."

I glanced to A.L. His hair had grown a couple of inches and I swear he'd sprouted a few more grays since Marionville. "So, this depression thing, does it last long?"

"Depends on the patient. Besides his physical therapy, we'll encourage your dad to get involved with support groups."

"Okay, but when do dudes get to feeling more . . . adjusted?"

"Varies. Some quickly, others, a while. Go on, say hi to your dad." I planted there; watched the interaction with his trainer.

"How's it feeling, A.L.? Getting easier?" the trainer asked.

A.L. slumped and exhaled a complaint after a weight crashed to the floor. Mr. Clark shot me a glance but the routine went on. After a while Clark said, "Okay, A.L., let's break. Looks like you've got a visitor. We'll keep this one short, but we've got some ground to make up, alright, good buddy?" Clark waved me forward.

A.L. turned his chair towards me. Scraggily beard gone, his sunken eyes brightened at the sight of me. Had he shrunk or was the chair a couple sizes too big? I stepped towards him. Things were awkward; I feigned upbeat.

"Hey, old boy, about ready for the Olympics or what?" I said.

A.L. spoke to a window. "Not even the special ones. How goes it?"

"Alright, plenty busy."

"Nothing wrong with busy." His head dipped, almost like he was searching. It rose again and he said, "Let's move to a place with a better view." I followed his slow revolutions to a large pane that overlooked the grounds.

I glanced around. "People seem friendly. This place is almost as good as Relaxo."

"It'll do, for now," A.L. addressed the window.

"How's it going?"

"Coach Clark surely trained Navy Seals, before this." A.L leaned in and whispered, "Likes his job a little too much."

"Play along A.L. and you'll be back to El Relaxo in no time. The animals miss you."

"I miss all you guys. What's up with you?"

"Same old."

"Holding down the fort, keeping up with the riding?"

"Ride's going good, and—"

"Is it?" His dark eyes bore into me as he drummed the arms of his chair.

"Yeah. I mean I haven't got out as much as I would like, what with . . . you know."

"Uh huh," A.L said, "and school? Still going?"

"No time. Commander's home schooling me."

"Sorry I asked." A.L. smirked.

"Everything's chill, man."

"Okay. So what's in the bag? Something for me, I hope."

I nodded. "Nothing much, just a little treat."

A.L. pulled the bottle out. "Yoo-hoo, huh? Well, life's complete. Thanks man. Follow me. Check out my digs."

He led an arduous pace to a tight, plain room with a single bed. The holeshot trophy had followed him and now rested on the bureau. He turned his chair and faced me. "I asked for the presidential suite and got it."

I walked over and hugged him, grateful my eyes didn't leak. He whispered, "Good to see you, too." He stared at the Yoo-hoo. "Best served cold." A.L.'s teeth clamped down on his lower lip as he twisted the stubborn cap. It didn't give, not at first, but I didn't interfere. Victory came with a satisfying pop of the cap which he sent in flight with a snap of his fingers; an old trick I'd yet to master. He raised the bottle. "To comebacks." He took a healthy swig and stared at the back label. Finally he said, "Pull up a seat; stay a while."

I brought a chair closer. "I see your holeshot trophy made it over."

"Ah yes, small concession for a larger dream. Take it when you go."

The dismissal surprised me. "Really?"

He didn't answer that. "A check should have come with it."

"Mr. Carter picked it up. It's home, in a safe place."

"Good. We're going to have to tighten our belts for a while." He downed what remained of his drink then absentmindedly began to peel the label with his thumb nail. The air grew heavy in the silence. "So everything okay, back home? The dog, the bird?"

"Yeah. Don't forget Billy the Kid."

"B.K., right . . . Anything from your mother at all?" he said to the bottle.

It struck me funny he'd ask. "I called her recently. Everything's the same."

"Yeah? How's life with Mr. Money Bags?"

"Didn't ask."

"What else? Electricity still on? Imagine there's a bill or two waiting for me."

"Done. Found the password to your online account and paid them all."

"Really?" He wrung his hands together. "Now don't be sharing anything about that account with anyone, hear?"

"No, sir." Didn't mention Demi or that whole drama. I'd ease those details in later. "Hey, guess what? Mark Beck called. Can you believe it? He asked after you."

His eyes narrowed over the rim of his tilted Yoo-hoo bottle. He lowered it. "Really? Our old friend Mark Beck, eh? Still hustling fresh talent?" He rubbed his face.

"I guess. All I know is he called your Georgia run the best amateur ride he'd ever seen."

"The part *before* the crash, I take it." His eyes lifted to mine.

I tried to divert him. "What else is new?"

"Well, I spoke with Jack. You came up. Your game was a little off at the last event?"

I shrugged.

"What happened?"

"Bad outing, I guess. Not worth reliving."

His eyes searched the floor. "Anything else I need to know?"

"Not about that . . . Mr. Drake checked in from the lumber yard. I got to thinking. Maybe you can work remote from El Relaxo when you get home."

A small grin came. "Colby, my planner. Those wheels are always spinning. Wonder where *that* comes from, huh? You work on your game; I'll work on mine."

"We're still a team, A.L., and—"

Three gentle raps cut my words short and the door eased opened. "A.L.? You about set to resume?" Clark stared coldly.

A.L. rolled his eyes.

I said, "Take it to the house. Fix yourself and come back, old boy. I'll have things ready."

"Alright, go find yourself a challenging trail. Don't let that winning ride get soft."

As Clark wheeled A.L. out, he began to chat, "Have I ever told you about my boy, Clark? One of the finest young dirt bike riders in all of Tennessee. I taught him. Now he's gunning to compete for the national championship. Think of that, Clark."

"That's awesome, A.L. Now we'll be tackling the pull up bar."

CHAPTER 19--RENOVATIONS

And so began the least exciting home renovation ever. As planned, Jillian and her dad had arrived to El Relaxo armed to the teeth with hardware, wood and tools. Mr. C. extracted a drill from the back of his truck and gritted his teeth like Eastwood.

"Well kid, can you only whisper sweet nothings to my daughter or can you drive a screw into a board?"

"Never doubt me Mr. C., even when I'm clueless," I said.

Drake's Lumber had generously donated all needed supplies. We extracted large sheets of plywood and hardware and placed them in the garage. Everything off loaded, Mr. Carter asked if I had any kind of plan in mind. With a slightly dry mouth, I presented my hand drawn concept of a ramp.

He scrutinized it for a moment before he looked off to think. I didn't know what to expect. Then he determined the slope and length looked about right. "Where's it going?"

I explained the garage door entrance looked good as any. Mr. Carter consulted the drawing and site again. "We'll take out those three stairs, maybe sacrifice a bit of A.L.'s workbench, if need be."

My hands went to my hips. "I was expecting that."

"We have a plan," Mr. Carter said. "Let's get going. After this, we'll install a bar in the bathroom so he can have easier access to the throne. Sound good?"

None of it did, but having the Carters here made the transition easier. I asked what I could do, and Mr. Carter said I could fetch him a glass of iced tea or anything cold. Jillian followed me into the kitchen and wrapped her arms around my waist as I pulled the fridge handle.

"This all feels awfully strange, J-Girl."

"A.L. will adjust. Time heals all, C-Boy. "

"Changes things, too."

Jillian's voice rose. "I just came up with a great idea. Why don't we throw a surprise, welcome home party? We should invite a mess of people. Call Jack. He'll get the word out. What do you think?"

"A.L. might go for that." I poured three glasses of iced tea.

Mr. Carter raised my cold offering without comment. As loud gulps dominated the garage and rivulets of tea dripped down his front, Jillian looked on with revolt. When the glass went dry, it was time to whip out the big guns. She slapped on some goggles and shamed me as she squatted and deftly blasted screws into wood.

Mr. Carter caught me ogling at her. "That drill of yours lost its charge, boy? Drag your butt over here."

I could repair a motor blindfolded, but woodworking wasn't a strength. Under watchful eyes, the pressure mounted as I clumsily tried to align the drill bit with a screw. After a few pointers and some botched tries, I found a rhythm. The garage hummed with power tools, and in no time, we stood back, marveling at the new addition.

"That concludes the ramp, Colby," Mr. Carter said. "Well, almost. You'll probably want to paint it."

Time and the effort had left us hungry. Jillian vocalized my thoughts. "Dad, I'm starved. All I can think of is Mom's lasagna we brought along."

"You're always hungry. How do you all stay so skinny?"

"I'm a wolf incarnate, Dad."

"Alright, lunch break if you must. You guys heat up the vittles, I'll cue up Phase Two.

Jillian and I hopped up the ramp and into the kitchen. While the lasagna twirled in the microwave, Jillian absentmindedly picked bits of wood debris off her front.

"Thanks, baby. This is a big help," I said.

"I think Dad's having fun showing you things."

"Yeah, he's not sneering at me as much as usual."

We filled the last twenty-four seconds with a kiss. *Ding!* Mr. Carter entered. "Oh jeez, stop all that monkey business you two. Dish up some of that grub."

Jillian served the steaming squares of lasagna onto our plates. After our feeding frenzy, she caught me up on the gossip. Lasagna devoured, he arched back in a stretch and sighed. "I suppose . . . Let's see about that bathroom railing."

A few quick snaps of his retractable measuring tape and he was good to go. Space in the bathroom was tight so he opted to work solo. The sunny day lured Jillian and me outside where we tossed a Frisbee and laughed at each other's errant throws. Sooner than expected, we were called in. "What do you think, Colby?" Mr. Carter asked.

Except for the debris and dust and on the floor, the railing seemed like it had always been there. "Looks fine to me, sir."

"When it comes to toilet bars, *I'm the greatest.*" His Muhammad Ali impersonation wasn't bad. "Okay," he returned, "mission complete for now. We'll wait for A.L.'s marching orders on anything else. He might want one of those chair lifts to get him upstairs. Let me know."

After I thanked him three times, Mr. Carter took his turn jumping on the ramp. "Colby, I'm going to leave you all a gallon of paint to slap on before he gets home. Thought the Battleship Gray would look nice."

"It should match his mood," I mumbled off.

"C'mon, doll," he said to Jillian. "No doubt your mama's got more jobs waiting for us at home." He gave me a wink.

Jillian shot him disgruntlement. "Can't wait, Dad."

She turned to me. "Our work here is done, sky master . . . for now. Coming to school tomorrow?"

A smirk was my answer. Jillian got a hug and Mr. Carter, an appreciative handshake.

Once gone, El Relaxo returned to the new norm: painfully quiet. I walked around and reexamined the new additions—feeling equal parts pride and dread.

I headed for my locker between classes. My thoughts were a thousand miles adrift, when WHAM! I was picked up and slammed against my locker by Prince Colossus himself. Students who didn't get Beach probably would have found the size mismatch and the sound of my body hurling into sheet metal unnerving, but most had seen this greeting before from Beach and moved on with hardly a glance.

"S'up, Beach," I said suspended, shirtfront bunched into my Adam's apple. "And what is the reason I'm up here?"

I mentioned that Beach's goal was to someday stalk MSU's gridiron as a lineman, maybe make it to the pros. Like all long shot dreams, it would take hard work, skill and luck, but also, in Beach's case, winning over a particular English teacher with an agenda who could help—or wreck his fate.

The ever gruff Matulis, the hall enforcer, reminded us, "Guys, you all need to get to your classes."

Red faced, not from embarrassment but lack of air, I nodded to the man before he continued on his rounds. My attention turned back to my assailant.

He released me and I landed with a thud.

"What's up?" I said.

"Dejon." Beach informed. "She asked me to be in the play."

"I think she's head-hunting jocks."

"What?" he asked.

"She asked *me* to read for a part, too. Course, I won't do it."

"Me neither, until she reminded me of my thirty-eight average in her class. She said if I took a part, even a small one, it might count towards extra credit. A *lot* of extra credit."

"Dude, why's she blackmailing you?"

"Maybe she needs black males. What I *do* know is English needs passing. No pass, no football at MSU."

"Just chill, suck it up and do it, seriously. I read some of it. Kinda funny in places."

"But not funny enough for you to do it?"

"I'm not the dude carrying around the 38 average. Play her stupid game; it'll be a clown-around. Pass English and it'll be back to more important business of hitting and tackling. Feel me?"

"Not at all," Beach said.

"Think it over, dog. Anyway, we best be getting to class or face more shit to boot."

"I'm not walking on any stage without back up." Beach stared at me.

"Look man, when A.L. gets home, there might be some serious ass needs. Dude's already brought up my ride, which lately sucks. Wish I could, but—"

Beach kept begging. "Do it for me, man. We'll split laughs between."

"Gotta go, man," I said over my shoulder.

On the ride over to rehab, I got thinking about Beach and the fix he found himself in. There's this long-standing, unspoken code in football: always reward those who make giant holes for you to run through. Maybe I could do it with him. He sure came off like a desperado. Why not? The part Dejon wanted me to read was small and might not take up too much time. So I decided, right then, if Dejon still needed me, I'd brave it with Beach. I texted him:

>You win. Broadway here we come! U owe me.

I met A.L. in his small room. He seemed somewhat better, closer to his old, fidgety self. We talked a bit about home, but I avoided any mention of doing a play. In no time flat, talk veered to motocross. I told him the mixed-truth that I'd been riding often and fine of late.

"Really?" He snipped, "Better not see grass growing on the sides of those hills when I get home."

I took him at his word. When I returned to El Relaxo after my visit, I broke out the weed whacker and went to town on those hills until they were shaved. I took Silver for a spin over them, too, but that only triggered another reality: The bold had tanked and everything felt stiff, at best. I didn't want him to come home to that.

CHAPTER 20—DRAMATIC ENTRANCE

Hands poised on theater door handles, Beach Moody and I exchanged what-have-we-committed-to faces as we paused before the open door.

"After you," the big man insisted before we took the plunge.

The two of us slowly plodded the aisle's descent like displaced astronauts on a strange planet. First impression—low-lit theater; no adults in sight; kids chasing each other; cartwheels on the stage; noisy anticipation—a freakin' teen bounce house by anyone's standard.

When we reached the middle rows, Beach said, "That's far enough. Let's chill here and check out things from a safe distance; wait for practice to start."

"I think they call them rehearsals, dude."

"So you know how things work?" Beach said.

"Well I did play the lead rabbit in a 4th grade production."

"You are experienced."

"If blowing your entrance and hopping in at the wrong times is experience, yeah."

Beach smirked. "Dump that tonky tronk."

The sudden clatter of an auditorium door spun our heads around. Framed in the doorway, was Dejon's unmistakable, robust silhouette. She stared in like a sheriff, sizing up the chaos in a western saloon. I scrunched down lower as the freight train stomped past us and braced for a killjoy holler that never came. She ascended the stage stairs and clapped her hands three times. "Have a seat at the table, please."

The cast's hasty, regimental compliance glowed with respect.

Beach giggled, "I found my place. Right here, on this velvet seat."

"Uh, I think she wants us on stage, bro," I said.

He sat with his hands folded on his stomach. "Real-ly?"

"Excuse me? You talked me into this dark hole."

He pawed his chin. "Remind me. Why did I agree to this?"

"I can recall two words: college and football."

"Now it's coming back." He vaulted up. "Shall we join the actors? Make room." He squeezed past me and I followed. Much of the scrubbed-face regulars locked in their doubt. Beach answered them with a quick lilt before taking the stage.

Dejon's beam went wide as a hippo's. Why wouldn't she? Beach and I were the latest recruits she had bagged. "There you two are. Welcome to JHS Theater!"

A friendly nod back would be the best acting I did that day. I paused to drink in all the empty rows of seats soon to be filled with hundreds of judgmental eyes. We hadn't even read line one and I was already nauseous and weak-kneed. I conceded to everything and prudently sat away from my buddy. I looked around. I recognized some of the cast, but there was no one I was really tight with.

Dejon congratulated veteran and rookie cast members alike for successfully *winning* a part. She didn't get far into her welcome before the next snap of the theater doors averted everyone's attention. If it brought a smile, it was because I knew these two clowns jogging down the aisle. Murphy and Austin were fellow football players, better famous for their locker room pranks than anything on the field.

They donned straight faces but my guess was this was some planned stunt.

"Sorry to interrupt, Mrs. Dejon." *Man, Austin was playing it straight.*

"What do you two need, boys?" Dejon snapped back.

From across the table Beach and I exchanged smirks as we half-waited for Dejon to light.

"Sorry, we were looking for keys to the light room," Murphy said.

What? Were these dudes actually involved?

"For the new cast, Austin and Murphy are part of our invaluable tech crew: lights and sound," Dejon announced. "Keys? You'll have to ask Mr. Benson. Try his room."

Beach and I swapped tight-lipped nods of approval. Instant allies, cool. Add to that, General Benson was also connected. Theater air got a little bit easier to breathe. As Austin and Murph bounded out, they were passed by another late incomer. *Untouchable!*

All eyes in the cast switched to Dana Raleigh as she bounded onto the stage then grunted as she twisted and appeared to fight off an unwilling book bag. It crashed to the stage with a decisive thud. "Sorry everybody," she said, frazzled but totally comfortable sharing her dilemma. "One of the problems with being the president of four clubs, you have to *run* them!" Her high-pitched cackle easily assaulted the rear theater walls.

Dejon's response was drought stricken. "The weight of greatness must be staggering at times. Sit Dana, please." Zeal returned to the old woman's eyes. "Now cast, let's begin our first read-through."

She promised that theatrical games and blocking would follow in future rehearsals. Beach's eyes widened to the size of half dollars until he later learned that blocking was theater jargon for finding your specific spot on stage.

I had no lines until Act Two. This gave me the chance to sit back and learn from the drama club veterans. For the most part, dramatics spilled easily from these guys. Some were able to ham it up and put great feeling into their part from the get-go. It all looked fun and easy and I almost began to look forward to my chance, even if I hadn't revisited the script since the first time I read it.

My concern was more for my wingman, Beach, whose lines were coming up. He flashed a look of panic as it wound down to his turn. But this was Beach Moody after all. Not only didn't he choke; the big man plowed into his script like he had acted his whole life, which in a way, he had.

Disapproving and bored faces now leaned in, captivated by Beach's bold delivery and masterful antics. In short, my man dazzled everyone. Laughter poured from the cast and Dejon. When he finished his first bit, *applause* broke out. Beach responded with a quick Moody Shuffle from his seat. "Thank you, thank you," he said as the applause died.

Dejon fawned all over him. "Fabulous, Beach."

At the break between acts, Beach was psyched and patted his chest. "Kinda liking the acting thing. It ain't so bad, dude. You're up, Weston."

Not to be bested, I was far from ready to yield the rookie MVP to the big man. But as my first lines neared, all confidence fell into the crapper. How did it go? In a word, horrible, and that's not being hard on myself. I became a panting, hiccupping, sweaty sack of a mess. I may have started with the same conviction as Beach but I couldn't sell it like Beach, or most of the actors before him. When my soliloquy finally grinded to a merciful end, I felt the judgment of seventeen pairs of dumbfounded eyes stapled on me. I slapped the table with the script a little harder than intended. "Whoops, sorry." I blasted off Dejon a telepathic message. *Cut me, now.*

"You'll grow into it, Colby. It takes practice to get good at anything," she said.

Oh reallllly? When the rehearsal ended, I only wanted to practice exiting. Now I had to endure watching Beach continue to entertain his ring of new worshippers who flocked around him! Beach gobbled up the attention, of course. When his fan club finally broke up, he began dishing out acting tips to me until Dana Raleigh sliced between us at Mach three and imploded his pointers, mid-thought.

"Hey, you missed me that time, Dana," I sneered, recalling our near-death collision in the hall the year before. Her mask was the most hostile I'd seen since. It contained all the Morning Show pep, just with more of a vile spin.

"Hey guys! You decided to try drama club? Wow. I don't know if you're aware at all—

"No," Beach cut in.

"Funny, Beach, but we JHS thespians have won numerous state awards."

Beach's confusion wasn't something made up. "Sorry, *what?* You're all gay? I mean I'm cool with it no problem, but it seems statistically—"

With batted eyes, Dana signaled she'd heard enough. "No, Beach, it's not a gay thing, it's a definition thing. It's *th th th, thespians.*"

"Say what?" he baited her on.

"You guys are football players, right?"

"Football, that's right," I said. "You may recall our last dance in the playoffs with—"

"Dance? My only dance with you, Colby, ended on the second floor hall—with bruises."

I turned to Beach, "Worst hit I ever took, dude." Then back to Dana. "Anyway, we're pumped just to be part of the show. Nice read up there."

She leaned in and narrowed the space. "Okay. Huddle up, you two," she said. "I don't mean to judge, but this production you've happed into? This is actually important to the rest of us thespians, remember the 'T-H,' sound, Beach. Try it."

Beach walked in circles, one arm extended to the ceiling, in a theatrical boom. "Th-th-thespians, gather!" Beach broke character. "Damn. So close. I almost felt like . . . Macbeth! 'Where art thou?' That it?" He donned confused.

Hand clasped to her mouth; saucer-sized eyes, all showed pure horror. "Wrong play, Beach. Also *never* say that name in the theater, *ever again*. Oh my god, you may have already doomed us and the play! I may never win the district's Leading Angel Actor award. Damn it!" Dana stomped off.

Beach's eyes followed Dana's exit right through the slam of the door. "She sure left me with a lot to think about."

"Or forget," I said. "I mean chill out a little, Raleigh. Whatever, bro, you're going to rock this stage. Me? I'm a disaster in progress."

"You're no damn disaster," Beach told me. "You're a damn th-th-thespian is what. Hey, y'all!" He addressed the empty rows like Caesar to a packed Coliseum. "I've got this!"

CHAPTER 21—A PACKAGE ARRIVES

Despite a wreck that would have killed most men, A.L., following his long coma, then rehab, was finally coming home. I paced the living room with a cup of coffee, kicking at four-dozen undulating silver and green balloons that Jillian had blown up. My noble warrior had fought off hyper ventilation in the process and rallied to tape them everywhere inside and out. While she did, I worked on converting A.L.'s pigsty of an office into a reasonable place for him to bed down. I piled his old paperwork in neat stacks on his computer desk and opened up the futon couch. Jillian peeked in. "Looks great, C-Boy! A.L.'s going to love this."

"Hope so."

"I'm excited to see who shows for his welcome back party. I called a few peeps and blasted out some invites."

"Same," I said. "Jack is spreading the word to the moto crew.

An arm circled my shoulder. "He's finally coming home. It's exciting, C-Boy, right?"

"Yeah." My fingers combed through hair that had gotten long. "Now if he can only make a clean break from Gremlin, everything will be just ducky."

"Maybe he'll move on no problem, C-Boy."

"Maybe, J-Girl. But we're talking a man who chose machine over wife."

She kissed my lips. "It's going to be all—what's that?" A growing, low rumble penetrated the place. "You hear that?"

I consulted a window and looked back to her. "Like bikes approaching?" I said. "Yeah."

Commander squawked and paced circles at the dozen bikes rumbling up our drive.

"What time is it?" I asked.

"'Bout eleven."

"I told everyone Two!"

Jillian bellied up to my side. "Them's bikers, dude. They party by their own clock. Chill, C-Boy. El Relaxo's ready to rock." Jillian's bare feet kicked up some balloons still on the floor. B.K. launched a sudden attack on one. Pop! This sent him airborne in fright. He scattered. Laugh therapy.

A middle-aged group of riders sat idling with their front wheels inches from the porch. In their prime, they may have been tough but now beer bellies spilled over their belts as they rubbed gray stubble and flashed bewilderment. "Look at them," I said. "Why bother getting off and knocking when you could announce your presence with a shower of happy bike horns?" I cracked the front door. A hero's cheer fell to collective grumbling when they saw it was only me. Doc Morrison, a close friend of A.L.'s yelled out, "Hey there, Colby. Where's A.L. at?"

Before I could respond, Amanda Triffle, straddling a pink Harley with plastic tits beneath its headlight, offered in a six-pack slur, "Yeah, I have a score to settle with that man," Miss Triffle's code for, I want to score with that man.

I said, "Hate to sour the vibe, guys, but you're a tad early. A.L.'s due at two." A collective murmuring broke out. "You guys are welcome to hang out here until he shows. Throw some horseshoes; toss a Frisbee; take on our hills . . ."

An approaching pickup truck stole their attention.

Doc smiled. "Hey! There's Hugo."

Hugo was Jack's go-to errand boy at the track.

Jack said, "I put my man in charge of the essentials, boys." Essentials being a tin tub crammed with ice and beer.

The gang also unearthed cards and gifts, including bottles of hard liquor, which A.L. hardly ever drank. This prompted me to set up our long, folding table on the patio. Jillian decorated it with more balloons.

"I've also got coffee and iced tea."

"Thanks, but it's almost noon. We're way beyond that," one of the riders chuckled to the next.

Another lowered his phone to ask, "Hey, Colby, mind if I invite a couple more friends over?"

I shrugged. "More the merrier, I guess."

He gave me the thumbs up and returned to his phone. "Sure, man, bring the whole gang."

Others quickly followed suit. Before long, tipped bottles and the clink of horseshoes striking iron gave El Relaxo a midsummer feel. Whooping laughter grew infectious. As the number of people swelled beyond what I could have imagined, so did the offerings of food, gifts and get-well cards. I fired up the grill and put on some dogs, sausages and burgers as tunes began to blast. Someone put an empty jar out on the table with A.L.'s name on it. By day's end the large jar would fill with cash.

The outdoor kitchen went to self-service after Beach and some other riding buddies of mine showed. With so many dirt bikes around and riders itching to check out our hills, I proposed a pick-up race. Young and old riders soon convened to the designated start line. Everyone else gathered to watch.

Just as the race was set to start, a cyclist pulled in gunning the engine. His rebel yell cut through everything as it converted festive faces into pensive ones. The crowd parted and my eyes widened at the site of this new arrival—or should I say rival.

"Damn it, make room pussy cats! What's this I see? A dirt race about to go and I wasn't invited? Shame on you all. Count me in, that is if there's room for one more!"

Klaus Ketty was the only man I knew who made my dad, and most others, openly seethe. The heavily tattooed ex-vet, ex-con and the region's present senior champion, feasted on all the negative energy aimed his way. His eyes shifted to me with a wry mouth as I instigated a stare-down with the devil.

Lucky for me, salty Doc Morrison took the lead. "Hello Klaus," Doc began. "Interesting seeing you at any social affair, never mind one for A.L.'s homecoming. Bored or couldn't find a fight?"

"Great seeing you, too, Doc." Klaus' gleaming gold tooth and dancing black eyes were more fit for an old western villain.

Jack said, "A.L.'s about to arrive back, and well, this was to be more of a *festive* occasion. Maybe you should be moving on."

"That's what I'm doing Jack, I'm moving to the starting line." A sly chuckle escaped him. "Relax, old man. I just happened to be passing by and, well, you know me, I can sniff a line of moto exhaust a mile away."

"Well, there it is," Doc said. "You had your sniff, now—"

Klaus waved a finger at him and smiled. "Loosen your belt a notch, Doc. This party is more interesting with me in it, and you know it."

My eyes fell Klaus' tattoo, *Faith, Motocross and Sobriety*. I ventured to guess two of the three had fallen victim. But the motocross part? Ketty was a solid competitor and culprit who had often made A.L. earn his wins.

"Hey, boy. Colby is it? Didn't get the invitation. Kind of hurts," Ketty spat. "Where's your daddy at?"

I stared a beat. "Coming, not long now."

"From rehab is it? He going to ride again or what? No offense, I never cared for the man, but compared to the rest of the clowns in these parts, at least he offered some competition."

"Yeah," I said. "Marionville spelled that out. Funny, you were right there with him when he went down." I didn't mind locking eyes for a second or two.

"That's right boy, shame about your daddy. All I know is you and I are off to the Regional." He smiled and stroked his bearded chin. "How 'bout a preview right now?"

An anonymous voice from the crowd suddenly sliced the air. "Ten bucks says you can't take the Weston boy, Ketty." Klaus spun toward the voice's direction.

Was that dude nuts? I was miles from top form, never mind taking on legendary Ketty and that bike. With demonic delight, Klaus said, "That greases my wheels. Are there any other brave fools out there up for lightening their loads? Klaus withdrew a wallet fat with bills and ran his thumb over them. "You know I'm good for it."

Though it was never a great idea to wager against God or the devil, most chose to. Soon a decent stack piled up. I became the defender of all things meek, moral and Weston.

Jack said, "Alright, Klaus, win and it's all yours. Lose to anyone and it goes to the A.L. fund."

Klaus feigned concern. "That's a lot of bikes to beat." He looked back. "What the hell, war on! Button up your domes, wildcats. Let's fire up this stogie!" Klaus squeezed into the sliver of space between me and Jillian, of course. When he ogled over her too long, he got rewarded with her lioness' growl and a stand-down stare.

I was motivated and harkened the rest. Idle engines began to gun.

"Alright, Junior," Klaus baited me over the roar. "Let's see if you got anything left after tearing up Marionville. I watched it. Your daddy taught you pretty well, but is it good enough?"

"Five laps around the course work for everybody?" I yelled over the zealous engines.

Helmeted nods answered me and Klaus's next quip was washed away by impatient throttles. I spotted Pastor Paul who I hadn't seen in months and waved him over. After apologizing for not making church since Mom had left, I anointed the pastor honorary starter and implored him to get God in our corner.

Pastor Paul uttered a short, controlled blessing skyward. I wanted this—for God, A.L., girlfriend, guests, and glory! Once Pastor Paul spiked his Titans cap on the ground, the line roared off. Quick start, I led the pack in the early going but I couldn't shake the roar of Ketty's bike right behind. No matter what I did to shoe him, he lingered close like an animal you regret feeding. Last lap, Klaus must have grown bored. He pulled even, offered a curt nod and overtook me for good.

Letdown.

After collecting his winnings and the ire of the disappointed betting crowd, Klaus made a quick stop by the patio where I exacted my revenge on a loaded hotdog.

"Winning is crack, ain't it boy?" he said over his ever boisterous throttle. "You can bring it, no doubt. Now you tell A.L. to get back on that damn bike of his and soon."

Like many, Klaus was uninformed as to the severity of A.L's plight. The rebel stunned me again as he eased the winnings from his billfold and tucked it into the jar. A finger touched his lips. "Don't be spreading a word about this, boy." He smiled. "Something like that could wreck a reputation." Klaus was diverted by the sudden hushed crowd when a van turned into our driveway.

He smirked. "Could this be the man of honor? My cue to retreat from this side show. Catch you at the track, boy—keep sharp. Semis will be upon us before you know it." Ketty's gunned throttle informed the crowd of his impending exit. He released his clutch and exploded past the van containing his once biggest, and perhaps most respected foe. After the last of Ketty's engine died, a palatable quiet followed. I quickstepped to the van as it came to a stop.

The driver's aggressive pull of the van's panel door echoed off the woods. A.L. emerged from the dark interior and wheeled onto a metal platform. He fought off a blinding sun as he tried to comprehend the large gathering before him. The lift's harsh mechanical whine of descent countered an otherwise sedate moment.

Jillian pulled close and squeezed my sweaty hand. "Damn, J-Girl," I said. "I should have had some music cued up or something." She didn't respond. Her camera possessed her as usual, and she pulled away and began firing off shots. I was excited but pensive. A package had arrived, one without instructions or guarantees.

After A.L.'s flash of surprise he geared back to neutral. Few would have known just then that his wheelchair was permanent, not transitional. Some familiar face in the crowd birthed a nod from A.L., but that was about it from him. Had this all been too much? I wondered. Once the van's hydraulic platform hit the earth, someone served up a single hoot. This put a pin in the tension and whoops and applause followed. The driver struggled with the wheelchair over a rough patch, so I hastily moved in to assist him.

I put a hand on my dad's shoulder and yelled, "Hey, everyone, what do you say? Let's hear it for my dad, huh, the best dirt rider ever to come out this side of Tennessee!" A rowdy cheer vaulted from the guests.

We moved him onto smoother grass and wheeled him to the patio. His first words to me leaked somewhat terse. "I take it everyone thought Taylor Swift was coming. What's all this?"

"It's for you, A.L.," I said and pushed him closer to the gift table.

A reception line formed. To his credit, A.L. held up and found it in him to greet each guest with some degree of charm. Visitors bent and gave him hugs; others shed a few tears. He took their hands and thanked them as brief and sincere as a campaigning politician. But his biggest, unfettered smile came when Bubbles burst through the woods and froze after spotting him. She then broke in a full sprint without regard for the strangers. When she reached A.L.'s side, she barked. She wanted her master all to herself. A.L. eventually quieted her with some soothing whispers and gentle strokes of her head. From then on, his eyes mostly stayed glued to his dog even as he thanked the last of the lingering few.

I drank all of it in. A sudden optimism flooded me. Everything would work out, somehow. The fun, games and laughter tailed off and the place emptied, save for Jillian. Most of the departed had promised to return for a visit soon. Few ever would. I'd struggle with that in the coming months until I grew convinced that most had come not to honor a legend as much as to bury one.

CHAPTER 22—ACCLIMATION

A.L. barely outlasted the diehard partiers. Jillian manned the wheelchair as I watched the last of my friends drive off. "We have a little surprise for you in the garage, A.L.," Jillian told him.

"A private jet?" he answered dryly.

"Almost as exciting." Jillian covered A.L.'s eyes with one hand. With the other, she yanked his chair into a lame spin. Jillian uncovered his eyes. "Ta da!"

After an expressionless stare at his new ramp, he pronounced, "Just what I always wanted."

I ignored his sass. "Thought it would work best here, A.L. and it only cost a slice of your workbench to fit."

A.L. sighed. "I was partial to that slice."

Jillian jumped in, "Colby researched the ramp, right down to the correct slope."

"*You* built this Colby?" A.L. teased.

"Nah, more researched it. The Carters did most of the work."

Jillian's pep still flew, "Oh Colby mastered that screw gun by the end."

"Uh huh," A.L.'s eyes rolled to me.

"Mr. Drake donated the wood," I added.

A clicked cheek and stoic drawl followed. "Could be a source of new thrills . . . gliding down at high speeds; seeing if I can stay up."

A giggle escaped Jillian. "Better use your bike helmet for a while, A.L."

"Mr. C. also installed a bar in the bathroom," I said.

"Wonderful," A.L. said. "He supply the booze as well?"

Jillian laughed. "You *wish* you had that kind of bar, A.L."

All this silly business was too much for Bubbles, who didn't understand human jokes and only wanted A.L. to herself. She filled the garage with repeated loud barks.

"Hush, girl," A.L. tried to settle her as he wheeled himself to the foot of the ramp. He paused and flashed that same look I had once given Jack's taller dirt hills when I was eight.

"May I have the honor, A.L.?" Jillian asked.

"No, I'll give it a try. But stay close, Jillian, just in case . . . Damn thing's like staring up at Mt. Olympus."

A.L. began a labored climb with a quarter turn of his wheel. A struggled groan left him as his hands snapped back to hold his gains. But his strength was still clearly not where it needed to be. He lost his grip on the subsequent try and began to roll back at us like a one-hundred and sixty-five pound bowling ball.

"Oh my god!" Jillian shrieked then leaped from the ramp.

I snapped ahead and brought it to a stop. "Whoa, horsie!"

"You were saying something about correct slope, Jillian?" A.L. panted. "Colby, your next project should be to install an electric motor on this chair."

"Okay, so the ramp might be a bit steep, but it'll build your strength. When he didn't comment or move, I told Jillian, "I've got it from here, J-Girl," and pushed him up.

Once inside El Relaxo, A.L. acted like he had entered a kitchen showroom. "Wait. This can't be my place. Where'd all the dishes and the rest go?"

I smirked with pride. "Dishes done, stacked and in their rightful place. Even mopped the floor." I peered down. "Well, kinda."

"I can almost see my reflection in those swirls." A.L. pulled at his new whiskers. "What's got into you, boy?"

"Demi's threats, mostly, so don't get too hopeful."

"I thought I had picked up her scent." A.L. rolled to the kitchen table. "Where's my mail?"

"Tossed, most of it."

"What?" He gasped. "But I heat the place in the winter with the junk mail, Colby."

"It's all in a box in your office with plenty more on the way, no doubt."

A.L. wheeled into the living room and paused. "Is it me, the drugs or is the floor . . . undulating?"

Jillian laughed. "It's balloons, A.L. Like five hundred of them!"

"That's a lotta balloons." He wheeled himself through Balloon Sea.

After a while Jillian bade goodbye and I walked her out. "What do you think?" I asked.

"He's got the old sass going. That's a good start."

"A restart, you mean."

We kissed and she sped off on Blue.

Back inside, time marched heavy with each tick of the kitchen clock. I didn't know what to do or say. I endured the silent awkwardness until A.L. broke it.

"People sure brought a lot of stuff . . . and booze."

"Yeah, they did."

"Where are we going to put all the extra food?"

I shrugged. "Garage fridge, should fit."

"Okay." He wheeled to some photos on the mantle. "Go on and do that now, then."

As I filled the fridge with food and beer, I dwelled on first impressions. A.L. definitely seemed a bit weak but not bad, considering. By the time I was done, he'd wheeled out to the porch and fixed on the riding hills. "Did you miss the view?" I said

He wheeled off without an answer. "Grab me a brewskie if one's left, will you?"

"We've got about a year's worth, any special request?"

"Pick me a winner, ace." I returned with an open one, and it went straight to his lips. He stared at the bottle with a sour face.

"No good?"

"It'll get 'er done." His eyes shifted to the birdcage where Commander had been pacing desperate circles looking for a way to rejoin A.L.

"He's raring for a reunion."

"Release the bird!," Al said.

I opened the cage and Commander immediately fluttered down to A.L.'s extended arm, then pulled himself up to roost on his shoulder.

A.L. beamed. "How are you Commander? Have you learned to hunt like a hawk?" Commander nestled his beak into A.L.'s face. Pure love. "I missed my animals. Even you, a little bit, boy."

"You got a great turn out, huh, A.L.?"

"Felt like landing in a Woodstock documentary. Did you invite the whole town?"

"Nah, just popped up like that. We even had a pick-up race on the field . . . I didn't even show you the money jar."

"Money, jar?"

"Yeah, a collection was taken up at the party."

A.L. nervously flicked at the bottle's label with his thumbnail. "Yep. Everybody got to see the new A.L.," he said and drew a long pull from his beer. "Not one comment on the chair, funny."

"Maybe they didn't know it was, you know . . ." I shrugged.

"Permanent? Say it if that's what you mean."

I shirked off his suddenly biting tone. "Well, old boy, I should tend to school stuff, I suppose. You good to chill with Commander?"

"Yeah, no need to be doting on me all the time, okay? Do what needs doing."

"Alright. Do you have any meds?" I asked.

"A lifetime supply. Going to try to manage without them, mostly." He slowly wheeled himself into the living room, closer to the TV. "Hand me the remote. Let's see if the Braves are playing." As luck would have it they were, and his team was down two in the eighth against the Mets. Even though it was a preseason game he still barked at the screen at some rookie's miscue. Better the Braves than me.

I left him to fend while I worked upstairs. It was hard to keep focus on school stuff. Thoughts of logistics and planning his needs distracted me. When I came back down, I found him asleep and wheeled him into the office. He came to and first noticed the unfolded futon.

"That the new sleeping arrangement?"

"For now, 'til we can work out something to get you upstairs."

"This will do." He looked around. "You brought in my fly fishing lure box from the garage. Been a while since I made one of those. That'll keep my hands busy, good."

"Maybe we can get out and test some of the new lures on the river, soon."

"Maybe." Then from nowhere, "Did you see it? See me go down?"

"Not really. Mark Beck and I were jawing at the time. He was singing your praises, too. You must have been sneezing distance from the finish. That's when I heard this ginormous exhale from the crowd. Helluva ambulance ride over."

"You see any nasty going on? Any contact from another rider? I don't remember."

"Nothin' obvious from where I was standing." Didn't mention Klaus' earlier appearance, or his act of charity at the end of our pick up race. A.L. might've set the jar's booty aflame just knowing Ketty's fingerprints were all over some of those bills.

I gave him a recap of what happened after the accident, especially the Demi highlights. That brought his first short but honest chuckle. But he couldn't let the crash go.

"Jillian filmed it, right?" he said.

"Yeah, but it kinda lacks one of those Disney-like endings, for sure."

"Have her burn me a copy."

"Why, A.L? What's done is done. I haven't even braved a look."

He was insistent. "I said I want to see it, okay?"

"You're the boss."

His tone shifted to edgy. "Correct."

I sucked it up and tried to reroute his mood. "I brought down your old guitar, A.L. It's in the office."

A.L. wheeled in and gazed upon the guitar propped in a corner. He wheeled over and picked it up, then attempted some strums before tuning it some. The strumming resumed and A.L. croaked out a few lyrics but didn't get far. He abruptly halted. "Hell, last time I played that thing it was to your mother, by the fire, way back when. He kind of raised it to me in acknowledgment before returning it to the stand. "These digits, like everything else, have gone soft."

I showed him the bathroom mod and I came up with a little used metal bowl he could keep within reaching distance on the tub. He nodded then wheeled himself back to the living room with a request to get horizontal. He stared at the couch for a bit. "Need some help?"

"No. I need to do this myself. They made me do it at rehab, though I still have a ways to go . . . but let's see what happens." A.L. struggled but his lion's heart wouldn't accept failure and eventually he made it onto the couch. Though painful to watch he pulled it off and that gave me hope.

CHAPTER 23—NEW AND OLD ROUTINES

I wasn't thinking about my day as much as running through A.L.'s logistics as my morning bagel began to smoke. I brought his phone from the living room where he had left it, plugged it in and placed it on the table next to him. I also left a sandwich and a thermos with coffee, all within reach. The last touch was the morning paper. That, I put on the foot of bed—even as he snoozed through my efforts. *There A.L., Santa came.* I opened the fridge and stared at the leftovers. No doubt he'd prefer them warm, so I placed the microwave on a wooden footstool and found an outlet within reach. His toiletries had to be placed within reach as well. All this altruism caused me to run behind. Phone and book bag in hand, I hopped in the truck and peeled off for school.

When I reached homeroom and calc, General Benson snickered as he handed me a math book to replace the one I'd left behind. No good deeds left unpunished.

After English I headed straight for the theater. I looked forward to the rehearsal even if I had yet to muster the courage to explain my new activity to A.L. I dashed off a

quick text telling him to chill—I'd be running later than usual. He shot right back.
>Late? Why?
>At school. U ok?
>Guess.
Sounded more lonely than in peril so I texted > Hang in.
Rehearsal ended. I had gotten into the habit of hanging out with a couple of sage-like seniors and other cast members, afterwards. They were always bringing up interesting worldly stuff and funny stories. I didn't add much; just let it all soak in. But this was A.L.'s first day alone, so I headed straight for home.
I found him on the porch watching his hills erode while nursing a can of beer. He came off annoyed, "Where have you been?"
"School, like I texted you. Everything okay?"
He shrugged.
"How'd you like your four-star room service this morning?"
"Beat rehab, thanks."
"Mrs. Dejon says hi."
"So time does heal all wounds."
"And old pranks apparently. How'd things go today?"
"Good, mostly, until—"
So everything hadn't gone to plan. He had taken a header trying to get from the futon to his chair which left him flailing like a dry-docked river bass.
"Damn, A.L., you okay?"
"Things only hurt from the waist up."
"Sucks, dude."
"I'm fine. It took a few tries, but I got back in the chair. These are the new, fun challenges I must embrace."
"Little steps lead to big leaps. Remember? You used to tell me that."

A.L. cracked his first smile.

"Bet you didn't lock down those wheels before you called it a night like the guy at rehab said."

"Probably not."

"You'll get straight. What about getting yourself up on the throne?"

"No problem. I pulled myself up and crapped like royalty."

"You've been crowned A.L." *Who would have thought a month ago I'd have such meaningful chats.* "Seriously, dude, something like that happens again, dial me up. I'm only an eight minute drive away."

"Eight? Takes me over fifteen."

"Cops will understand."

A.L. pondered a bit. "What kept you so long, anyway? I was hoping check out your ride before dinner; see where things are at."

There was no getting out of this. "It's been such a freak show lately; I haven't had time to tell you."

His eyes narrowed. "Tell me what?"

"Beach kind of suckered me into joining this club, see, and—"

He smiled. "Ah! Doing a little off-season weight lifting? Great. Never hurts the moto any, either. That reminds me; I jumped on a buy that will benefit us both."

I welcomed any veer from the inevitable. "Did you break down and get one those fancy jet tubs? Hell with that and a box of Mr. Bubbles, Jillian and I'd be pretty much set on a Friday night."

"Fat chance," he said. "We have all the Bubbles we can handle. Don't we, girl?" *Thump, thump, thump* went her tail. "No, I went ahead and ordered us a workout gym."

"Boring. Just kidding. That's great."

A.L. looked off. "You made me forget what the hell I was going to ask you."

"About the massive allowance raise?"

"No, no. We were talking about Beach and after school clubs," he said.

At light speed, I fessed up about the whole drama club entrapment. A.L. slipped to a bitter hue then smacked the chair. "You did what?"

"Don't spin out, A.L. It's not a cult group."

A.L.'s chair charged unnervingly close to me. "Be serious! Did you really sign up for a play?"

I shrugged. "Well . . . yeah."

All the good air left him. "But why, especially with MX Regional coming up?"

"It's a bit part. It's not a tragedy; Beach asked me."

"Beach? Well boy, I'm seeing a tragedy in the making about a talent who squanders his chance to be a motocross national champion over a silly play."

"Are you really that mad? It's cool. The cast is great, and dude, wait until you check out Beach. Fun-ny."

"I'm so proud of you both!" He rolled in tight-wheeled circles.

"I'm not selling Silver, dude. Look, you're edgy, I get it. This was your first day of being alone and—"

He snipped, "Don't patronize me, Colby. Poor choice, bad time."

"A.L., the regional is more than a month after the last show. Chill."

"I wonder how many other of the thirty-nine riders are prancing around on a stage in tutus or whatever it is."

"Tutus? I think that's ballet, dude. Also my character's a badass, you'll be all in."

"And you're going to be all out."

"It may have slipped your transmission, but those thirty-nine other wannabees in

Marionville? They're the ones with ground to make up."

"Knives dull pretty quick when not regularly sharpened," he said.

"I'll sharpen it," I said.

"But that ain't the same as obsessing about it." A.L. tapped a finger on the arm of the chair. You need to talk about it?"

I went to the window." Talk about what?"

"Your ride. What happened? Sounds like you've been finding time for everything else but Silver."

"It's been fighting me a little, maybe."

A.L. stared off. "How often you seen a rider go down in events?"

"One too many."

A.L. paused. "Eh, maybe I pushed too hard there at the end . . . I knew the track was crawling with pros and . . . I needed to impress them."

He waited but I offered nothing.

"Now I gotta live with it. We both need to, son. All the same, what happened to me was a freak thing. You're a special talent. It's always come easy and sometimes that can be a problem too." He sighed and rolled off to his office.

I stared through the milk film at the bottom of the glass, wondering if I would ever feel A.L.'s level of obsession about anything. Annoyance slipped to pity. Why had fate robbed him? Was everything just stupid luck? I slammed my glass to the table, clomped down the ramp and mounted Silver to prove a point.

Three laps in, just when I thought I'd found my old rhythm, things got away and I went down. Again. I wanted nothing more than to walk away, but a glance caught him spying from the porch window, how he often had done. I pulled Silver up, had a quick chat between man and machine and climbed back on and resumed. That evening the clink of silverware on our plates was about the only sound shared between us.

In the coming days, the old coach in A.L. couldn't hold back. He insisted on filming my workouts and fine tuning my technique but there's a fine line between motivation and desperation. The latter was what I began to feel from him. Rants became frequent and long, not his old self at all. Fortunately, I had my castle in the sky where I sought escape. The stairs acted as a protective moat when things grew pissy. Among other things, I worked on memorizing my lines. Figured I might free up on stage if I could get my nose out of the script. When I got overly dramatic on certain lines A.L. would yell up and ask if I had lost my fucking mind. I absorbed his sass and tried to steer from confrontation when he got irrational. That worked for a while.

One late afternoon, a woman with prizefighter arms pulled into Relaxo and emerged from her car with two bags. I intercepted her to ask what she was selling before it occurred to me, she was the physical therapist that had been scheduled for home visits. I whispered her arrival to A.L. who was in the office, glued to his computer. "Hup to, A.L., the lady with the whips is here."

A.L. cautiously emerged from his study. I caught his eyes when she introduced herself as Mrs. Beard. A.L. attempted his old charming ways with an extended hand towards her. I had seen enough and wanted nothing more than to return to my castle upstairs and an online battle with some friends. But A.L. asked me to stick around and listen. So with crossed arms I stewed the whole time.

Mrs. Beard proceeded in a professional and cold manner. She presented options such as further modifications to help A.L. jump back to normal life. *Good luck with that.* He nodded along and began his new beard-twisting thing.

Pleasantry time inevitably eroded to torture time. Mrs. Beard pulled out some resistance bands and other gear as A.L. looked on helplessly, eventually releasing the nervous proclamation, "Uh oh, here come the colorful whips, Colby."

I'd seen all I could take and booked out of there.

When I reemerged downstairs for a snack, Mrs. Beard had cleared out and A.L. was well into his first beer of the day.

"Did you earn that?"

"God, and I thought the guy at the rehab lacked a soul. Her biceps alone should have tipped me off."

"Don't get bleak. It'll get easier. I heard that somewhere. Meanwhile, I agreed with her on the whole you finding something new part. Maybe hook up with one of those wheelchair basketball teams or get one of those special chairs for road racing. Seen those? They're slick, man. You need some action, some competitive release, old boy."

"Talk is cheap. Where's your action at?"

I reigned in the divisive. "It's coming this weekend at the next event. I've got some things figured out. You'll get to see it firsthand."

CHAPTER 24--DAWN BEFORE THE RACE

Saturday morning I woke before the alarm. I was anxious to prove myself—for me and A.L. I fed the animals and checked the forecast: clear skies and little wind. Reason enough to put this motohead in a whistling mood. I cracked open my racing folio and reviewed the venue as usual, but time ticked down and there wasn't long to get too lost in the data. It was getting late and new routines now sucked up the mornings faster than ever.

I entered A.L.'s office, cracked a window to chase the stale air and commented on the sunny conditions. All the while A.L. snored on. The last half inch of whiskey in the glass betrayed his activities from the night before. My positive attitude wavered, as priorities shifted from my game to his.

I heralded, "Motivate, old boy. It's race day!"

Nothing. A shake of his shoulder finally yielded a few grunts. A dazed head rose, looked around, and then collapsed back.

"Partying late to the tunes last night, A.L.? I had to plug my damn ears, old boy. But no worries, coffee's on. Are you hearing me?"

He jerked and looked startled, then seemingly tried to swing his legs out of the bed. Old habits, the last to go. I immediately regretted having even uttered, *Race day*. He'd be a grounded spectator at a track he once dominated. All I could do was turn on the cheer and shake the pom-poms. Odd how the roles had reversed or so it seemed.

"C'mon, man, let's get those morning needs out of the way. After, I'll fix your favorite race day egg sandwich. I even bought muffins to go with."

He clawed at his pillow. "Great, man, go. Do what you need to do to get ready."

"I have. Now you need to get ready. The Carters will be swinging by soon, so . . . you want a piggyback ride to the can or what?"

A bitchy eye rolled my way. "Alright, help me into the chair, I guess." Once aboard, he sarcastically clapped his hands and said, "Yes! Yes! Yes!" to a morning he clearly despised. I dunked a wash cloth in the stainless steel bowl with warm, soapy water and handed it to him so he could hit all the essentials. Marine bath, he called it.

All thoughts returned to the importance of the race. I was hell-bent to make it a comeback run. Breakfast done, I lightly knuckled the bathroom door. "Almost done?"

He tried to speak through his electric toothbrush. "Thith whole deal ith a wonderful . . . Roy-al pain in the ath, ith what." I cracked the door. He rinsed and dramatically spat into the bowl. My eyes rolled to the ceiling. *Thank you A.L., and fate, too, for all you've done.*

A.L. finally emerged, still this side of shipwrecked.

"Ready to eat?" I said.

He said he wasn't hungry and felt off; said I should get ready. But what did that mean? Was he too sick to go? Was it a hangover or something more serious?

"What is it, A.L.?"

He took one bite of the sandwich and let the rest drop to the plate. I tried to stay upbeat. "Warren Mills should be crawling with your old riding buddies dying to see you."

"If they were dying to see me, they'd pay me the odd visit."

"Have you invited anyone?" I asked. A.L. didn't answer. I debated not telling him but broke the news. "Look, I wasn't going to spoil the surprise, but Jack arranged a little gathering after the event for you."

He straightened. "What? That's odd. Why did he call *you* to discuss this?"

"Because he wanted it to be a surprise?"

"Eh." He belched.

"Gross, A.L. Anyway, it'll be fun." It was like trying to get good speed on deflated tires. His gloom prevailed. The sound of Carter's truck stepped up the urgency. "That's them, A.L. Showtime!"

"Christ, not so loud," he growled.

The spirit oozed out of me. "What's wrong, man? Are you that hungover?"

"No, I'm just not back, I guess. Look, finish what needs doing. Load up your stuff and get going." He began wheeling for the sunroom then ordered, "Release the bird!" I dropped my plate into the sink, too hard, I guess. It shattered.

"Get a hold of yourself Colby! You're acting childish."

"I wasn't trying to break it!" I spiked the shards into the garbage. "Maybe I should sit this one out, too."

"You're not sitting anything out," A.L. said. "You need reps against real opponents; that's obvious. You'll race and you'll win, with or without me. C'mon man, you're almost seventeen, same age I struck out on my own and had to learn to do everything, myself."

"Until now," I mumbled.

"I heard that!" He wheeled back towards me. "Sorry I'm not a hundred percent after a wipeout that put me in a wheelchair. Deal with it!"

The hard rap at the door went ignored. "I'm trying, A.L. You've never missed an event of mine and you haven't been getting out at all. You need sunlight and someone to talk to beside a parrot and you've got friends expecting you."

"What I need is more time. Now respect that."

"Fine, but cuddling up with a whiskey bottle wasn't on the doctor's list."

He thrust a finger forward. "Don't get in my wheelhouse, boy!"

"Bit hard these days."

"The Carters are waiting. Get going. Release Commander, *please*." I did. A.L. produced his wallet and removed two twenties as the next series of raps came from the door. "Here, buy the little lady something and give Ned a ten spot for gas." I reached for it but he drew it back. "You've got this. Make me proud." I grabbed the money.

Jillian cracked open the door with a confused look. "Coming, guys?"

Jillian didn't get my usual warm greeting. She got rolled eyes and I got back a look of understanding. I clomped down the new ramp to fetch Silver and my gear.

Jillian entered the garage. "Hey. What's going on? Is something wrong?"

I talked to the floor. "A.L.'s not feeling up to the trip."

"Sure he'll be alright alone?"

"He thinks he'll be. Let's just load and go."

Bike and gear packed, I entered the cab and endured the cold stare of an impatient Mr. Carter. "Good morning, sir!" I said with false cheer.

"Where's your dad?" he asked.

My gaze shifted to El Relaxo's peeling paint. "Looks like just the three of us, today, sir. Hey guys, clear skies, I see."

But the only fake smile came from me.

CHAPTER 25—PARTY OF ONE

Even from the Carters' idling truck I could hear the tunes leaking from El Relaxo. I had a hunch there was more to A.L.'s cure than that blues shuffle punching through the walls. I looked over to the trophy Jillian still clutched. Yeah, I was a little pissed I hadn't earned one, too, but I was surprisingly satiated by my girlfriend's success. I hugged Jillian and congratulated her on her strong finish. "Keep this up baby and it will be me filming you at these things." She told me not to get down, which was hard after back to back subpar showings. I thanked Mr. Carter, who wouldn't take a cent of gas money, hugged Jillian and left. I pulled Silver and my gear into the garage and clomped up A.L.'s ramp to brave the music's visceral sonic assault—and maybe his.

I found him, head teetering, bathed in an infomercial's sickly blue light and surrounded by cans and a shot glass. I retreated back to the kitchen to rummage and it hit me how it had regressed to its dirty dish despair. After grabbing the other half of an old wrapped sandwich, I propped myself in the open space to the living room. Seems quite the party had happened. Commander had stayed stoically loyal on his master's shoulder. A.L. was oblivious to the long, white streaks of blue and white guano that ran down the back of his shirt and chair. Bubbles and B.K. remained conspicuously absent.

Commander roused. His squawked greeting blasted A.L. into reentry. He fumbled with his wheels and labored to pull an about face. Commander was spooked by A.L.'s sudden moves and launched himself for his cage. A.L. stupidly lunged for the bird in flight, a potentially disastrous reflex move.

"A.L.!" I wailed.

Luckily, his attempt was errant. Commander reached his cage, free of harm, and tucked himself in through the open cage door. A.L.'s sheepish mask of shame was brief before his shit-faced grin replaced it. I'd never seen him more wasted. I flexed a wrist, a plea to lower the volume. After a spastic struggle, he located the knob and dropped it some. Pity found me as I witnessed a man desperate for anything to celebrate. But besides Jillian's success, there wasn't much cause to rejoice.

"You made it back in one piece, thank God." He slapped himself, maybe an attempt to stop the room form spinning. He narrowed his brow and waved a finger, but his attempt to play the wise elder was futile. A nonsensical slur betrayed him.

"You've been on my mind all day, *baby*."

He never called me that. "Partying with all your friends, A.L.? No wait. They were all at the track; disappointed you didn't come. My mistake . . . or was it yours?"

"Oh I'm going to have a big party, invite them all over. Right now though . . . uh, is there any beer left? Grab yourself one boy . . . Everything I need is here . . . my music, my bird, my boy . . ." He looked around. "Wait. Where's

Bubbles? Girl!" He moaned before he pulled off a couple of pumps toward the basement door.

"Watch the stairs, A.L."

"Bubbly!"

Nothing. "Where is she, A.L.? Out?"

"Wait. That's right I let her out. She's fine. Let's talk about you!"

"Chill out a sec." I turned for the door and pierced the midnight stillness with a two-fingered whistle. Nothing, at first. Concern finally dropped with the sounds of familiar trotting paws. Bubbles burst into the circle of porch light and accepted my rub. She barked towards the dark she had returned from. I kneeled and offered caring strokes. "You been out all day, girl?" She licked my face a couple of times and followed me in, tail flying.

A.L. threw up his arms. "There she is!" Bubbles went straight to the master, who doted on her. But the dog's ultimate priority was food so she skidded around the corner, into the kitchen, soon as I poured kibble.

I returned to A.L. "The cat in?"

A.L. shucked it off. "I don't know, I don't think so. He's fine wherever he is. He's got nine lives; more than I fucking got. Get us some beers. I want to hear about your race."

"We're all out of beers, A.L." I lied, then went to the bottom of the staircase and called to B.K. without success. "A.L., look, we've talked about leaving the cat out after dark. The area's swarming with coyotes. I heard them yipping the other night when you were gone. Think I'm going to blast off a couple of shells in the woods with the twelve-gauge. Scatter their coyote asses."

"Don't be an idiot. Plugging the empty night air with holes won't bring B.K back. Find us some damn brewsky and pull up a chair, damn it."

"Wait a second, A.L." I went outside and yelled for B.K., but cats don't obey like dogs.

A.L. mocked, "Lose your kitty?"

"Not funny, A.L."

"Fine." He slapped his chair handles. "Down to business, then. Tell me about the day."

"Well, good news. Jillian got herself a first place trophy."

"Awesome, man!" He rubbed his chin. "What about Team Weston?"

I looked away. "I took a tumble coming down one of the hills. Nothing bad, but too much lost time, I guess. There were some good moments." I exhaled. "So yeah, I got shut out in this one."

A wedge of silence. "You let this morning get in your melon didn't you? I can't be holding your hand no more."

"Fine by me. Don't sweat it, I'm not. This was a pick up race, won't hurt my standing much. Come the Regional, I'll be tippity-top, wait and see."

"If you can salvage the old confidence." He slurred on, "I'm trying to say . . . no one cares if you win or fall on your face. That's why you better care." He half sung, "Oh dear bread and beer. If I was dead I wouldn't be here." He took the last long pull from his can. "I'll get you all coached up like I do."

"We'll see," I said.

"See what?"

"So I talked to Jack a little at the event. He said I'm welcome to use his track much as I like, no charge. I know what needs working on. Might as well use a pro track, right?"

"Generous of him." A.L. looked down then back at me. "Guess we can do it out there, long as you can get your back; impress the pro scouts."

I wasn't thinking we, but I let it slide. I gave a final shout outside for the cat. Still nothing. A.L. said he would try again before bedding down. It grew stone quiet.

I started upstairs but didn't make it more than a couple of steps before I heard my name called out; once, then louder a second time. I returned down and asked, "What?" Something was wrong. His color had turned ghoulish. He attempted to wheel himself to the bathroom but lost strength. He began breathing deeply and grabbed his middle.

I rushed to him. "A.L., you don't look so hot. Talk to me, man."

"Under the sink! The pail. Bring it. Hurry!"

"A pail? What for?" Then I realized. Oh shit.

I bolted to the kitchen and snatched up the plastic bucket. Everything, including the *Living Gloves*, scattered onto the kitchen floor. Out of the corner of my eye, I spied what I believed to be A.L.'s true culprit: a whiskey bottle under the sink, its contents way down from the last time I'd seen it.

A.L. ripped the pail from my hands and buried his head in it, his guttural moans reverberating into the plastic. Nothing came up. I parked by his side, put a hand on his back and turned away. "Breathe, man. Slow, easy breaths. Feel better, old boy?"

From the bottom of the plastic bucket the muffled voice came. "Sorry, Colby. I'll get better. I'll be better."

"Counting on it, man. You're still part of the team." A profound sadness overtook me. Both of us had lost our shit.

He lifted his head, and oddly his tone went from panicked to very matter-of-fact. "Why Colby, I believe I've been over-served." A not so dignified, wretched gush of foul stew flooded the pail with a most repugnant smell, a mix of beer, whiskey, bile and who knows what else.

"Oh god," I said. I wheeled him into the bathroom, poured cold water on a rag and handed it to him. "You take any meds with your drinks tonight? Should I be more worried than I am, old boy?"

"No pills, don't think so . . . the worst is over."

It wasn't. The next round left him like a fire hose. I flushed the horrible, stinky mess down the toilet and rinsed out the bucket. He began to shake. "I'm cold." He was gaunt and pathetic, leaving me in a rare moment of wishing to God, Mom was around to make things right again. I dropped to my bottom next to his chair on the cool tiles.

I said, "So this day's sucked for both of us. Guess we try again, tomorrow, okay?" He nodded. I put one hand on his arm. *What if this is the new norm, A.L. Version 2.0.*

I helped him out of his chair, onto his futon. He shook with chills so I added another layer of warmth. I placed the rinsed-out bucket by his bed, in case. I stayed by his side until his breathing became as rhythmic as the machines that had recently kept him alive. I brought his blanket to his chin and killed the tunes in the living room. Bubbles padded in, paused for a brief rub, and took over the watch at A.L.'s bedside. I called out the door for B.K. No trace. Everything felt hopeless and beyond my control.

Upstairs, in my kingdom in the sky, a surprise lay sleeping at the foot of my bed. "B.K.? I thought you'd become Mr. Coyote's snack. Why didn't you answer?" But B.K was a cat and answered to no one. He, at least, slept soundly.

CHAPTER 26--A BETTER PATH

"Maybe you can do something with him!" Mrs. Beard almost flattened me as she lumbered past, straight for her car. *What happened?*

"Colby!" Commander and A.L. both hailed my name from different places. I steered for the one I thought was at the root of Mrs. Beard's anger. That would be in the kitchen where A.L flipped through the paper. "Well, well, the drama king has returned," he uttered blandly before snapping the page to the next.

"My drama is nothing compared to what blew out the door. What's up with Mrs. Beard?"

He played the fool. "Don't know for sure, besides our chemistry never clicked from the start." He folded the paper and rifled it into recycling. "Whatever. Her services won't be needed. I let her go."

"You fired her? She didn't seem that bad around me."

"She never made you beg with one knee cocked into your back," he said.

"True . . . so, are you getting someone new, or—"

"Not someone, *something*. It has arrived." A.L. zipped down the ramp at daredevil speed, right up to a tall box tipped against the wall.

"Is this the new gym equipment you ordered?"

"The game changer has arrived. I could use a hand putting it together if you've got a sec."

"You mean two hours?"

I had planned to run over to Jillian's. Recent domestic needs had robbed me of J-time and I'd been missing her. Out of duty I followed A.L. Parts were soon unpacked and splayed all over the cool, cement floor. Diagram in hand, he directed me from his chair and cracked jokes. It was the closest thing to enthusiasm I'd seen from A.L. since his return. Finished, the workout station loomed like a grand prehistoric bird with ropes and a seat.

"Wow, looks great . . . hope it gets good use," I said.

"That's why I got it, for both of us. Twenty minutes a day is all it takes!"

I wanted to ask what his plans were for the remaining twenty-three hours and change.

He got himself onto the bench and began pulling the cables like a mad fool. His breathing grew heavy and he petered out quick. "I feel more powerful already!"

"Awesome," I said dryly.

He let the last weight clank. "I've got a way to go, pal."

"The thing had to come with shortcuts," I said.

"Alright, wise ass, you hop on and give it a try."

I helped him off, hopped on and took a few tugs. "Wow. I can get into this." I cycled through some of the options. "Who needs the weight room at school? I can get ready for fall ball right here."

"Won't hurt the riding, either," A.L. said. "Hey, I want to show you something inside."

His AWOL deal at the last moto event had left me pissed. But even if I didn't want to be there, at least the old boy flashed some flame. Maybe this was a turning point. He rolled to the base of the ramp and paused. I took a step forward to help. "Let's see if I can do this alone," he said. A.L. refused help and with labored determination ascended to the top without assistance. He led me to his office where he showed me some new fly-fishing lures he had been working on. He held one up; a true beauty with blues, greens and reds weaved in. "Think any bass will be able to resist this?" he asked.

"Hey, *I'm* even tempted to bite it." A magnifying glass allowed a closer look. "One of your best to date, A.L."

He implored me to watch him put the final touches on another lure with surgical-like precision. There was a slight shake in his hand, not seen before. A.L.'s brow narrowed as he spoke in halts. "I just have to . . . pull this little thread through . . . there we go." He began to tie the knot with a pair of tweezers and clipped off the excess. "This one's ready to hunt."

"Let's take out the little sucker and see if we can catch one."

"Like now?"

"Why not? There's plenty daylight left."

"Maybe you should hit the hills for a bit."

"I'll get the time in, A.L. I'll have us packed and on the river in no time."

He thought, then nodded. "Alright."

It was mid-week, so few cars dotted the parking area by the river and the bike trail that hugged it. I toiled like a Chilean mule to get A.L. and his chair onto the smooth blacktop. But once there, everything turned idyllic. A chirped greeting from a songbird sounded. The dappled, spring light penetrated the new green leaves. The river churned a reddish brown. Returned to nature, A.L. immediately relaxed. His head darted this way and that like he'd never seen any of this before. Energized, he waved me off and began wheeling himself along. When he petered out, A.L. grew a little peeved at himself.

"What's wrong with me?" he hissed through his clenched jaw.

"You commit to this and your new gym, before long you'll be showing up the marathoners." It seemed like the perfect time to revisit the lightweight chairs made for long distance runs on smooth surfaces. He didn't respond but maybe the idea would rattle around some.

The sound of the falls beckoned us. We reached our old favorite fishing spot. As we readied our gear, light chatter returned us to easier times. We settled on the remains of an ancient dam that rose high above the river. Being there returned me to the boy who regarded his dad as a hero; one who could show me everything about life.

"See that?" A.L. screamed towards the bass that leapt from the churn. "Ha! Hungry and waiting for us." We launched our first casts and let our flies drift on the calmer waters away from the churn. Naturally he teased me with an old story I wanted to forget.

"You caught your first fish here, remember? Smallmouth bass, pretty good size. It had swallowed the fishing hook pretty deep."

"Yeah, that was a long time ago." I nodded then launched my next cast.

"Not to me," A.L. said. "Time speeds faster with age, I guess. Anyway, you couldn't get the hook out."

"Don't remind me."

He laughed. "You panicked when I took out my pliers. You begged me, *Don't hurt him, don't hurt him, A.L.* But with the cool of a surgeon I inserted the pliers. After a few gentle wiggles the hook popped free."

"I was like, what? Seven? Eight? Standing in about the same spot I am now. We climbed down to water's edge to release it. It sank and struggled to right itself. It couldn't get upright. I panicked."

"You actually shed tears for the little thing!" He chuckled.

I shrugged. "It popped back to life and darted away like some miracle. You were the miracle man."

A.L. chuckled. "Weren't them the days?"

He began whipping his rod. Fighting off the breeze, he found his mark. I followed. On the third try, my fly skimmed off the top of the swirling waters close to his. Side by side, we fell into our own thoughts and the rhythm of our casts until a hard tug snapped me back to real time.

"Got a customer?" A.L. asked.

"Let's see." The next hit bent my rod's tip. "Oh yeah."

A.L. yipped playful encouragement as I overplayed my lean back. The smallmouth bass exploded from the water and splashed with a smack. After a fun fight, I landed a decent sized fish.

"I want some of that action," he said.

In time, luck found him and he reeled in a good-sized bass of his own. With plenty of frozen fish home, we released our catches. Sunset cued us to pack up the gear and head back.

He whistled a slice of a tune before he admitted he needed to get out more. I was half amazed when he requested I reserve him a ticket for closing night of my play. I prayed all this was the start of his turnaround.

But back home, after a second glass of whiskey, his mood turned surly again. He teased and provoked and insisted we sit down and watch tapes of old rides Jillian had taken. I did not indulge him and moved upstairs. Halfway there he stopped me.

"Hey."

I sighed. "What, A.L.?"

"Why did you cover Gremlin?"

"What? Oh that. I just did," I said.

A.L. held an accusatory stare before rolling off. Thirty minutes later, when I returned down for a drink, I found him in the garage, beer in lap, mesmerized by a now unveiled Gremlin.

CHAPTER 27--NOT TWO SWEET

"Good morning, sir." The high-pitched breeze that followed us through the sliding door could have toppled the dinosaur greeter. This was fidgety A.L.'s first shopping excursion since his return, and at least we agreed on this: it felt like penance. We endured long aisles filled with joyless faces who paused from filling their carts to check out A.L. He'd insisted on coming dressed like a celebrity trying to skirt the paparazzi. The once affable and striking athlete entered the place dressed in Mom's ginormous left-behind shades, topped off with a dorky white fishing hat drawn down to the bridge of his nose. We hadn't even reached the personal hygiene aisle before everything gnawed at me like red ants. Here I was, stuck in a Big Mart in Buffalo, Tennessee, a place A.L. specifically requested we visit in order to avoid detection.

After ten minutes watching him mull deodorant options, I kind of popped. "Feckin A, A.L.! Look at all the money we can save by buying the Dri-Day Super-Saver Three-Pak! Can we speed this up a little? I've got peeps to see." A glare from the stupid shades was hardly intimidating. I ringed a three-pack in the cart from three-point range.

"Also, my man, when are you going to break down and get yourself a customized van so you can drive yourself around?"

"Then I wouldn't have your fine company," he teased. "Push on."

Swinging into the next aisle, a familiar face made a bad scene worse. *What was Miss Ritz, my history teacher doing here in Buffalo?* Sure, she was most famous for making time stand still, but at least I agreed with her when she once proclaimed mankind hadn't learned squat from history. Mission Avoidance: My term paper on the Prussian War was overdue, mostly because I'd been busy fighting my own war. A.L.'s chair could draw her attention and the last thing I needed was an impromptu parent conference to break out.

I cranked A.L.'s wheelchair sharply around and down the next aisle. Too sharply. He shrieked after I clipped a display of condoms! After a lame effort to restack a couple boxes, I squashed the idea and fled. A.L. grumbled and seethed until he mellowed enough to jump into one of those classic father and son talks. He became reflective. "Actually those rubbers reminded me, are you and Jillian having sex? Maybe we should talk about that."

"You're so right. Let's talk about it here, just be loud. Why just the other night, after a couple of kegs, you started covering all the best positions before your chin hit your chest for good. But yeah, go on."

A.L. stared wildly and started yanking his beard again. "You've been awfully snippy lately. What's wrong with you?"

I whisper-shouted. "Really? I feel like dancing." I swerved his chair with the basket in front side to side, down an aisle as I hummed a waltz.

"Stop that!"

"Stop what? You were saying something about sex? THERE'S NO NEED! I might as well make balloon animals out of the rubbers you gave me for the amount of time I've been spending with my girl."

"See, that's the drama stuff dripping from you. We have no control over nature.

The weird thing is the older and wiser we get the less nature wants us spilling our seed all around." But his nonsense utterings fell to the floor as we entered the sports section where towering above all else stood—

"Rods!" He pointed with reverence as we rolled closer. The vertical sticks acted like some honing beacon for him. "We need to get out and do more fishing. Test some of those new flies I've been making."

"Uh, okay, I'm all over that." The great thing about pushing someone from the rear is you can flip them the finger without them knowing, and still get along fine. Soon, we had enough animal food, T.P and disinfectant to last through the next plague. I granted him a final indulgence and wheeled him through the electronics department. A game-changing move.

"My lord, I can't believe how big TV's have gotten since I died and was brought back," he said.

"What if we're actually dead and have gone to retail hell?"

Just when I started to believe A.L. had committed to the magic of MasterCard, he regrettably returned to his senses. "Ours works fine." He sighed. "Let's make like birds and get the flock out of here."

I was good with that until I turned down the next aisle and a familiar, hyena-like laughter set off alarms in me. Yep. Two identical redheads, same purpose in life: repel all others. Apparently, the Sweet Brothers were no less idiotic off the football field than on. I had played them and the rest of the Buffalo Buttocks each of my three seasons with JHS. They could be down thirty-eight-zip but the Sweets would still trash-talk you like *they* were ahead.

A.L. didn't get a response when he asked me why I had ground the chair to a halt. But it was too late. The twin cackle fell to muted, stupid looks. The two heads stiffened. "Eh, what the . . .?" one Sweet said.

"Why did we stop?" A.L. asked."

"It's okay, A.L. Remain absolutely still."

Horrible luck. A.L. had chosen a distant store where he wouldn't be recognized. In doing so he had placed us smack in the middle of enemy territory.

"Hey, Harley! I know that kid pushing around the dude in the wheelchair."

The other twin narrowed his hyena eyes. "Wait, he plays for Jefferson," Marvin said.

"We hate Jefferson," said Harley.

"Just because they've gone to state finals twice, they think they're hot shit."

"Whoopdeedoo," said the other.

When we advanced, the Sweets held their ground and blocked our way. I resisted getting snarky. "Hey dudes, my dad and I have a plane to catch. We'd like to get by."

"They have a *plane* to catch? Where to, I wonder?" Marvin's eyes rolled about.

Harley said, "Did I get all the brains? The asshole's kidding, you dope."

A.L. cleared his throat. "Uh boys, we really need to get by if you can make room."

"I don't know," said Harley. "Can we?" Another deviant cackle.

Enough. A.L.'s chair conveniently doubled as a battering ram if needed. I whispered, "Hang on, A.L.," and set him in motion.

Harley, the slower of the two, got his leg grazed, which I hadn't really intended. "What the hell, A-Hole!" he howled and lashed out, which launched an uppercut from me. I connected and pretty hard. He bent to his side, held his face and peeled off an F-Bomb. It became double trouble when Marvin came at me. A hard shove sent him to the floor where he flailed like a beached walrus on his back. Harley rebounded and came at me, knuckles flying. I ducked and my fist snapped up and clocked his jaw. He dropped like a sack of concrete to the floor beside his brother. I felt no glory.

A.L. yelled. "Colby, stop it! Get us out of here before the cops come and drop the net!"

As one twin clutched his jaw and moaned, blood could be seen on the shirt of the other. A woman coming around the corner looked on in horror and ran off, presumably to wail for security. I grabbed the wheelchair handles and we bolted away, goods and all.

A.L. barked, "Colby, get in control. Slow down!"

I did but zigzagged A.L. between aisles to avoid detection. Once back up front, we saw an empty express lane. "Did you find any Big Deals today?" the indifferent checker asked with a pop of her gum.

A.L. barked when I slammed the truck into reverse and screeched off just ahead of the approaching Buffalo cop car, cherries whirling.

"Slow down!" He said for the second time in five minutes.

The sound of the sirens bent as they passed us. "He's in a slight hurry. Wonder what's up?" I said to the mirror.

"Don't even joke about this, Colby. You're in big trouble. These places have cameras, dude!"

We finally hit the freeway but A.L. was still agitated. "I've never seen you this out of control, Colby. Not cool. Probably should have stayed, faced the music."

"Look, I didn't mean to hurt that two-headed clown, but you saw for yourself. Self defense, dude."

"I don't like any of your choices lately."

"I wish I could change a couple of things, too. I didn't choose to take out the sour Sweets. Just because I ended up getting the better of the deal, does that make me guilty?"

"Just don't talk, even if I ask questions . . . and watch your speed!"

Back home, I helped A.L. into his chair, dropped the plastic bags in his lap and wheeled him up the ramp and inside.

Bubbles greeted us. "Look at Bubbly, A.L. She knows we got her Dog Bites."

Thump, thump, thump.

"Give her some, then. And give me a drink"

"No you don't. It's not happy hour, A.L."

"That's why I want one."

I poured him a discounted shot. It wasn't long into unpacking and sighs of pleasure after A.L.'s first sip when five aggressive raps on the door froze us. A.L.'s shot glass smacked the kitchen table as he released a loud exhale. "What was that?" he said from the kitchen.

I braved a peek through the door's peephole. Though the nose was distorted to the size of a raccoon, the rest of him looked quite familiar. The good news: it was my back-slapping, old soccer coach from middle school. The bad? He'd come dressed as a cop, something he did when not coaching. I shook my head at A.L. "Uh, it's Mark Delvin."

"You're kidding. Someone grabbed our plate and called it in."

"What do you want to do?" I said.

"Well, let the gentleman in before he breaks out his damn battering ram."

Shit. On. Me. The last time Delvin was here, he was complimenting the delicious hot dog I had fixed for him at A.L.'s party. His look now definitely spelled cop business. I composed myself, gave it another second and yanked open the door.

"Coach!" I sold him a broad smile.

He didn't dance a jig and greet me with a hearty, "Hey, goal tender!" which had been his tendency. But those were simpler days—when I was winning. He looked at me deadpan, already exasperated before his first question. "Colby." He curtly nodded. "Your dad around?"

A.L. rolled in, charming as ever; reeking of his new favorite cologne, Jack Daniels for Stationary Men. Either Coach Delvin didn't notice or ignored it. He gave A.L. all the polite cheerfulness usually afforded a friend with a terminal disease. "A.L., nice to see you, brother. How goes it?"

"Living the life, Officer Delvin. You?"

"That-a-way, me too—say you all have a second or two?"

"Maybe three," A.L. chortled. "Grab you a beer? My bad, you're working. Iced tea, coffee?"

"I'm fine, thanks." While the stout officer crumpled on the couch, I stared at his belt and mulled the fourteen ways he could disable me.

The short of it was the Sweets' parents had reported our little scuffle. A bit ironic when you consider the history of those jailbirds. My stomach churned. I tried to paint myself the victim before some ridiculous charge fell from Mark's lips. As I died slowly inside, I settled on A.L. who began wheeling his chair back and forth in quarter turns.

"Colby, I'm utterly flattened," Coach said. "You clocked one of the boys pretty hard according to one witness."

"I wasn't trying to hurt anybody. They were hassling us. One pushed and I just reacted, Coach."

"Well the good news is neither of the boys was seriously injured. Tell you what. Buffalo isn't too far from my place. I may just pay a visit to those Sweets. See if we can't come up with some kind of out of court settlement and—"

"What's to settle? It was self-defense, Coach. You should be charging them."

"Be respectful, Colby, it's Officer Delvin," A.L. said.

"Yes sir. *Officer* Delvin. "

The next evening Jillian and I sat on a knoll by the duck pond having a rock-skipping contest. I retold the Big Mart thriller but I didn't get the expected return I was hoping for. As I spilled details, she listened without comment as her rock throws intensified. I got the message she didn't approve, so I switched subjects to things like my play's progress.

When Jillian pulled into El Relaxo to drop me off, both our eyes froze on the return of Mark's black and white.

"Now what'd you do?"

I stayed light. "Don't worry J-Girl, that's just Officer Delvin. I bet he brokered a deal with the Sweets, and in record time, too. Wanna come in and hear the verdict?"

"No more than come to your hanging. Here's where you get off and I move on." I kissed her on the cheek and was repaid a quick smile, but a second after I slammed the door, her truck sped away and I found myself fending off the small flying debris.

"Perfect timing, son." A.L. clapped his hands repeatedly, way too peppy.

Officer Delvin took the same seat where he'd laid down the law before. He explained the Sweets had agreed not to press charges but their counter demand was absurd. "They want a fifty-dollar gift certificate to the High Star Diner in Buffalo." He didn't even break a smile.

"What? Fifty bucks, Coach? Bull crap! I wasn't even in the wrong."

A.L. said, "Calm down, boy, we're takin' that deal."

Mark's attention shifted to me. "Listen to your dad, Colby. You'll avoid court; attorneys—and their two-hundred dollars an hour fees."

"Two hundred bucks an hour? Change of plans, A.L. My next jump is to law school!"

"We have all the law we need here," A.L. said

I offered a compromise. "How about if I buy them all a Happy Meal and we call things even?"

Officer Delvin stayed in top-cop character. "Take the deal, goal tender . . . One kept raving about their famous mini sliders."

"I've tried those. They are good," A.L. said.

"Oh fine. I'll buy them a couple of weeks of grease . . . idiots."

"Jesus embraced his accusers, Colby. Just don't get flagged again," Delvin said.

That night A.L. parked at the base of the stairs. The Big Mart ordeal and his next round of booze had left him surly and combative. He shouted random complaints about me and faults with my riding. Fortunately, my headphones had come equipped with the PNR feature: Parental Noise Reduction. I lay on my bed, listened to tunes and let my thoughts soar beyond the ceiling to Jillian, distant places and better times—having no idea just how soon they'd come.

CHAPTER 28--BIRTHDAY BOY

Ah, seventeen. The last year you have no real freedom or legal rights, but you're expected to man up. I slumped in Benson's homeroom, doodling on my notebook and feeling anything but the party animal as Dana Raleigh babbled on with the announcements. Though we were actually starting to click on stage, I viewed Untouchable's wry smile with dread. Here it came: the recorded drum roll and . . . "Today's birthdays!" Horns squawked and a little confetti was thrown from behind Dana. Highly low tech.

She cheered: "Let's give a big shout out to Colby Weston! Not only can this birthday boy leap mountains with a dirt bike, turns out he could be Hollywood's next matinee idol." Oh my god! There was a cutaway to a photo of me rehearsing with her on stage. Could I ever forgive her for this? The hype continued. "You can see Colby and the rest of the talented JHS cast in, *Lost Gifts*. Don't forget to get your tickets soon!" For once I was grateful when Benson hastily extinguished Untouchable with the remote.

"Listen up, troops. I have the test results from Friday, and some of you have suffered heavy losses I regret to inform."

Tamitra Goings pouted. "Feed my test to the recycling bin, Mr. B, I beg you."

Benson smirked back. "At least your shreds will not lie alone in the trough of despair, Tamitra." Groans were common after tests slapped desks. He made it to me and held a deadpan look. "Will it be a happy one, birthday, boy?"

"Hit me," I said. Slap. My eyes rolled down to it, then back to Benson. *Ninety-six.* I nodded.

"You're on a roll, Weston." Benson wasn't a man to cavort with his troops, so any praise was something to lock away. He added, "Have you signed up for the SATs?"

I fed him what he wanted to hear. "Been thinking about that, Mr. Benson." The reality? I hadn't given it a thought. No SAT would help Silver get more air.

He became emphatic. "Do it. A good score means more options. Options are good. You have potential for skills very much in demand. It's only an afternoon to take the SAT, a small investment."

I shrugged but was playing coy. I had great respect and admiration for the man and Benson's words felt like a royal blade had tapped both shoulders. Maybe I'd go online and sign up, see where mine stood against other brains. I was left to contemplate his words until a crumpled test ricocheted off my head and extinguished my big man on campus fantasy. The culprit was Caroline Baker, two seats away.

"Hey, birthday boy, I could use a private tutor like you," she said. "That could be another option."

Bold is good, I thought, before thinking the better. "Sorry, Baker, but I'm tutoring someone else at the moment." I underhanded her crumpled test back to her, then eased her playful pout. "But, hey, I'm just across the aisle if you ever get stuck."

As luck would have it my scene wasn't being rehearsed that day. As planned, I pointed Silver straight for Jillian's place. A.L. duties had acted like a wedge between us of late and I craved her company. We had planned a birthday ride. As I approached the Carter's front steps, I was hoping this wasn't a trap. I didn't feel like being led down her basement stairs to a hoard of crouching buddies ready to leap and detonate a "Happy Birthday!" bomb. I just wanted to hook up with Jillian and play, and feel seventeen like her.

Mrs. Carter welcomed me, dressed in a flowery kitchen apron, chatty as usual. A luring, sweet scent of baked treats hung in the air of the spotless home. Jillian's younger sister, Ann, stood near her mother, her silent, dark eyes evaluating. Mrs. Carter asked after A.L. and his progress. I painted a rosy picture, of course.

"Are you messing with my man again, Mom?" A voice in motion suddenly appeared from the stairs, grabbing my behind as she passed.

Mrs. Carter turned mom. "Jillian, your little, eh hem, science experiment you abandoned in the oven? The buzzer went off about ten minutes ago."

"Crappola! Did you—"

"Everything's taken care of." Mrs. C. sighed, then rolled her eyes towards me. "Teen girls."

I played along. "I know. It's hard."

Jillian returned with a picnic basket wafting fresh-baked enticement.

"Whatcha' ya' got there, Little Red Riding Hood?" I said.

"Maybe a little treat for Mr. Wolf." Her eyebrows snapped up and down a couple of times. Jillian turned to her mom. "Sorry to break up the fun, Mom, but we're late for a very special date."

"Headed for Harriet Pond?" Her mom's smiling head bobbed madly.

Jillian's was pure sass. "No, Mom, the justice of the peace."

Her mother brushed it aside. "Jillian, that basket was a special wedding gift, you know. What if it falls off your motorcycle and breaks?"

"You'll have to get married again?" Jillian said.

"I'm serious."

"I'll protect it with my life, Mom. I've got this."

"You best. Home by eight, Jillian. School night and all."

"Tell you what. Make it nine this time and I'll love you an hour more."

Mrs. C. caved, like she always did, unlike Jillian's dad, whose demands poured like quick-dry cement.

Outside, Jillian said, "I like freedom, don't you?" She tilted her head to button her helmet. "I'll shock cord this baby down . . . like that, and hopefully the shit won't spill out all over Route 9. Let's hit it, birthday felon!" Apparently she wasn't about to totally let me off the hook regarding the Big Mart thing. Jillian was artistically free, loved a risk, and was always up for a little mischief. But she hadn't been raised by Hell's Angels.

Past the outskirts of town, Jillian led me up a dirt road that wound into desolate woods I hadn't visited for a long time. I took the lead under a shimmering canopy. By the time I realized Jillian's engine had faded, a snatched look told me she and her bike had vanished.

I pulled a one-eighty to find her. No sign. Suddenly she leaped from a bush! She looked ever the hot traffic cop as she held up a hand and I ground to a halt. Taking the lead, she pushed Blue until the thick brush shrunk the trail. A ways in, unseen from the main path, Jillian removed the basket from her bike and we plunged the rest of the way on foot. I didn't know what her plan was, but I was just fine following her lead. At last the last branch slapped my face and it opened up to . . . railroad tracks? I became a bit overcome by the smell of crude oil as I picked off burrs from my shirt.

What was she thinking? The defoliated gray and brown zone was stark, and heat shimmered off the tracks on which were parked an infinite line of forgotten boxcars. Jillian spun, threw up her hands and shouted, "Ta da!"

Confused, yeah, but I played along. "J-Girl! You got me boxcars. You shouldn't have. So what's the *ta da* part?"

"Trust me, C-Boy." Basket in hand, she led me a short distance to one with its door slightly ajar. She stood erect and launched into conductor mode. "Club Seventeen, all aboooard!"

"So where does one get tickets for this train, Miss Conductor?"

"It's a birthday express so everything's totally free. Your lucky tour starts," she mimed retrieving a pocket watch, "now."

Sure, it was just days following the Sweet episode, and I was a little gun-shy about running afoul of the law, twice in a week. But who could resist Jillian's subtle pose against the train with outstretched arms like she was modeling for Amtrak. The breeze approved and tousled her hair as she correctly read my hesitation.

"Don't worry yourself, C-Boy. These boxcars haven't budged in a week and there's not a soul to be seen." She must have caught my darting eyes, which combed up and down for any signs of authority. "But," she shrugged, "if you want to play it safe and listen to ducks quack on the pond, it's your birthday, baby."

My answer? Hands coupled in the shape of a stirrup. "After you, m'am."

Once hoisted up, Jillian reached for her basket, then me with an outstretched hand. It was dark and cavernous in there—a place that bred excitement, even standing still. She vanished into a dark corner with her basket. The space was cool and smelled of the hay thinly scattered over the wooden planks. Blackness had all but swallowed her though I could hear her rifling through the basket for something. A sudden, struck match brought a wise, luring face into view. She had planned well, my girl, and I flooded with nervous anticipation. She touched the match to the wick of a large jar candle, similar to the one we had enjoyed moments before Demi had chased our love away. This time there would be no Demi; no parent tromping onto the scene bellowing, "Don't mind me, just passing through."

Jillian's illuminated gaze offered a pledged commitment as her pursed lips blew out the match. I wanted to frame this picture forever but her heat tested my patience. Wordlessly, she removed a Mexican blanket from the basket and spread it out. The candle's sensual light flickered all over her and up the nearby walls. Love nest complete, I slid the cargo door shut harder than intended. It coupled with a large clang that startled both of us. But Jillian's relaxed smile returned when it became the two of us isolated from all others. Finally. No adults. No A.L. issues. Just us.

"Enjoying the tour so far?" she asked.

"Best seat in the house. This is the kind of private club car I always dreamed about, J-Girl."

But Jillian gasped when the boxcar released a creak and broke the chill vibe.

I reassured her. "We're cool, J-Girl. Just old boards squeaking in the wind. How'd you find this rig?"

"Out riding, poking around, hunting for a good photo . . . the usual."

"I love the usual you." I smiled. "Helluva find."

"So were you, J-Boy. Sorry life's been dealing you low cards lately."

"Higher ones are coming, I hope."

I joined her on the blanket and ran my hand through her hair. Candlelight bounced off her curled, dark locks. A yellow blouse topped the denim shorts, and sculpted legs were drawn to her chin. We didn't say all that much. I wanted her as much as a championship ring, but I didn't want to rush.

All of a sudden some inspiration hit which sent her crawling on all fours to the basket. She withdrew a couple of bottles of ginger ale and two chocolate cupcakes. Each was pierced with a candle she lit. She held them up and sang the birthday song. A wish came to me fast and I blew the two flames out.

I scooped off a tiny amount of frosting and painted her lips with it, then kissed them clean. The cupcakes went fast, along with everything that followed. We stretched out and gentle strokes gave way to hot breaths of gratitude. Nothing else mattered. Things transitioned quickly from one great option to the next. No brakes on this buffet with wheels—until a small logistic sobered me.

"Damn," I said and frowned.

She propped up her head with one hand. "What's up?"

"Confession, I was expecting Harriet Pond, not this. I have no uh, protection."

Now she went theatrical. "So you came unprepared, and now everything has to grind to a halt. Is that it?" She rolled over and balled up. "Damn it."

I flung an arm over her. "So sorry, J-Girl. Why didn't I see sex on an idle train coming when I left this morning?"

She popped up. "Wait! Just kidding. I forgot your big present." She crawled on all fours to the basket. "You can open this now."

With the deftness of a magician she presented a foil package pinched between two fingers. It glistened in the candlelight like a precious jewel.

"J-Girl, you ultimate cruise director. I love you."

"Toot -toot! Take me somewhere. Everywhere," she said.

My tongue explored hers for a delicious while before we undressed and caressed each other. I fumbled for the pack and ripped the foil eagerly. We had reached the top of the roller coaster, so eager for the plunge! But then . . . a sound. Another creak in the wind?

"What was that?" Jillian sat up, nakedly beautiful, but halting the rocket launch at T-minus 10. Sure, I had heard it, a low, rhythmic bumping sound, but damned if I was going to let anything get in the way this time, short of our boxcar catching fire. But Jillian's practicality—Okay, call it survival skills I didn't possess—were piqued deer-like. "Colby, listen! What *is* that?"

CHAPTER 29—THE WHEELS SPIN

I paid no heed to bad fate's rhythmic pounding as my once gentle strokes turned into a flurry of groping desperation.

"Stop!" Jillian snapped. I got it. She needed humoring the same way I needed denial. I placed one ear against her bare chest. "Yep, ma'am. That's just your heart beating a little harder."

"No, LISTEN, C-Boy," she said. "That puh, puh, puh low drum-like sound." Each *puh* was accented with a punched fist two inches from my face.

"Yeah. Kinda sounds like some T. rex stalking us. Probably just some distant construction going on."

"I've got a bad feeling, C-Boy."

"Like what?"

Bang! The boxcar lurched like it had been struck, triggering Jillian to shriek. Soon a second jerk followed, this one louder and more wrenching. Our car released a tired groan. It was awakening. Panicked looks swapped, Jillian cried out, "Not a moving dinosaur, dude, a moving train!"

My open palms slapped the floor. "Why, why every time?" I cried.

Being frustrated and panicked was one thing. But two teens panicked, naked in a dimly lit boxcar was definitely pile on.

"Jillian, the candle!" It had fallen over and was rolling around, ready to ignite the loose hay. "But don't—"

It was too late. With Jillian's quick puff and a "Whoops," we were left to grope in the dark like blind moles. Jillian let go a scary shrill. "I can't see!" The noise built as our love nest turned into a wood and iron jail on wheels.

"I am F-ed if I don't exit this joy ride and fast, C-Boy." Her voice trembled.

"Stay cool, baby, we're fine." But soon as I spoke, the train's next lunge slammed me into the wall. "Ow!" I panted and wildly rubbed my head. "Don't worry. These things take miles to reach good speed. But we should jump soon, sweetie."

"Wow! Who knew you were such an expert on fucking trains!" she said as she hopped a full circle, trying to get a second leg into her jeans. "Find. The. Door. C-Boy!"

"After I get my pants on, thank you." I did and groped frantically for the handle. "Where *is* the damn thing?"

"Aim for the little slit of light!" Jillian said. "And if you do get it open, don't dare jump without me."

Churning wheels drowned out her choked apologies for choosing this spot. I blindly clawed along the wall until I pawed the curved steel handle. A little late, Jillian found and struck a trembling match and relit the candle. The latch felt jammed and wouldn't budge! After a roar of anger and some brute force, the door sprang loose and I pushed it open.

An explosion of light, wind and track noise flooded our once serene space. I instantly became dumfounded by how quick a mile-long train could find speed. The sharp, crushed gravel below began a blur.

"Hurry, J-Girl!" We finished dressing and she gathered the rest of her gear. Once set, it was Jillian who seemed ready to throw caution to the wind. She didn't give one thought to our speed and how badly maimed one could become by jumping off a moving train this high above jagged ground.

From behind me came, "Move, C-Boy. We are a go!"

"Uh, Jillian? Wait." I mumbled toward the ground streaking by.

Either she didn't hear me or mistook herself for a super hero. She clutched her basket, closed her eyes and yelped, "We jump and roll. Got it? Ready . . . set . . . go!"

Only my snap reflexes saved her from becoming a wrecked, mental vegetable. Both my arms wrapped around her as she shrieked and her legs kicked wildly in the air. "Let go of me, Colby!"

"Are you nuts? We can't jump now, Jillian. We're going too fast! We'll break our fool necks diving on that rocky ground, not to mention your camera."

Jillian found a dark corner, buried her head into her palms and tore off the next f-bomb. I staggered to her side, wrapped my arms around her and whispered sweet lies. "We'll be fine," I said. Of course, what the hell did I know? Nothing, particularly how far freight trains ventured once they started to roll. Her face collapsed into my chest. "I know, baby. We'll keep trying until we get this right." Of course everything had to be half yelled.

"Yeah, great," Jillian said, "but right now I'm a little more concerned about where this love train is bound."

"Trains stop frequently, like buses, don't they? Why, I bet in no time we'll be laughing about our latest interruption. Until then, what can we do but enjoy the free ride, or, uh—"

"How can you even think about that now? I wish I'd jumped . . . headfirst. It would have been quicker than what faces me when I get home," she said.

"Oh, your dad will laugh his ass off."

"After he flushes Blue's keys down the toilet."

"Nah. Look, this is the sickest birthday I've ever had. You and me on a rolling train? Can't be beat." I meant it. But when Jillian took out her phone, I reached to grab it.

"Colby!" she snapped back like it was some violation.

"Jillian, you can't call your folks. What are they going to do? Drive alongside us and wave?"

"My dad can have the train stopped."

"Did he build this railroad? Does he own stock in B and O? He ain't got the brass to stop a train in full stride. It'll stop soon, for something. They always do. When it does, I'll call one of my go-to boys and we'll get scooped up, that easy, that quick. It's early, yet. We'll get back like nothing this strange ever happened. In fact, things just got more awesome."

"What'll A.L. say?

"Whatever it is, neither of us will understand it. He's probably paddling down Whiskey River by now. Anyway, he can't drive in any condition."

Jillian's red, swollen eyes rolled to the ceiling. "Can you at least figure out what direction we're headed?"

I looked out. "Well . . . got the sun in our eyes. Moving left of that . . . I'd say south, J-Girl. Good news in a way."

"Why?"

"Less room to roam than north." I offered a lame chuckle.

"Great, C-Boy. Maybe it'll be party in the French Quarter tonight."

"This birthday boy's down for that."

"Woo-hoo!" Her mock clown face imploded. "I'll be fried Beignets when I get home."

"Like I said, nine's the deadline, baby. Hours yet to get things straight."

I held Jillian as my eye surveyed my birthday gift within reach. Since trying to jumpstart my girl's love engine would be near impossible, I grabbed it, blew it up and set it to the wind. A gift for some farmer to puzzle about as it bounced along over his field.

She squeezed my hand and, despite her swollen eyes, chuckled as she waved at it. "Bye, bye. So close. Again."

As our train chugged on, we came to accept our fate, whenever and wherever that would be dealt. We watched silos and farmhouses stream buy. Jillian grabbed her camera and began snapping off shots of the boxcar's dark recesses and the rolling countryside. Eventually the lens fell on me, something I never cared for. I flashed a series of stupid faces which at least made her chuckle. When I stopped clowning and gave her serious, Jillian said, "Yeah. That one. Good." She tucked the camera away in the basket and drew close to me.

She squeezed my hand and kissed my cheek. "Hey birthday boy, you're my star, don't forget it."

I pulled her close and for a while we just held each other. Jillian used my lap as a headrest and at some point, she was rewarded with merciful sleep that dodged me. I texted Beach a picture as the day faded.

>We're rolling. On a runaway train. Seriously.
>For real?

Thoughts about my future were no clearer than the details that blurred by. It was my birthday; I was seventeen; we were miles from Darin; and the truth was I was no longer certain where this train or life was really taking me. The sun slipped behind the horizon and after a while, I followed Jillian into sweet oblivion.

Pitch black greeted me. The rumbling had stopped. Had it not been for what sounded like distant traffic crossing a bridge, I might have believed I'd rolled off and died. Fact was, we were in another train yard, somewhere, but where? I pulled out my phone. "This is interesting," I said and nudged Jillian.

She mewed and stretched off her stiffness. The night air was cool so she cuddled back into my body's heat. But not for long. Her head rebounded and she blinked rapidly as she tried to interpret reality. "It's quiet. We stopped, C-Boy?" Jillian sprung up. "Wait! What time is it? Where are we?" Her face turned ghostly when I turned my phone around for her to see. She hissed a whisper, "*Memphis?* How far is that?"

"Not far. About a hundred miles, is all."

"What?" She stood up and proclaimed, "I'm officially dead. Also, I need to pee, like a monsoon. After that, I'll vomit. Where's the damn ladies room on this rig?"

"Can't you hold it until we're off?" I asked.

"Literally, C-Boy, no. I'm not squatting out there in some spooky dark place with grubby rail men stalking about."

"Have another option?"

"The only one there is." She disappeared into the boxcar darkness.

"Wait," I said. "Oh no, Jillian, don't . . . don't . . . do it . . ."

It came, not like some elegant, gentle tinkle one might expect from such a beauty. The sound of her jet stream power-washing the boxcar's floorboards is indelibly etched on my brain. Every time I see a boxcar, I hear it.

Through a heaved laugh, I said, "Damn girl, *awful*. That's some pee-cutting super powers you got there. You could put out a freaking four-alarm with that blast. I, for one, am bailing this rig."

Jillian returned with a new smile. "All better. Needed to mark my territory, C-Boy. Ain't no one going to mess with our club car now."

"I can imagine. If they reach New Orleans, they'll take one whiff, uncouple this thing and roll it straight into the freaking Gulf of Mexico."

A distant train horn serioused us up. "Hear that, J-Girl?"

Her face flashed alert. "Yeah. What are you trying to say, C-Boy?"

"Jump!"

CHAPTER 30—LAND OF KINGS

A guttural blast of air left Jillian when she hit the ground. I hurried to her side. "You okay, baby?"

She grimaced as I helped her stand. She tested her sore ankle. For the moment, she cast it aside. "Hey. Where's my mom's basket? God help me if that got busted."

"Over there, behind you."

She hobbled to it. The basket sat on its side, contents splayed. The first thing she did was test her camera. When it lit up, she held it to her chest and thanked the Nikon gods. Then she repacked her unscathed basket. But after a couple of painful hops, she sagged to the ground like a helpless fawn. "Damn, C-Boy, Feels like I broke the bitch."

"You best be kidding."

Great. I pondered our predicament. I fixed on the red lights of the caboose as it disappeared around the bend.

"Bye-bye, love nest," Jillian said.

"Heck of an idea you had there, J-Girl. If only it stayed where we found it."

"Now what, C-Boy? We need to escape this train yard of horrors and get our butts back home."

The eerie place lived up to its potential when a couple adult of male voices approached. Security? Possibly. Either way, this was our cue to exit. "Can you run?" I whispered to Jillian.

"Run? Don't know if I can walk," she hissed back.

A man's voice hopped up. "What are those kids up to?"

"Yeah," said the other. "That girl's holding something. Maybe lifted from one of the cars. Let's git'em! Stay right there, you two!"

Including my best break-away runs on the gridiron, I was never prouder than outpacing two men with a girlfriend on my back clutching a stuffed basket. Our stocky, pursuers couldn't keep the pace, but they emitted joyful yips all the same. A utility shed off to the right seemed the best option to duck into. Jillian slid off and followed me in through the unlocked door. A large, ancient relic of some kind became the perfect place to hide behind. After a tense couple of minutes Jillian found a wry smile and whispered, "I think we lost them, C-Boy."

BANG! The door kicked open and two flashlight beams glided off the walls and floor as they sucked air and we held ours. I covered Jillian's mouth before she could gasp. Finally, they abandoned the shed. Once outside, their muted voices mulled their options.

"Did you happen to catch that young fox draped on that boy?"

"Funny," said the other. "He still flew like a greased cat for sure. So now what?"

"I think we scared them off. C'mon. Already cost us half our damn coffee break."

It grew quiet. Jillian began to rise but I pulled her back and shushed her. I hadn't heard footsteps. After a hard couple of minutes passed, sure enough, a voice returned. "Yeah nothing. Kids must have made it to the gate," one said. "They're at the mercy of the neighborhood wolves now."

Jillian's head spun with concern. I gave her a confident nod even if I was feeling anything but.

The men's footsteps and grumbling voices faded, this time for good. Jillian's sweaty hand tightened in mine. "Well played, my prince."

"With age comes wisdom, I guess. How's that ankle, Gimpy?"

"One way to find out."

Once clear of the train yard, I said, "Give me the basket. We'll head for downtown."

"But what about those neighborhood wolves they were talking about?"

"Plaster on a tough face, J-Girl. Let's try to find some ice, cool down the swelling."

Jillian still favored one ankle but at least she could hobble along, unassisted. The buildings around us were dark, old and in disrepair. We said little, kept our heads down and walked as fast as we could motor. Between my phone and the distant skyscrapers, we navigated the streets to downtown Memphis. A quartet of rowdy teens hassled us from a stoop but no harm came from it. Through sheer will, Jillian kept up until we reached a 7-Eleven, purchased an extra-large cup of ice and cooled down her swollen ankle a bit.

Entering the touristy section of Memphis flooded us with relief. Memories returned from my last visit here, two years before when I had arrived via more conventional means with A.L. and Mom. That fun weekend vacation also proved to be our last, together.

Now, though still slightly panicked and with no plan to get home, a certain festivity took me all the same. I was smitten with the city's bright lights, evening energy and people still bustling about on a weeknight. Live music spilled from bars and we window-shopped our way to the heart of the city. "Memphis, J-Girl." I pumped my fists. "Who would have thought? Ever been?"

"Sure, but it's been a while. I'm excited—could be the last place I see before my parents end me. My ankle, C-Boy . . . can we rest a bit?"

"Yeah," I said looking at options on my phone. We're close to a place we can chill and score a burger. Now I'm doubly glad I took some of that cash Demi had given me."

"You and me both. Sorry, looks like the birthday boy's buying."

I wrapped my arm around her, and acceptance for our plight settled in. I felt as exuberant as I had been since my win at Marionville. Our tourist necks craned around at the skyscrapers, the city folk and the storefronts.

"J-Girl, I could move here. Like tonight."

"We may have to, C-Boy," Jillian said.

"No more worrying about the folks, okay? Wasn't our fault. They'll understand, so will A.L. Hell, he's probably shouting a laundry list of needs thinking I'm upstairs." That drew her first smile in a while.

Fate served us a big convenience when an antique trolley approached and halted just ahead of us. We jumped on. The ride and spring's evening breeze lifted her spirits. We reached burger Mecca. Dwyers Burgers on Beale Street was still open and just as I remembered it.

"Great call, birthday boy. All this swollen ankle walking, jumping on and off trains and evading rail security has burned off the cupcake."

"You're a cupcake," I said.

Once seated, Jillian went right for the menu. "What are you thinking?"

"I'm decided. Bacon cheeseburger and shake for this birthday boy."

"Ditto for me. Think I'll visit the ladies' room to freshen up and pluck out the hay that's still stuck on me."

"Mighty fine, porcupine. I'll get the order in."

I did just that, and a request for a kitchen rag with a large cup of ice for Jillian's ankle was also granted. I figured the time was ripe to drop the bomb to A.L. When he picked up, nervousness turned to annoyance as I tried to get beyond his new-normal slurred state. Little could be reasoned from the man's wandering babble. After having to repeat Memphis eight times as annoyed eyes parked on me, I silenced him.

Jillian emerged looking a little closer to city. I was more grateful than jealous at the glances from the other booths. The food arrived. Ravenous, we attacked our offerings in a wordless feeding frenzy. Afterward, I sat back, bloated and reborn.

"Think of it, J-Girl. Here we sit in Memphis, home of Gibson guitars and The King."

She grinned as a stream of chocolate shake split her lips, causing me to forget the next thing I was about to say.

"You call A.L. by chance?" she asked.

"Yeah, though explaining things to Commander would have been the more sensible choice."

"Give the old man time, C-Boy, his plane has crashed."

Giddiness returned with the rise in blood sugar. Jillian joked, "Whoever said birthday parties had to go to plan?" She leaned over and rewarded me with a birthday kiss. Some guy in a nearby booth sighed a mock *awe*. "Hey man," Jillian fired back, fearless. "This here's my birthday boy."

Outside later, after debating all options, Jillian paused on the sidewalk and braved her phone to her ear. "Stand back, C-Boy. My daddy could explode from the receiver end. It's ringing. Here goes. "Hello, Daddy? How was your day? . . .

That's awesome . . . Uh huh, yuuup. What? Oh, the birthday boy's having himself the time of his life . . . Of course he isn't . . . Uh huh, uh huh. You're too funny, Dad . . . Why did I call? Well, see, that's another funny story—or unfunny depending how you look at it . . . No, we're fine, but it's getting on and I wanted to let you in on a, well, unusual circumstance. You've probably heard of aliens abducting teen girls so they can juice up their race. It's about that bad . . . Where are we? You're quick to the point. We're down the line a little, south. Memphis, actually . . . Correct. Memphis, Tennessee. Hello? Daddy . . . Dad, you make no sense when you're yelling like that . . . No, we didn't plan it."

Jillian offered rolled eyes and tilted her dad's squawk my way. It took him a bit to find his calm, but once he did, Mr. C. promised to begin the retrieval soon. So, like two escaped cons on borrowed time, we strolled big-eyed through Memphis and all its storied history. When it got too much for her ankle, we took our next trolley for a sightseeing tour. A souvenir shop seemed like the perfect jumping off point. I probably overpaid for the sterling silver Gibson guitar key chain for her, but it seemed the perfect something to remember this unusual night by. Perhaps my final deed, I thought, before some orange-vested highway worker discovered my bloated ass in a ditch between here and home. I expected all blame to fall squarely in this boy's lap.

We began to laugh at everything and nothing. She grabbed me to a halt in front of a Justice of the Peace's office. "Marry me," she said.

"What? When?"

"Right now. Marry me. Look. Sign says, *Emergency Weddings 24-7*. We'll run away and get a jump on all the great places we've ever talked about. You'll ride to glory and fame, I'll sell the pics."

"Tempting," I said. "We could find ourselves a nice, cheap apartment right here on Beale Street." We played out the whole fantasy. We'd travel the world, she with her camera, me with a hot bike.

But all too quickly, the clock sped to the moment of truth. Her phone's chime launched a fresh round of panic. I heard her tremble out a dry okay. She held it tight against her and said low, "Fifteen minutes 'til doomsday." She raised the phone back to her ear. "What's that?" she said. She lowered it again. "He wants a pickup point, C-Boy."

"Tell him Beale and South Main, I guess." I checked my phone. "Your daddy does make good time."

"He's a contractor, C-Boy. Always about the getting there."

Anxious feet shuffled as our thoughts sailed us in different directions. Not much time passed before Mr. C. announced his arrival with a screech of tires around the corner. He was already mid-sentence by the time his passenger window lowered. No doubt, we missed the friendly greeting part. "Listen, you two," Mr. C. said. "See that red light? When it turns green I'm going, with or without y'all."

I sent Jillian in first, not so much because I was the gentleman, but mainly as a human shield between us. I began to crawl in after her. "Colby. Why don't you slide into the crew cab, in the back, *if you don't mind?*"

I gave a quick peek. "The back, sir? It's pretty tight and full of your carpentry tools, and open bags of nails and things," I muttered more to myself.

"Oh my bad, guess I didn't have time to tidy up, son. Well, squeeze in and do your best before that light changes."

"Ouch!" I said, as he mashed the pedal and something pointy found my butt.

"Comfy back there?" Mr. C. flashed a wry grin.

Jillian scowled at her father's inhospitality, but quickly backed off after his rebuke.

"So tell me what happened, little girl."

"Dad, I am soooo sorry. We were exploring this abandoned train—"

"Wait, let me guess, and it turned out *not* to be abandoned? Got it. Great town, Memphis. Haven't been in a while. I'd stay for a longer visit if I didn't have to be on a job site in about six hours." Jillian and I shrank lower. He waxed on. "You know, guys, we have a great town, too. In fact, you may recall we have a lovely park. And in this park exists a pond, where the legendary Tom Swan and other majestic wildlife can be seen floating about. It was designed preeee-cisely for situations like yours. You don't have to hobo to Memphis for whatever. You just find a nice, grassy knoll, spread out a blanket, watch some swans or something, do what teens must do, then get your asses home. You don't have a problem with *swans,* do you, Colby?" Two steel gray eyes burned into me from the rearview mirror.

"Uh, no, sir. I'm definitely cool with swans."

"You see, Jillian? The birthday boy is cool with swans. No need to hitch a ride on an empty train like a pair of depression-era hobos. What were you thinking? Your mother's home worried sick." He glanced over. "That picnic basket best be intact. That was a wedding gift, you know."

I offered, "If you need a snooze, Mr. Carter, I'd be more than happy to take a turn at the wheel."

"Nooo, you're fine right there, Colby." He jacked up the country music and I turned my gaze skyward out a small window. I stared into the abyss of the Milky Way and its stars that barely outnumbered the questions I had for them. I watched the truck's clock turn from 11:59 to 12:00, then 12:01. I was seventeen plus a day old, far less sure of everything than I had been at sixteen plus one.

On arrival I apologized a final time to Jillian's dad and bade farewell to Jillian, this time with an abbreviated hug. Though it left me on pins and needles, I agreed to leave the bikes in the well-camouflaged brush until the next day. I was dropped on the road and walked the driveway's length then eased through the front door. A.L. had tucked in but not before leaving the better part of a six-pack of empty cans in his wake. I wished I had the magic to fix the man, but I needed some of my own back, first.

CHAPTER 31—SOUTH SLIDE

The next day after school, I picked up both bikes and dropped off Blue at Jillian's. She greeted me at the door but seemed distant. Maybe she'd taken some heat from the folks. I was back on a train with her, preferably one that kept going. Or maybe lying next to her at Harriet Pond, making out; blowing dandelions and tossing our thoughts to the sky. But she had plans so I took Silver to Jack's for a workout before I summoned the courage to return to El Rlaxo.

"What up, A.L.?"

He grumbled, "Find your bikes wherever the hell you left them?"

"The very spot. Took mine to Jack's; had a good ride."

"Uh huh. So you hopped a train to the birth place of rock and roll." When I didn't answer he moved on. "I got you something for your birthday."

"Seriously?" I said.

"Yeah, a pizza."

"I could get into that about now."

"Seeing as you were *detained,* I ate most of it. Might be a slice left in the fridge."

"Any chance you had a cake delivered or did you eat that too?"

"Cake should be the last of your worries. Memphis . . . could be interesting, if the one thing you were put on the planet for wasn't falling apart before our very eyes."

"I wouldn't say falling apart A.L. Off some, but you should understand that reason."

"Sure I do. Between the school clubs, legal tangles, hanging out with your playmate, I'm not surprised to see your technique in the shitter. Clock's ticking boy. You're seventeen—the same age I struck out on my own. Time to step up." He retreated to his office.

That night, after I made dinner, he rolled in, buzz well in progress. I didn't set out to hurt him, but I guess I kind of launched an offensive. "What's going on A.L., huh? I don't see you using the new gym much. And what about work? Are you doing it remotely; are you returning any time soon?"

"Aren't we full of questions," he said through bloodshot eyes. "Pass the damn spaghetti."

"It just seems there's been a lot more partying going on than anything else."

"You don't know nothing." A.L. fixed on his plate of food.

"Sure seems that way."

"So seventeen's the magic number that gives you the right to cross a parent?"

"Or maybe it's the age when you get tired of the bullshit. A.L. You've been drinking too much. It's messing you up and everything around here."

He snapped back, "Shut your mouth, boy and fix your own shit. Yeah, let's talk about that. Lousy showings at events, getting into fights, joyriding trains. No, all I've done is spoon-feed you opportunities so you could make something special of yourself." He slapped the arms of his chair.

"I think I've made the best of them."

"You call one lucky weekend in Georgia making the best of things? That ain't reason enough to swagger. No, sir, real winners are consistent, in practice and outcome. They also aim for the bull's eye and you've got a big one on your back after Marionville. Who was that weird blond kid, the one you edged out, the one with the Yamaha sponsorship?"

"Tooley Cumberland?"

"Yeah him," he said.

"I've got more than a bull's eye on my back these days, A.L. I'm carrying the weight of your problems, too."

"So this is my fault? You think you can call the shots because your daddy is in a wheelchair, huh?"

"No. I'm not trying to call any shots. I'm concerned about your wellbeing, dude. I have to live with this new guy, and I'm not talking about the wheelchair, but your lips that are wrapped around the fucking nipple of a bottle every night."

"Watch yourself. The facts are I have a couple of drinks at night," he said.

"A couple? Tell it like it is old boy or don't tell it."

"Tell? I'll *show* you something."

Hard as it was, I mostly held eye contact. "You're not getting out, seeing people, following up on the rehab. That ain't you, A.L. Guys in your shoes adapt and lead decent lives all the time. Of all people, I expected you to do the same—sorry, that's why I'm frustrated. Reliving old times with photos and tunes; banging the booze, ain't going to bring back the past."

A more sedate tone from him suggested calm, but piercing black eyes implied something else. "Are you done, Colby? Best be. Who's still paying the rent? I'm the one in charge. I make the decisions. Here's an option. You can pack up your gripes and move north, I don't care anymore."

Defiance won out. "Don't I know it. Year from now, come graduation, I'll know where to point the ship. The question is do you still believe you have options. You had heart and class. My friends and almost everybody looked up to you. Where is that guy? Still sprawled on some dirt track back in Georgia?"

I wasn't afforded the time to apologize for my last remark. Stars. The explosion of his fist snapped my head back. The metallic taste of blood filled my mouth. The only life, the only sound, came from the milk glass that continuously spun in tight circles. His gaze became equal parts shock, anger and remorse. When the glass neared the edge, I calmly stilled it, up righted it, and stood over him. A.L.'s head slumped as he wheeled past for the sanctity of his office, hit-and-run fashion.

I went outside and took Silver off the truck and brought her to life. A couple of loops around the yard did nothing to dilute my anger so I tore off for the open road with only one intent: just to keep riding. Was Team Weston dead?

The play's tech week arrived. This meant rehearsals every afternoon stretched deep into the night. *Hell Week* they call it, but it sure felt more like heaven to me. Marty, my character, talked and pleaded into the dark abyss like it was a confessional, though his problems were wimpy and vague— nothing like the actual real shit I was living through. There, I escaped into this other world where outcomes were pretty much known, good or bad. In one of the final rehearsals I felt I had really nailed him. When I finished, hoots and applause erupted from the cast watching from the seats. I chugged it all down like sweet milk because I knew these guys had my back.

Beach never failed to bail me out of any slump, more with his antics than actual advice. He always maxed out his part with the famous *Beach Ease* that entertained us all. His big reward would come with the spike in his English grade that got his collegiate football dream back on track.

Another boost came from Untouchable of all people. One night, Dana lingered after the rehearsal and approached me to let me know how much she felt my character was coming along. I offered back a *whatever* shrug but inside I felt like I had been knighted.

That night I floated home. As I made dinner in the kitchen, a question came: How was A.L. restocking his poison? Liquor and beer had been pouring into him at the pace of a hydrant, yet the party offerings couldn't have lasted this long. He couldn't get it and Bubbles was no St. Bernard. Coincidently, I got my answer later that evening as I was cleaning up the living room. A blonde on TV was leaning in, wrapping up her ad pitch, "Southside Liquors of Darin. When you can't make it to us, we'll come to you!" *Light bulb.*

When A.L. rolled out to the garage to sneak a glass from his private stock, I ducked into his office and delved into his online bank records. Southside had been taking the man's money all right, and at a good clip of late.

During the next drama practice, with time to kill before my second act appearance, I braved a trip down to Southside Liquors to possibly cut the flow at its source. "Uh, may I help you?" A middle-aged man at the counter looked at me suspiciously. He was far less peppy than the buxom blonde on the TV ad, who was nowhere to be seen.

"Sure. Is the manager around?"

"Mr. Carlyle is in the back, but he's busy now. Is there something I can help you with?"

Dude, I wasn't asking for the great and powerful Oz. "No," I said, "my question's for Mr. Carlyle. Should be quick."

I got all the love of an intrusive cockroach. After a painful sigh, he said, "Wait here." He locked the drawer to the cash register, disappeared, then reappeared to wave me into the back space. It wasn't refrigerated but dank and chilly. Beyond the cases of beer and wine, Mr. Carlyle sat staring at a computer screen. A fan of moto, I remembered him from events at Jack's track. I was ready to make my point despite a churning stomach, but he waited a hard thirty seconds before he looked up. The counter guy grew fidgety. "Mr. Carlyle? This is the young man with some kind of question."

Carlyle's eyes scrolled over me with indifference. "Alright. Mind the counter, Bill. What's up, boy?" He finished typing in something on his laptop than flipped down the screen. His neutral look upped my uncertainty until he donned a look of recognition. "Hey, wait, I know you. You're A.L. Weston's kid, right?" A loud creak left his office chair as he leaned back and locked both hands behind his balding head.

"Uh, yes, sir. Colby Weston."

"Right. How's your dad doing?" he asked.

"We're all trying our best, sir. Tough times."

He shook his head. "Nasty luck, that crash. I was a fan, you know. Even sponsored some of his runs."

"Yes sir, he wore *Southside* on his back."

Proud eyes lit then narrowed,"You call your dad A.L.?"

"I get that question a lot. Long story."

"Yeah, quite the sky walker, your dad, a real shame what happened. But based on what I've heard some of that hot dog has rubbed off on you, huh?" I nodded. "So what brings you down? Looking for an endorsement, perhaps?" He sized me up then his office chair groaned back to upright. "Tell you what, son. I can't sponsor minors, but if you're as good as they say, maybe we can work something out, down the road. Hell, someday, you might just find yourself on my Southside billboard. How'd you like to be riding into town and see your head the size of an elephant?" He followed that with a big belly laugh.

"That really would be something, sir." I had no clue where to start, but time, including mine, was growing short.

Apparently he felt the same way. "I'm kind of busy. Anything else?"

Seconds hung like ten-pound bags of sugar.

"Just a quick question. I was wondering if Southside's been delivering beer and whiskey to my dad, by chance?"

He dropped his once playful demeanor to defensive. "What?"

"Southside came up a few times on his bank records."

"Wait. You went into your dad's *bank records?*" He snickered. "Yeah, well, I don't discuss my clients' accounts, not even with their nosy teen kids."

"Okay . . . but he is a customer and you did make some deliveries, right?"

"What if we had?"

I exhaled. "Mr. Carlyle. My dad's been zipping through the stuff and uh, it's setting him back. That's why I swung by."

He framed a tough guy look. "I'll keep it short. I'll admit to delivering to your dad, which is no crime in itself and certainly no business of yours. But he must be the one to tell me to stop. You're the kid, he's the adult."

"I understand that, sir, but he's been bummed out and not following through with his rehab. Your stuff isn't helping any."

"Noble to look after your dad, but he decides." He gave a dry chuckle. "Wanna call him right now."

I shook my head. "No, sir."

"Didn't think so. Your dad just lost the use of his legs. Who wouldn't need a few stiff ones after that?"

Flustered and out of time, I blurted out, "Mr. Carlyle, I don't think you understand. I'm asking you to stop delivery."

Amusement filled his eyes. "No, *you* don't understand. There's nothing you can do, kid."

Needless to say, I railed every ounce of emotion into Marty like never before. As usual, Mrs. Dejon had notes to share at the end of the rehearsal. She saved mine for last. "Someone's ready to kick down the barn door and that someone is Colby Weston, folks." A collective hoot came from the cast. "Keep up the intensity, Colby. And cast? That's the way JHS Theater is done."

But as the rehearsal broke up, the weight of Carlyle's words hung heavier than the director's praise. I barely noticed Dana at my side. This time she wasn't in her usual panic to rush out. "What up, Dana?"

"Weston. Don't ask how, but I think you found something besides riding dirt bikes you might be good at. I only hope you haven't peaked too early." She winked and gave me a light punch on my shoulder. "Later, gator." I halted, confused. Dana bulled ahead for the exit.

Beach filled the space she had left at my side. "Weston, dude! Did you get flirt punched by Untouchable?"

"What, Beach?" I was still trapped in a negativity storm. "I think she was aiming for my nose, man."

I didn't hang afterwards with the seniors like usual. I made for the truck and contemplated the dying sun from an empty school parking lot. Carlyle's words still boiled inside of me.

CHAPTER 32—FULL HOUSE MINUS ONE

Opening night, everybody taut as the curtain ropes. "Fifteen minutes, cast!" the backstage manager yelled. Dana Raleigh chanted syllables into a corner to get her risqué mouth loosened up, I guess. Others walked tight circles, pounding out their lines. Beach and me? We didn't need a new thing. We already had one, even if it left the cast a bit confused. We pounded on each other, locker-room style. I head-butted Beach's massive chest. In turn, he barked obscenities and shoved me hard with open palms on my pad-less shoulders.

"Okay, I'm ready, dude. Stop before you break something I need."

A small tear in the curtain provided a peephole to the audience. Like spies, we took turns peering through it to search for familiar faces. *Show yourself, J-Girl. There. Sweetness! Look at you, all dolled up and pretty.* Seated next to Jillian was a friend, no surprise there, but on her other side, her parents. I was touched.

"Places!" the clipboard-toting girl with the headset barked.

I was caught up in the beehive of nervous energy, even if I had no action until Act Two. Dialing up some tunes and helping the prop girl place her stuff on the set helped push back the opening-night jitters. I cautioned the freshman, "The fruit, Em, don't forget to set the fruit." She slapped her head and dashed backstage to retrieve the bowl.

The first half zipped by with very few kinks from the cast. Naturally, I was proudest of Beach, who had entered these halls fueled only by bribery but was now stealing scenes. He kept it as big as he had in rehearsal and was rewarded with big laughs from the audience.

Intermission came and flew by quickly. Techies flooded the stage with fog to set the scene for my first high school play entrance. Was I ready for this? Hell no. Nevertheless, like a man with a date with a guillotine, I took some deep breaths and anchored myself in the wings, just beyond the fringe of lights. Untouchable, now dolled up as the Fairy Queen, waited wordlessly beside me. Then, just before Act 2, a trio of friendly pokes in my back came from behind, and with them the words, "You've got this, Weston. Now move out of my way. I enter first."

The stage manager swooped in. "Stage is set. Ready, guys?"

Obviously she took my horrified expression as a yes. "Houselights down, stage lights up," she said calmly into her headset. The lighting crew bathed the stage in soft light.

Without hesitation, Dana fearlessly split the ankle-deep fog at curtain's rise and pounded her solo diatribe. I was impressed, almost hypnotized watching her from the wings until it hit me: I couldn't remember my opening lines! *Please God. Punish me double another time, but not tonight with my girl in the house.* A wave of offensive perfume hit me. What was Dejon doing back here? Whatever. Hers was good timing—what theater and such was all about. She whispered encouragement. "Your first stage entrance, Colby."

Yes, I know this, butta . . . "Mrs. Dejon, hate to ask, but you wouldn't happen to remember my first line?" Nervous chortle.

"It's just fear of the unknown."

"Then I'm the unknown and the fear is winning."

"Jump in. You know the lines. Trust yourself."

"But—"

My cue. "Who is this approaching from the mist? A stranger?" Dana said in her theatrical boom.

Dejon's hard shove cast me out into a new world. I found my spot and gave myself a last reminder: *Don't lock eyes with Jillian.* Clunk! The spotlight kicked in. POW! I peered into the yellow light. "Just a lost soul, ma'am, in search of some food and shelter for the night. What brings you out here on this foggy eve?"

I delivered the rest of my lengthy soliloquy without a hitch.

I was an actor.

Safely backstage, I was showered with love—not unlike for a well-timed stunt for crowded stands. Who would have thought? Not me, but there it was, and I liked it. "Quick!" I whispered to the prop girl, "Get me more lines. More lines!"

After Beach's final appearance, he tromped off to raucous applause, the likes not heard since he had sacked the opposing QB in the final down of the state playoffs. Later, he would muse that all this would help when he got to the NFL and had to do thirty-second soda commercials at two million a pop. That's when I knew Beach couldn't miss. When it came time for bows, I emerged to a few loud whoops from Jillian's gang. Riding a wave of bliss, I blew a kiss to the crowd like an idiot. The cast came together hand in hand in a single straight line and bowed in unison as the crowd came to their feet.

Energy soaring, most of the cast and crew headed for the Spanks Diner after our opening night. Jillian joined us for the late-night feast and laughter. She seemed to enjoy the scene and afterwards I got rock star treatment in the truck.

Closing night had come too quickly. It was about as nerve-wracking as the opening, though for different reasons. Everyone wanted to go out with a bang. I was surprised at the melancholy wave that came over me. I dreaded to see it end. A.L. had actually expressed enthusiasm for seeing the play. I was anxious to show him I was more than just motocross.

I arrived early to help set the stage, as usual and to lap up the cast's energy. People were flying around no less excited than on opening night—everyone's last chance to climb into the skin of their character. Ten minutes before curtain, the house buzzed with chatty folk. I pictured A.L. in the spot I had reserved for him in the back by the rail. He'd be searching the program for my name. Maybe he had reached the place in my bio when in a sentimental seizure I had dedicated the performances to him. Maybe the blurb would show him that even if his recovery had been slower than planned, and had strained us, there was always hope for the future. I peeped through the small tear in the curtain. No A.L., no Jillian. Jillian I knew about. She'd already seen it twice and had made other plans. But I didn't understand A.L.'s absence. I couldn't dwell on it. I needed to get ready. The first act had pretty much followed the script. Now it was my turn, one last time.

Second half: I was a boxed-in rodeo bull ready to romp. From the fringe I watched as Dana split the fog. My cue would soon follow. I looked out, ready to say my line, until my eyes drifted to the empty space where A.L. should have been sitting. And he wouldn't be the only thing that abandoned me.

BANG! Spotlight! It was all me now, but this time my opening line may as well have dropped to the floor for the night janitor to push away. Panic! I was left to scramble. I stood there, rendered in a cage of mute bewilderment as a dead-silent, crowd ogled. My queen stood frozen, never losing her high chinned nobility. I had to do something, but what? To her credit, during my brain wipe, Raleigh never lost her cool. She advanced closer, her satin dress billowing to the rescue, and delivered my cue another time, "What news do you bare?"

It didn't help. But one thing was in my favor: Marty was an agitated, nervous wreck of a guy, so I played that up, right down to the heaving sighs, groans and paced circles. Trickles of amusement leaked from the crowd. *Were they mocking me?* Probably not, but it all felt like an ill-fated moto jump in progress. I needed to right these wheels, fast. That, or exit the back stage door, hop on Silver and explode out of town.

So what I did was reach for the first prop I could grab from the fruit bowl. Surely the bright, plastic lemon would prove the perfect choice to channel my rage. I paced back and forth, shouting nonsensical psycho-holler. "No lemons, no person, will defeat me!" What did it mean? Nothing, but who knew outside the cast? At least it fed the laugh track that grew louder by the second. Dana swooped in and improvised deftly.

"Marty, no lemons, limes nor ego-driven kings will swerve you from your path of purpose . . . and just what is that?"

"Exactly, Lady of the Fog!" I rage-dumped every bit of emotion that had dogged me for the last six weeks on stage and for all to see. I ended my diatribe with an unplanned, dramatic flair: I gunned the freaking lemon into the audience.

It just felt right, and best of all, my actual lines came roaring back so I said those too. Only the outburst from some woman, about ten rows back caused some scuffling, and for me, mild concern.

Dana, too, momentarily dropped the regal and backstroked from her character with a horrified look. But as fast, she reeled it back in. She stared out into the crowd, her hands shielding her eyes. "Yes! Free your lemons, Marty. Everything is now free!" The crowd responded with shouts of approval and lively hoots. But during the final bows, there would be no kisses blown to the crowd from me; only a weak smile through the hard stare at the empty space A.L. never filled. Backstage, plenty of yips, tears and bouquets of flowers were doled out as I crumpled to the floor by the curtain ropes like a defeated boxer.

Beach quizzically leered at me, totally juiced on fame. "What up? I caught your shit from the wings. Coach might start you at QB throwing like that. Word is you nailed an old lady pretty good."

"Really? Like is she . . ."

"Dead, nah. Concussed, maybe. Gotta hunt down my new fans. Catch you at the Wyatt's cast party." I nodded, unsure if I was even brave enough to go. Soon, anger at A.L. drifted to concern. I texted him and got zero response.

I texted Jillian. She was about to leave for a friend's. I begged a favor: could she stop by and check on him?

Dana Raleigh's pose became a backlit silhouette. She smirked towards what probably was a ghoulish face, lit by my phone. "Shining another spotlight on yourself, Mr. Hyde? What are you doing, Weston? Play's done, props are away, nothing left to throw."

I rose. "God, Dana, I let you down."

"I'm over it and ready for the post fun. You juiced, *Lemon Drop*?"

I told her I wasn't sure I was going.

"Not an option, Weston," she said. "What I say goes."

"You saved my ass out there, queen."

"Oh, I've been known to throw an occasional line to a desperate sailor. You shined like a star. Now don't flame out, it's party time!"

Jillian's text back came in the form of a photo of A.L., head bent, passed out in his chair.

"Problem solved. Looks like I'll be joining the guys after all," I announced to the near empty seats.

CHAPTER 33--TOUCHABLE

Soon as I killed the truck's engine and glanced up, my insecure mood switched to awe. *Holy balls.* So it was true. El Relaxo could fit into the Wyatt's three-car garage! The only thing keeping this from being a castle was a moat and a drawbridge. The wafting music and laughter lured me. I was ready to take shit for the lemon and whatever.

The place was already en fuego as beach balls flew, marshmallows flamed and the cast danced under strung lights on the lawn. Some also splashed around in the pool, beating each other with foam noodles. Not knowing where to begin, I poured a Coke and mulled the sprawling buffet options. But conspicuously propped in the center of the cold meats sat the infamous lemon. *Great.* Immortalized, but at what cost? No doubt my night would be peppered with a fair share of ribbing.

As I sampled some chips, my eyes fell on the volleyball game and Dana Raleigh's bullet serves. So she had some jock in her, too, huh? In cut-offs, tee and a loose smile, she modeled a new version of herself—one that actually fit in closer with the rest of us. After serving consecutive aces, she readied herself for the next explosion until her eyes met mine and she fumbled the ball for a moment. Had she caught my teasing grin? She retrieved the ball and casually fired her next ace. *Take that, Weston!*

A curious rustling steered me towards a nearby bush. Grant, the captain of Philosophy 101 post-rehearsal talks, emerged looking a bit wobbly already. His checkered sports coat covering his bare, hairy chest and swim trunks were another reminder I had fallen way behind the party curve, at least in fashion. He held a blue Solo cup with one hand, while his other stroked the sage's full beard in contemplation.

"Bang-up job tonight, Weston," he said.

"Back to you, Grant. I dropped a line, but wasn't entirely laughed off the stage."

"You take what you can get. Your improv with the lemon was something for the ages."

"Thanks. Your idea to place it on the centerpiece in the middle of the food?"

I got a smile and sideways glance. "I see it as a symbol, an antithesis best actor award."

"Call it the Drop Alotta Script Award. On behalf of my shamed ancestors I accept this honor."

"In the end we're summed by our finest and most notorious moments, Weston. Not the shit between. You're JHS theater legend now. Cheers." Our Solo cups touched and side by side we surveyed the wide-angle folly.

Grant suddenly raised an index finger and blurted a subtle reminder. "But . . . you are aware it was Paige's grandmother you plunked, dude"

"What?" I drew in. "I should probably backstroke out of here."

"Stick around. Everyone's anxious to see how things play out."

"Like me dying?" I said.

Grant glanced around; extracted a silver flask from his sports jacket. "This will return your swagger. Imbibe, Roman." I couldn't refuse my mentor as he unscrewed the top and glug, glug, glugged therapy into my Solo cup. "Consider your ticket stamped," Grant said. "Now it is I who must answer to an ancient calling, to wade amongst the theater minions" He sighed like a reluctant hero, towards the pool with five bikinis in it. "We'll talk, Weston, we'll talk." Grant sauntered toward the pool, tossed his suit coat onto a chair and plunged into the water, all without breaking his easy stride. A flurry of colorful noodles mercilessly descended on him until he sank from sight.

All sins and worries lifted. When someone left their spot in the volleyball game, I was quick to fill the void. Dana was still there, bumping balls and looking the part. The action and the laughter came freely. After a couple of games, I decided it was time for the next option. I floated off, giddy, my cup still half-full.

A voice nabbed me from behind. "Hey, Lemon Drop, where you headed?"

"Dana," I said. "So honored by a royal following."

"At least bow to me when you say that."

At the buffet, Dana opened her bun and I dropped on a dog from the grill. I took one too, and both became smothered with an absurd amount of condiments. We shared a laugh over each other's painted lips and faces after a couple of bites. "Whoops. Your makeup is running, Dana. Here." I dabbed a napkin in cold water.

She flinched. "Oooo, cold!"

"Next time I'll use the garden hose. Geeze, learn to eat," I teased.

As we enjoyed the hotdogs we looked off without words. Finally,"Hey, Weston, are you the curious type?"

Two hard blinks. "Depends."

Dana playfully probed. "My question has no depends. One is a searcher or isn't."

"Put me down for a yay, for now."

She drew in like a cold war spy. "Good. I found something interesting in the Cabbot's' house."

"I bet . . . Like what?" I said.

She shrugged. "Want to check it out?"

"I don't know. Everyone's outside."

"Up to you." She turned and started to head for the sliding glass doors.

Grant's elixir had left me squirrelly enough to roll on the unknown. "Hold up, Dana." I prattled after her.

Only atmospheric music swirled and followed us throughout the rambling place. I paused before a large abstract painting on the wall. "What would you call this, Dana?"

She glanced over. "*I Can't Paint #6?* Dunno, but it's not why we're here. Follow me." I was led to a grand staircase, which she began to ascend like she owned the place. Near the top she realized she had lost her audience. Dana turned, annoyed. "Coming, Weston?"

I whisper shouted. "I don't know. What is this little discovery?"

"It's a show-don't-tell kind of thing. Trust me. You won't be disappointed. Up to you. Paige's folks are chill. "

I bounded after her, a faithful terrier. We tiptoed to the end of the hallway, into an expansive library neatly pocketed in dark walnut shelves. Beside two comfortable looking leather chairs, French doors opened to a narrow balcony. We stood there, two wordless voyeurs, overlooking the fun raucous scene below. I spied Beach, fresh arrived and entertaining a throng of fans with sweeping gestures.

"Beach," Dana dismissed. That haughty tone almost tripled her age.

"Awesome view, Dana. I like the floating candles on the lake. Do they own a boat?"

"Oh yeah. A fast one. I've been on it."

"Cool. So is this the little secret?"

She said blandly, "No, but this is where our little secret starts." A vague smile found her before she turned. "Follow me." She sauntered over to the far end of the bookcase. To hype the drama, Dana splayed her arms with her back to the books. "Turn around and count to ten, slowly," she said. "Do it!"

At around seven I heard some kind of muffled scraping sound. I parted my fingers and opened one eye. Dana Raleigh had vanished! I drew close to a leather bound copy of *Moby Dick* and whispered like an idiot, "Dana?" Call me Ishmael, but this was way too weird. "Dana?"

Sudden adult voices from down the hall dialed up my panic. No way did I want to be discovered and cornered by Paige's folks where I didn't belong. Dana's faint voice called as if from a dream. Desperate, I quickly discovered the cleverly disguised lever. The choices were simple: stay and face a double-barrel dose of lemon inquiry or take refuge with the ever bold, Ms. Raleigh. Believe me, the choice wasn't a gimme, but I soon was swiveling the stack inward. Once inside, I closed the door. *Thub*. I entered an insulated world, tight, about the size of a den, dark mostly with a bubbling sound.

Dana stood by a red leather couch, thumbing through an old *Popular Mechanics* issue as if unaware of my entrance. "Can you imagine living back then?" she said to the hastily flipped pages before boredom prompted a haphazard side toss. "What took so long?"

I didn't answer at first, still trying to figure the unique space. My eyes glided over everything but Dana. A few sketchbooks sat open on a drafting table. Besides that, the red couch sat atop a plush, white, shag carpet; a rather strange ensemble of work and play. My favorite was an illuminated, long, clear tube with living seahorses. The bluish aquarium light gave Dana's face a bit of a demonic sci-fi look.

"You like sea horses, Weston?"

"I do now."

Did you know male sea horses carry the babies in their pouches?"

"Wow. I always wondered what was hiding down there." After her smirk I asked, "What does Mr. Wyatt do?"

"He programs microchips that run entire city grids or something."

"That explains the swinging bookcases and a place in the country the size of a mall. Is this like his thinking room you suppose?"

"Who knows? It's got me thinking," Dana said.

A prolonged hiss of air oozed from the red leather sofa as she dropped onto it. "Oh my god, Weston, you've got to give this couch a try." Her flat palm did slow circles.

"I will." But I didn't. I stayed upright and tried to stay chill, even as my confused chemistry wreaked havoc and battled over mixed messages. "When did you discover this?"

Dana pulled in her knees. "Hanging out with Paige. Hey, behind you? That staircase? It leads to a wine cellar. Want to check it out?"

"Nooo, thanks. I'm more of whiskey guy. This is great, but maybe we should be headed back."

Dana's hypnotic gate wouldn't compromise. "There's no heading back. You can't leave until you experience this couch, seriously." Dana said.

The thick cushion sighed and pulled me in like quicksand. It prompted giggles from her while I nodded straight ahead with a tight-lipped grin. "Yep, this is one comfy couch." I reached for an ancient copy of a *National Geographic* and feigned a sudden interest in Jane Goodall's monkeys. I held the cover up and mimicked the monkey face next to it. "Ooo ooo ooo." I tossed it back on the table.

She laughed. "You're such a nut." She covered her face with both hands then showed a conflicted smile. Promise you won't laugh at me."

Now *I* was amused. "What?"

She looked me in the eye. "Can I kiss you?"

I forgot how to breathe. "Really? Wow, um."

"I didn't plan it," she said. "I just thought—"

"Dana, I've had so much fun being on stage with you. But—"

"Don't say it. It's okay."

Not to disappoint . . . it's just, well . . ."

"What?"

"Among other things I'm worried about running out of air in this tight space."

"That's the part I like, don't you?" she said. "Being sealed in our own world."

"But what if it locked behind us?"

"We'd eventually suffocate but we'll die in the presence of seahorses. Also, stairs lead to the outside, silly boy." She leaned over. A hand combed through my hair and slid down my face. *Why couldn't I just say it? No.*

Head-on assault. Her lips mashed into mine. I went with it. The couch sighed every time Raleigh squirmed and shifted. I was being devoured like a Spanks meatball sub. I didn't know what to worry about more—the guilt storm to come, or waking up the next day all black and blue.

"Weston, you're not scared are you?" Dana teased. She pushed me over and I became her next cushion. I flailed from underneath her straddled knees. "Awe, Colby, you're trembling." She shot a manic laugh towards the ceiling as winged sea horses continued to wander into and get sucked upward by the violent stream of bubbles. "Relax, will you?" Dana said.

It figured this would be the one time no one interrupted the foreplay. I needed to take charge and did—a little too aggressively. When I arched up, Dana got rolled off the couch, onto the soft shag rug. "What the hell, Colby?"

With total disregard for the low oak beam I jumped up too fast to assist her. Bang! "Fuck!"

"Owee!" she cackled. "Bet *that* didn't feel good." I fell back on the couch and rubbed my head. Not forty seconds later my phone buzzed. Dana took my side and cuddled close. "Who could that be?"

Jillian. Oh god, why did women always sense these things? This space, Dana's laugh, I was now that expendable actor in some indie horror movie. "I gotta go."

"Is it whatshername?"

I was already having guilt attacks. Now I felt pissed. "I'm splitting this chicken coop."

I sprung for the latch but nothing gave. "Am I doing this right?"

Dana remained back running her fingers through her blond strands. "Do I have to do everything?" She traversed the shag on all fours then slapped my fumbling hands away. She feigned panic. "Oh my god. It does seem stuck! We're trapped, forever! Thousands of years from now they'll find us balled up, all shrunken and gray, a couple of huddled teens!" Dana's chin jutted toward the *National Geographic.* "Can you picture the cover? *Teen Sex in Ancient Darin.* We'll be immortalized, Colby!"

"Thanks, but I was shooting for *Motosports Weekly* before I'm mummified. Let me try the latch again."

As my trembling hands fumbled with it, Dana studied her dark blue fanned nails. "I might keep them like this." She sighed. "Give up, Weston. It's futile."

Suddenly, the latch freed. I tumbled into the study, which was still void of humans, but I needed out and fast. I looked back to Dana. "Coming or what?"

"No one really likes me, Weston." She closed the passage and her pout became just another bookcase. I spoke through the books, told her performances had shined. It didn't work. After a hard ten seconds, hearing nothing back, I left.

Relief came with the night air. Beach broke from a circle of peeps. His face fell to something closer to curious. "Yo, Weston! Where did you sneak off to?" But his voice fell to a whisper as he pulled me aside. "Dude, you look like you just lost a fight with a lipstick tube." He rotated full circle. "You best clean up before J-Girl makes a surprise showing." He smirked.

Damn! I quickly plucked a napkin off the food table, poured a cup of water and madly attacked my face in cleanup mode.

Beach's hearty laugh. Stares from others. Guilt. I bolted the scene.

CHAPTER 34—GLASS HOUSES

I flipped down the visor and examined myself in the mirror. From the truck's glove box, I unearthed a napkin in an effort to rid my face of the last of her lipstick. *Fool.* That evidence was easily tossed out the window, but the guilt dried hard like paint. I fired up the truck and punched it into reverse. Town was mostly dark and lifeless as I looked around. My patience couldn't outlast the red light so I mashed the truck's pedal and burned rubber through the intersection. Towards the outskirts of Darin, the tall Southside Liquors sign stood dark and taunting. I thought back to Mr. Carlyle's arrogance and how powerless he had made me feel. He had profited when A.L.'s star burned high, and was still profiting from my father's habit after the fall. Carlyle's parting words still etched into me. *There's nothing you can do, Colby.* We'd see.

The truck seemed to steer itself. I pulled into Southside and killed the headlights. I silenced the chime and killed the interior lights with a quick slam of the door. It was easy to sell out reason in a moment of despair; the absence of good judgment cleared my path. The cinder block waiting in the empty adjacent lot beckoned like a gift-wrapped present. An approaching car gave me a chance to think but didn't change my mind. When the car's red taillights vanished, I walked over to the cinder block and hoisted it up. I wanted to punish Southside, punish A.L. and Raleigh. Punish me in the reflection.

Block to my middle, I trudged to the giant window behind which towered a pyramid-style display of whiskey bottles. The perfect mark. I cocked the cinder block back and heaved it through the glass with everything I had. The night's stillness ended in a frightening cascade of shattered glass. Shards of the large pane were now scattered inside and out of the store. Shocked, yet exhilarated, fear spun me towards the road for a check. Besides a distant dog's bark, the night resumed its pall. The whiskey, with its now, sweet caramel vanilla scent that had taunted me before, ran in rivulets over jagged shards of glass.

Greed for greater revenge would cost me. With outstretched arm, I poked my hand through the shattered opening to clutch the neck of an unbroken bottle. My intention was to let it fly towards another undisturbed display but was only rewarded with a flash of excruciating pain from a sliced-open hand. I recoiled. Glass collapsed and shattered to the ground. Blood, wine, whiskey, everything ran like prohibition. Bleeding and bent with pain, I staggered to the truck.

I entered the house with a hand wrapped in blood soaked paper towels. A.L was still passed out in the exact pose Jillian had sent me earlier. Bubbles' keen senses picked up my distress and probably the scent of my injury, too. Her ears pointed and she whined. I put a finger to my lips, launching another jolt of a pain. *Not that hand, fool.* I retrieved a first aid box from the utility closet and bee-lined it upstairs to the bathroom for some self-triage. B.K. appeared from my room and arched off his stiffness in the open bathroom door. He cried for a dinner he probably never got. I whispered, "Chill, cat. I can't now."

I slammed the bathroom door harder than intended. I unwrapped the soaked paper towels over the sink. The wound still oozed. An excruciating sting came when I patted it. There had to be glass in there—glass that would have to be plucked out with tweezers, one agonizing piece at a time. So with the other nervous hand, this is what I set out to do. Pain and involuntary tears came with every attempt, but I eventually cleared out the pieces from my palm. Done, I braved a squirt of antiseptic. F-bomb! It said *No Sting!* A.L. heard it, and his bleated cry followed.

"Colby? Is that you? Are you home?"

"Yeah, I'm home!" I barked.

I barely caught his mutterings. "Bubbles wants to be let out. Do you hear me?"

"Then do it!" I said.

"C'mon, help me."

"Not now, A.L., deal for once!"

The next round of pain sprouted as I attempted to apply butterfly bandages to close the wound. What hurt more? The pain or the thought I may have also ended my shot at the national semis over a stupid deed? Minus a strong grip, I would not be able to control Silver, especially over high jumps at competitive speeds. This would cost me practice time and the next heap of the old man's wrath.

Bandaged hand, elevated and close to chest, I descended the stairs with hungry B.K. weaving perilously between my feet. I ducked into the kitchen quickly so A.L. wouldn't see the damaged goods. My left hand took over where my right left off and I poured BK his chow.

Collapsed in a living room corner, A.L.'s attempt to lift his head was half-hearted. A string of drool oozed from his mouth as fresh lines of rancid bird guano ran down his shoulder. This time, though, Commander had retreated to his coop and put himself to bed. A depressed wave overwhelmed me: Maybe both of our dreams had been washed away. Now what?

I wheeled him into his office and helped him into bed, not easy given the injury. A.L uttered a stupid apology for nothing specific. A batted light switch was my only answer. I let in Bubbles. A note from Jillian lay on the table. Each loving word about me and about the play only jacked up my self-loathing.

Sunday morning. I was jolted awake, not by my alarm, but persistent pain. There was no getting back to sleep. Coffee soon dripped. I stared off in a cloud, unsure what to do about anything. I poured two cups of strong brew and entered A.L.'s cave. "Get up, Poo Pot," I said.

His eyes finally opened and he came to. "What? What time is it? What's happening?"

"Take this," I insisted.

He complied with his new, just-arrived to Earth look. "Ah, room service. Just leave the cup on the table." He fell back with closed eyes.

I said, "C'mon, turn your sorry ass engine on."

"Sorry about your show . . . Couldn't be helped. I'll explain later. Leave me be now."

"We both have some explaining to do," I muttered towards the window.

"What time is it?" he said.

"Time to see Pastor Paul."

Everything left him like he was down a quart. "Now? Wait you're not proposing church. We'll talk later. I need to lay low."

"It's called a hangover. It too will pass. You're coming with."

He barked, "Stop trying to direct my life, boy!"

I deserved a medal for getting a protesting dad in a truck. I sarcastically thanked him for his no show and how it launched an improv that almost wrecked the play.

He hissed only sass, "Well you should improv some fresh moves from Silver while you're at it." He apologized for missing, but placed the blame squarely on Amanda Triffle and her blown engine.

"Her engine is blown, alright—from the neck up. Not buying the BS, A.L."

Eventually he noticed the bandage. "What happened to your hand?"

"Can you believe this? I nicked it when I ran into an old window the Wyatts were storing by the garage."

Of all times to find clarity. "That's odd. The Wyatts recently built a new place by a lake. We provided most of the lumber. Strange to have old windows sitting out."

"Who knows why?" I said, hand throbbing. "I don't want to talk about old windows,"

"Hey! Shit man, you got blood all over my seat! Am I getting the real story or what?

"Sorry I cut myself. Next time I'll stand outside bleed out. I'll clean it up when I get back."

He rubbed his face. "Fuck, Colby. That should have been done last night. Also pal, that's your throttle hand. Maybe a better option would be the ER, huh? A couple of stitches might be in order."

"I told you, I dealt with it."

"I can't believe the bad run you're on, Colby. It's one damn distraction or poor decision chasing the other. No mystery why your game's headed south. Idiot!"

At least church forced us to endure each other, side by side in silence. The pews and the rich stained glass offered reflection but little serenity. Persistent throbs of pain pulsed to the beat of the hymn, while my insides became a category four hurricane of worry. When I should have been reveling in the play's success, I was instead consumed by a potential drama of bad outcomes. I prayed for a simpler life, say that of a Macaque monkey. I looked over at A.L. whose head began to nod ten minutes in. I nudged his foot with mine, forgetting the action was a wasted move. I let him be.

Head bowed and clenching an achy hand, I had some favors to ask. I began my pact with The Man, begging forgiveness. *I promise to repay Southside somehow and never again be led astray by another woman. I will grab the reigns of life again, not slip off the honor roll; heal to return pride to the Weston name and dazzle with showmanship in moto events in your name. Also, if you can just sober up the old man a little, cool? Guide him . . . well, you know what to do with it. Your go-to servant, Colby. Amen.*

The organist nailed the last chord and people rose to exit. In the reception area everyone gathered for treats and coffee. I munched a chocolate chip cookie, snickering at the uneasy but forced-to-be-charming A.L. as he mingled with the crowd.

"Colby," A.L. said out of one side of his mouth as I filled a plastic cup with lemonade.

"A.L., you're a hit. Cookie?"

"Get me out of here."

"What's the rush? Hey, there's Pastor Paul." I ignored my dad's snips and wheeled him straight to the man in black. I whispered, "Remember why his one arm hangs lame like that?"

A.L. muttered, "Of course. A Kodiak bear surprised him in Alaska. You may have parts of you hanging like that before the day's through—Pastor Paul, hello!"

"What's this? The Lord finally jostled the Weston Boys from hiding?" the minister said. "Welcome back, guys. And what about you, A.L.? How's it going?"

"The speed of life's a little slower than I'd like, Pastor, but otherwise no complaints. Very nice service, sir. There's just something about singing to God, huh?"

At least A.L.'s penchant for BS hadn't dulled any. So why didn't he fake that degree of sweetness to me?

On the ride home, we were silent. A flash of optimism entered me. Everything would be fine. Monday after school I would head down to Southside and admit to Carlyle what I had done. I'd write him a note promising to cover the damages. To appease A.L., I would brave the bad paw and try some laps after my attempts to scrub his seats clean. Then, I'd pick up Jillian and steal her away to the pond for catch up. Maybe I'd tell her. She'd understand. Or maybe I'd say nothing and skirt the whole issue. In short, there was maneuvering to be done but for now I had a battle plan and a hopeful feeling about things.

All optimism crashed in a heap at the repeat appearance of Officer Delvin in our driveway. He stood leaning on the trunk of his patrol car, rubbing the back of his neck, looking every bit the enforcer whose lazy Sunday had been interrupted. A.L. stiffened as he connected the dots from the seat's bloodstains, to my bandage and my now blanched face. No nonchalant shrug from me was going to change any of this.

CHAPTER 35--HARD TIME AND RESCUE

"Don't know, A.L."

"Seriously? You can't tell me why *for the third time this month* Officer Delvin is here? Damn it, Colby!" A.L. yanked the door and swung his shoulders like he'd forgotten his plight then quietly added, "Help me down."

A.L.'s niceties with Mark were brief this time. While they mulled the weather, I weighed escape into the woods. The two men moved inside. I followed. My old coach didn't seem that upset. Maybe it wasn't about Southside or some follow-up to the Sweet thing. I lurked in the kitchen, clinging to hope this was the case. "Colby, you still there?" A.L. said. "Bring us out some iced teas."

I did. Officer Delvin took a slug, nodded at his glass. "Guys, I swung by with a couple of questions about something that was brought to the department's attention." He let a slice of time hang, took his next sip, and said, "Something last night."

My legs went closer to boiled spaghetti.

"My questions are mostly for Colby, A.L."

"Feel free to fire away, Officer Delvin." By now, A.L. probably meant with his gun.

Delvin asked, "What happened to your hand there, Colby, if I might ask."

"Nothing, just nicked it at a party last night, Coach."

"Tough party." Mark cleared his throat. "Have a seat, son."

Like on an electric chair? I sat calmly, once again fixing on his lethal belt, my brain, an assembly line of lies. When he reached the part about the store's security cameras, I was anointed Darin's next king of fools. Mark never formally pointed the finger at me, just respectively allowed me to slip my own head in the noose.

"Have you heard the expression cameras don't lie, Colby?" he asked.

I recoiled like a trapped snake. "I only heard they add ten pounds."

A.L. barked, "Colby, stop yanking the man's chain!"

Officer Delvin's leg pumped a few times. "I'm kind of at a loss here, Colby. You're the last kid I would have guessed would vandalize a storefront."

"You *vandalized* a storefront?" A.L. said.

"So it would seem, A.L. Southside Liquor. Didn't they sponsor you?"

"*Southside Liquor?*" A.L. was incredulous. "Why?"

"My question too Colby?" Delvin said.

I was that hissing trapped raccoon I had cornered in the garage one time. "You know why, A.L."

A.L.'s fidgety hand went to his chin and he said in a controlled tremble, "Mark, I'm not making excuses for my boy. Lord knows there are none . . . But Colby hasn't adjusted since I got home from the hospital."

"Me?" I said and rolled off a villain's three-beat chuckle.

Mark saw that A.L. was ready to blow so he served his next point up with matter-of-fact calm. "I get it, A.L. It's been a rough patch for you both. But the fact is Mr. Carlyle insists on pressing charges." He scratched at his neck. "Don't think sliders are going to do the trick, not this time."

Sarcasm dripped from my defeat. "Imagine that, A.L., after all the business you've been giving that guy?"

"Quiet!" A.L. hissed. "He was a sponsor. A sponsor!"

I fired back. "Well he's been sponsoring a bad habit is what." I looked to Mark. "Coach, I tried to talking to the owner and well—"

"You confronted him?" A.L. asked.

"Yeah I did. I asked him to stop delivering. I was trying to help."

Mark said, "A little remorse might go a ways, Colby. You were cut some serious slack after the Sweet episode, but there's a bad trend developing."

A.L. seemed content to throw me under the bus. "I agree, Officer Delvin."

I turned to Mark. "May I add my two cents, sir?"

My old coach cut me off. "You've had your nickel's worth. A.L., bottom line is I have to take Colby downtown for processing. We'll try to arrange some kind of bail, then y'all can expect a court hearing to follow."

I slapped my knees. "Oh c'mon, Coach, I'm no damn felon. You *know* me, man. I'll settle this with Mr. Carlyle and pay for the damages with my own money. Made that pact in church this morning."

My plea didn't soften Delvin's steel gray eyes. "I do know you, Colby, and that's why I'm as surprised as your dad about all this. Deciding in church the day after is too late. Last night at 12:05 a.m., when you paused in front of the window with that cinder block? That was decision time. And, son," he paused, "you made it. Let's go."

A.L. looked stunned. I rose, unsteady.

I overheard Delvin whisper, "A.L., I know in his heart Colby's a good kid. I'll see if I can't get him back by nightfall. Let's see where the chips fall."

A.L., who had rolled off, snapped his chair around and closed his distance to me. Rage consumed him and he exploded. "You'll do nothing of the kind, Officer Delvin! Take him away! Let him cook in there for a good while until the son I raised is ready to return with straighter priorities. You hear me, boy?"

Even I was shocked at the level of my father's emotional outpour. Still, I tried to stay as blank as Jillian's lens recording the chaos of a pit race. Mark took my arm. A last visual check over my shoulder showed that A.L. had already turned his back on me, probably for good. His head was in his hands. My god, how we had fallen. He wanted nothing more to do with me, nor I with him.

I was led out. The sudden outburst of glass breaking paused Mark in his tracks. He took my arm and said, "He'll be fine."

Juvenile detention. Never thought I'd get the pleasure of the tour. Despite my promises to the woman at the desk not to hang myself or dial up my escape posse with my cell phone, they confiscated all personal possessions. Mark made me recant my devious deeds for his written report. All such bullshit. The clerk was a jerk. Mark, A.L., Untouchable, Carlyle . . . all assholes. I was stripped of allies except for Jillian.

I was escorted through threatening stares to a closet-sized concrete cell with nothing more than a cot and a place to piss. Maybe my sad dad would ease up and spring me from the joint. *The Joint. I was in the joint!*

Sunday night came and went. A.L. kept his word. He left me there to sleep and stew. It was chilly and dealing with the wails of the crying kid in the next cell hardly helped. Occasionally someone howled at him to shut up but it did no good.

Monday came and I pushed back the tepid plate of scrambled eggs for a cup of something hot they claimed was coffee. I was allowed access to a common room where dudes blankly watched two women whoop up on each other over a cheating husband on a daytime talk show. I stayed low-key, said little and kept one eye on the clock. *C'mon, A.L.* Even if I got sprung soon, I would never tear free of Darin's gossip line. *Seven-forty-five.* General Benson would be silencing Dana but only after she unveiled a new wrinkle to *The JHS Morning Show: Confessions from a Teen Seductress.* While a few rooms down, Jillian would calmly stare and entertain the idea of castration. And to think my biggest fear had been Monday bringing lemon jokes.

I only poked at the lunch that came and went. I looked up from my back; surveyed the patterns and cracks in the ceiling. The next shouted voice was for me.

"Weston!" I jolted up.

"Let's go. Someone gives a crap about you."

About freakin' time, A.L. I wonder who he'd sent. Pastor Paul was the obvious choice. Knowing him, he'd be cool, and the only thing I'd have to endure on the ride home was another retelling of his bear attack or having to hunt seal with Inuit. Ooooh, better yet, it might be Beach's mom with a greasy bag of her fried finest. Either way life looked brighter.

Expectation buckled to utter befuddlement. The sight of the lone, engrossed man flipping through pages of *Seventeen* made no sense. I turned my back to shield my face. The woman behind the desk stared at me funny but stayed with the script. "Colby Weston, that gentleman has come for you. It will take a moment to process your things. Do you understand me? Hello?"

With one thumb pointed behind me, I whispered, "He must be here for someone else. Do you know who that is?"

"Yes I do," said the lady. "Klaus Ketty and I go *waaay* back."

"Then you must understand, Klaus isn't exactly, um . . ." I nervously rubbed my palms trying to complete the thought but ultimate avoidance was futile. His nose rose from the issue of innocents.

Klaus boomed, "Colby Weston! There's the little felon!" He rolled up the *Seventeen* and tucked it under his arm. "Why, Linda! Didn't know they transferred you over to juvi. Poor kids."

"Difference here, Klaus, is these kids might grow up."

I said to Linda, "You know, I'm good walking. It's not far."

"No, you're coming with me," Klaus grumbled. "Per orders of your daddy."

With a hard thud from a stamp I was free. "Off with you both," she said. "Oh and the magazine, Klaus?" An extended palm held patient before the rolled issue was slapped into her hand.

Outside, Klaus turned towards the sky. "Ahhh. Take time to bask in the sunlight, son. I'll never forget that first time after hard time."

"Yes sir, Mr. Ketty."

"Call my dad that, if you can ever find him. For me? Klaus will do."

"Yes sir, Klaus."

"Stop trudging along so, boy. I need to get back to the body shop. Mine's that new silver Mercedes over there," he chuckled.

My new version of freedom consisted of being imprisoned with Klaus Ketty inside a 1997 Pacer, mostly eaten away by time and rust. It did nothing for my assurance seeing the passenger door lacked handles for my window or escape. This felt more like a hit than an act of charity. Once the ominous thing sputtered to life, Klaus fired up a choking cigar. I waved away the smoke. "What's wrong? Hot? I'll turn on the AC." It clattered to life like a mouse wheel.

A ways down the road, we cruised by the yellow-taped front of Southside Liquors, the root of this whole mess. "That your masterpiece, kid? You did a pretty thorough job, though I would have finished off Balloon Boy as well. Did the owner have it coming or was this a more a recreational matter?"

Why the hell had A.L. sent Klaus? "Guess he had it coming, Klaus, I don't know." Klaus shrugged and hunched close to his steering wheel as he zeroed within striking distance of a motorcycle he was tailgating. "Right at the next light, Klaus."

"I know where you live," he said.

"Mind if I ask you a question?"

"Like why did I bail your ass out of jail?"

"Yeah."

"It's kinda funny, springing the son of the son of a gun. There was this one time—"

"Klaus, look out!" I screamed. A sudden horn blared from an Old Dominion freight truck whose path Klaus had wandered into. It shook the entire car in a near miss. Only Klaus's last-second swerve abated extraction via tweezers.

After we swapped f-bombs, Klaus said, "Damn service is to blame. Ordinance hit my tank."

"I feel like I'm in one . . . Wait, you drove a tank?"

A smile found him. "An M1 Abrams in good ole Afghanistan. Fun in the sand until the tread rolls over a fat mine. Oddly, it hasn't affected my moto reflexes none." Klaus's hand playfully jostled me.

"Just drive, Klaus, please," I said.

"What the fuck were we talking about?"

"Before we almost died? Why you were chosen to pick me up?"

"Oh right. Anyway, I was on my bike, heading towards Jack's, when I risked a route, rarely taken."

"The road past our place?"

"Precisely. Damned if A.L. wasn't outside, by the side of the road, slumped in his chair, looking grumpy. I raised a hand and—"

"Waved?"

"No, shot him the finger, but the damnedest thing? Something made me stop."

"Next mailbox is ours, Klaus," I said.

"I know." He pulled in but was in no hurry to exit. I didn't know if I wanted to sit there or get out. I let Klaus ramble. "Anyway, we ended up having a decent chat about things and old races . . . The man's gone and got his passion stripped from him. I can't imagine."

"I can imagine what he'll do to me," I said.

"You just open that car door, walk inside like nothing happened."

"Oh, that'll work," I muttered to the dusty window.

We both stood staring at El Relaxo. Klaus finally said, "Suppose I could duck in and say hi. Might cushion the blow."

"Like a human shield? Lead the way," I said.

I walked up and tugged the door. Klaus appeared hesitant. "Comin'? I said

"Kind of strange entering the lion's den."

I smirked and motioned him forward. Inside, the TV played to an empty couch. Bubbles emerged but clamored down the basement after Klaus said, "Git."

"A.L., I got your boy." Klaus's bellow filled the place.

A.L. emerged from his office slightly less deranged looking than I left him, still grandfather-strict. He halted his chair short of Klaus who acted as a wedge between us. I reckoned he'd be more tense, but A.L. joked, "Never pictured you standing in that spot, Klaus."

"So this is El Relaxo." Klaus looked around. "Nice."

A.L. asked, "Any trouble springing the delinquent?"

"Not a one. Wish my sentences had been that short," Klaus said.

A.L.'s face tensed up when his gaze settled on me. "Yeah well, hard time's just begun for this youngin."

"Boys will be boys, A.L."

"You ever raise one, Klaus? No, that's what I thought." A.L. paced one of his curious tight circles. Eventually the chair stilled. "Winning anything these days, Klaus?"

"Without you around? Shit, I'm a fox in a hen house, brother. Almost miss our hard-fought battles."

A.L. sneered. "I bet. Give it time. Eventually some young lion will appear and knock off your crown." A.L. talked through Klaus' rolled eyes at me "Maybe even this guy, someday, if he can get his act together."

Klaus gazed at me. "But first, Junior and I will be watching each other's runs, hopefully all the way to the Loretta Lynn Championship." A.L.'s look suggested more doubt then pride. Klaus grew fidgety. "Gentlemen, duty served, I leave you two to catch up or whoop up on each other." He paused at the door. "Say, A.L., you should make your way down to Jack's sometime, check out the action. You've always liked doling out tips to fellow riders." He offered a teasing smile.

A.L. smirked. "We'll see. Until then, thanks for plucking the jailbird."

Klaus left. Wordless, we stood side by side at the open door and watched his dust settle. "Klaus doesn't seem all that bad," I said.

A.L. retreated inside without comment.

CHAPTER 36--A.L.'S SENTENCE

A.L. fetched a beer and planted himself on the porch. He called for me but avoided eye contact. "How was lock-up?"

"I'd give it half a star, maybe; loud neighbors, lumpy cot, rude staff."

"Your mother and I talked last night," he said.

"You called Mom? Why? Did you mention where I was?"

"Yeah," he said.

"Damn it, A.L."

"So now you care what she thinks," he said.

"Not really. So what's going on?"

His eyes met mine. "You tell me. Your wheels are coming off."

"I wonder why?" I said.

"It's easy to point blame away from yourself but it all circles back."

I raised both palms. "Guilty, I'll admit it. I can't seem to take two steps without putting my foot in the dog shit, but I know what needs fixing . . . You and I just need to work some things out. It'll get better A.L. Think of the old times."

"I do, that's what's killing me," he said. "Colby, I'm trying to figure out what's best for everybody now, so is she."

"What's best is gone. You know that A.L. We'll put a shine on Plan B and run with it. I'm sorry I've been trouble for you. We'll figure it out. Right now I just want to chill, I'm tired."

He said, "What I've figured out is she's willing to take you."

More out of denial than anything I said, "Great. Mom and I talked about that while you were away. Maybe after the Regional I'll visit—check out the new house, meet Moneybags and his rugrats. Maybe take in a Reds game while I'm up there."

"Or buy season tickets."

I hesitated. "What are you saying?"

"It's not a bad deal, son. She's living in big place, nice neighborhood. She's already discussed this with—"

"Wait old boy. Are we talking about me *moving* there?" I framed a funny face. "Like for senior year? No chance."

He turned bad salesman. "Think about it. They have a beautiful house, walking distance from a newly built high school, solid football program . . . I didn't ask if they've got a . . . *drama club*."

"Stop, A.L. You've lost the big picture. I haven't."

"It's been a bad stretch, Colby. You're not adjusting to the changes."

"*I'm* not adjusting? Who do you think caused all these problems? Your idea of therapy is getting wasted daily and shutting out everything and everybody else. You wonder why I've been a little upset, why I'm a little off my game?"

"Oh no, don't you blame me for your problems as Silver rusts in the garage and people forget the Weston name."

"Look, the national championship has been an important goal for me. It's still doable."

"How is it doable when you haven't put in the time and now you've messed up your throttle hand?"

"Lots can change in a month . . . apparently. But hey, plan on me to be in the mix like before. With all the recent shit that's come down? Yeah, it might've cost me a step. But I can get it back. If that's what you want, I'm good for it."

"If you're doing it for me than you might as well sell Silver now, don't matter."

"Course it matters, just saying. And do you think Mom would let me run my routine up there? Guess again. Silver's knobbies wouldn't even be allowed to touch that garage floor of hers. Hell, she probably waxes the damn cement. I also have Jillian to consider. No, I'm not leaving. I'll sleep in the woods if I have to. You live your life the way you want, I'll live mine. We both got hills to climb."

A.L. took sip of his beer. "You still have a court date, my boy. You're downplaying the hole you've dug for yourself."

"No, I'm staring at the fucking shovel."

"What did you say?"

A.L. began to roll away but paused before the door of his study. "Anyway, you were interested and that's what your mom and I discussed. All parties agree it's best for you."

"So you didn't hear a word I said. Never took you as a quitter until now, but that's what I'm seeing. You're quitting on us both."

He erupted, "That's a lie. That's a lie!" A.L.'s chair spun and he cocked the bottle above a deranged face."

I shook my head. "You don't have the balls, A.L."

But he did—and a true arm. The rotating glass missile zeroed in on my nose and only a last second duck spared me. The glass exploded on the wall next to me as beer splattered and ran down. Weston, Inc. was officially bankrupt. I slammed the door behind me and bolted on Silver for a long escape in the country.

Tuesday morning, first bell. This time as the students thinned and the busses pulled away, Jillian didn't emerge with a longing look. I dreaded every step to homeroom. So much had happened since my lemon throw; Untouchable, my arrest. I didn't know what J-Girl knew or what rumors were flying around, only that I didn't want to face them.

The mere appearance of Dana on the homeroom TV caused me to cower in my seat. What if she lost it and started a new reality, tell all segment "And now, morning confessional!" Thankfully she didn't reference us or the town's police blotter but followed the script, bubbly as sea horses.

Before I could feel too much relief, Benson loomed over my desk. "Since your reliable assistant didn't pick up your work yesterday you'll have double duty . . . Oh and Colby, guidance called and wants to see you."

Now what? My sneer wasn't intended for Benson and I hoped he understood that. I promised I'd make up Monday's work and check out guidance. He shot an inquisitive look but didn't bring up my bandaged hand.

After pre-calc I made it as far as my locker unscathed. I began a redial after I messed up my combo. Locker door barely open, an interruption came with a light tap on the shoulder. With a warm smile I spun expecting a forgiving Jillian.

I fought off fleeing at the sight of The Secret Chamber Queen. Still, I greeted her with a playful bob of the head. "What up, Dana! So you escaped the mystery nook. Interesting times, huh?"

"Cut the bullshit, Weston!" Dana attracted the one thing she coveted beyond all else: a riveted audience. To better make her point, she kicked my locker door shut. Spectators stood gape-mouthed before scattering.

I said, "Uh, I still needed something from that locker, actually."

"Remember that sticky latch at the Turner's?"

"I do. And?"

"It got stuck again. After you *abandoned* me."

"I didn't—What? How?" I said.

"Who cares? You never answered my cry for help."

"Because I didn't hear it. Sorry you got stuck, but you're the one who pulled me in. Hell, I would've been down with small talk by the lake view."

Dana obsessed. "I want you to know, I had to grope my way down that dark, dusty staircase, past cobwebs and old wine bottles until by some miracle I found the door to the outside."

"Was the volleyball game still on?"

"What? Who cares?"

"Dana. Let's just move on."

"Great idea!" Dana did a one-eighty and charged down the hallway like I'd yanked the fire alarm.

I shrugged and turned. I reopened the door. But just seconds after Dana fell from view Jillian sailed in from the opposite corner. "Hey C-Boy, I think we need to chat." I'd never seen this defiant and icy.

"Good morning, I love you. Sorry I couldn't call . . . I was somewhat detained. I had a funny weekend."

I lunged to embrace her but only caught air after Jillian's matador sidestep. She said, "Funny? The shit I heard wasn't funny." She kicked my locker door shut. "I've been texting all weekend. Where have you been? There're some strange stories flying around. Some kind of wilding spree with the cops getting involved and things getting a *little* out of control at the party?"

I was that wildebeest with two lionesses on my back, bleating for fate's reprieve and forgiveness.

Her face turned disgusted. "What happened to your hand?"

"I cut it. Meet me at the pond after school and I promise the full story."

Jillian framed exasperation. "Can't wait," she said.

Last period, one step out the door, Dejon said, "Missed you yesterday."

"I was auditioning in New York."

"Ooooh. Punchy are we? Did you offer your Hamlet impersonation with a lemon? Hamlet chose to reason with a skull not treat it like a fastball pitch.

"To be or not to be, *what* was the question, Mrs. Dejon? Sorry, I have to be somewhere."

"Like I told you, make sure the props stay where they belong next time."

"Yes, Ma'am."

"Another thing, Colby. Make sure there is a next time." Dejon then beat her fist rhythmically on a desk as she said, "Fortitudine vincimus!" I'd later discover the master survivalist Captain Shackleton motivated his crew with the same words—also after the ship had sunk. Now I needed to whip up some fortitude, and fast. After dismissal I headed off to collect Jillian for a talk at Harriet Pond and a heap of chin music. What should I tell Jillian? What should I omit? Mess this up and I might lose the one friend I couldn't imagine life without.

Jillian's mom didn't seem her usual rosy self when she answered the door. I cemented my feet to the stoop where she told me to stay put—not a good sign. Jillian's signature, rhythmic clomp down the stairs was uplifting, but proved short-lived. A whispered squabble busted out between mom and daughter. Jillian blew past me without greeting hopped into my truck, crossed her bare arms and glared out the window.

As we rumbled toward the duck pond, all my efforts at small talk netted zero traction. Once there we looped water's edge until her interrogation began to dominate the conversation. For a while I took my deserved beating like a man; then I decided lap three would belong to me.

I promised her honesty and that's what was served. It almost felt like a first date, with me desperately trying to sell myself to Jillian all over again. In the end, I offloaded a boxcar's worth of sins and let Jillian sift through all the shit, including the near-death experience with Ketty, the only thing she laughed about. What I didn't share was A.L.'s pending eviction. I wasn't a total fool. If she was even considering second chances, she wouldn't be tempted by an already condemned man.

The net result? I was rewarded with a torrent of confusion, sadness, and basically everything you don't want to hear from anyone you love. Jillian couldn't cast away the incident with Untouchable, no matter how meaningless. I had broken the trust. My pleas ultimately sunk to the bottom of her pond with the rest of the skipping stones. All I could pray for was eventual forgiveness.

My heart wanted to rupture on the mostly silent ride home. I expected her to bolt the second my truck pulled up to her place. But she sat frozen with a cold straight ahead gaze with hand on the door handle. I broke the dead air. "What do I need to do, Jillian?"

Unexpected words followed. "Get back on Silver and win out, Colby. That was when you were at your best."

"It's always been the plan, J-Girl, it just got derailed over . . . well you know. It would make preparations a lot easier if I knew you were there to see and film it when I do."

"I'm not taking requests right now," she said.

"You've got film camp coming up. Can I drop by before you leave?"

"Maybe. I don't know. Try me." She yanked the door handle and exited in a red-eyed trot.

CHAPTER 37—VISIT TO A HAUNTED PLACE

A.L.'s ongoing coldness suggested his desire to have me move to Mom's in Cincinnati remained real. As friends began talking fun summer plans, I stared stoic, wondering how I might turn my life, my ride and my dad's perspective in my favor. Meanwhile, texts from Mom began flying in at record rates. I think she was thrilled with the idea of having a live-in babysitter for her young step kids—as long as I left Silver behind.

>Hi Colby! A room awaits. What color would you like it?

>Hi Mom. Midnight Mansion? No done deal down here. Will keep in touch.

Between Jillian's cold shoulder and A.L.'s delusions, life didn't have a lot of soft spots. I wasn't ready to leave A.L. to die; give up my friends; lose Jillian, nor my senior year at JHS. I also hadn't given up my moto dream which remained parked in the garage. Somehow I needed to change the old man's mind, and quick. He might put me on a bus to Cincinnati within hours of the final bell—coming soon. Jack seemed be the obvious choice to intervene, but when I gingerly approached him he only shook his head and mused to the horizon, "That's a tough one. Time heals everything." I couldn't get him to understand. Time was something I didn't have. My options were wheeling away from me faster than any bike on his track.

A few days later, I ran into Klaus Ketty taking some practice rounds. I flagged him down and thanked him again for picking me up from juvie. Eye contact with Klaus was intimidating so instead I stared at his tattoo. *Faith. Sobriety. Motocross.* It hit me: despite their differences, they had shared similar dreams and setbacks. There must be a grain of mutual respect, and A.L. needed someone other than me to set him straight. Maybe this was the guy.

Sick with nerves, in the middle of nowhere, I paused atop Silver before a hand-painted mailbox that read *665 Turban Lane*. This was nothing less than a desperate swing for the fences trying recruit help from an ex-felon; ex-rival of my dad. Even if he knew I was coming—and I had called him, all sorts of things could go wrong. But then again, I wouldn't have come if all kinds of things hadn't gone wrong already.

Was it the dark woods? There was a palpable spooky vibe that swirled about the place as flashes of late afternoon sun exploded through agitated leaves. To the side of the long, ascending, dirt driveway ran a tumbling stream. A wisp of wood smoke suggested I was close. I reached a plateau where a rusty work shed, dead cars, sawhorses and half-completed projects spoiled the pristine surroundings. Atop the next incline sat a modest cabin with torn porch screens, through which dogs began to bark. My gut tightened even more. Klaus was nowhere to be seen.

I slipped Silver into neutral but couldn't brave a dismount. "Klaus!" I shouted. That only riled the dogs more. I weighed immediate retreat, but desperation cemented me. I called out again. This time the cabin's flimsy screen door forced opened. Not Klaus, but two Dobermans headed straight for my jugular. "Klaus! It's me! Colby!" I cried to no one.

Their owner's quick, bounding descent through the brush arrived seconds ahead of twin jaws of death. *"Heshtje!"* the bearded one bellowed, crossbow in one hand and a completely random violin in the other.

This man sure had control of his hell hounds, something I was immediately grateful for. The dogs grounded to a halt like they had smacked into an electric fence. Like a pair of statues they sat up, perky and obedient, pink tongues panting, hoping beyond all, the stand down order would be lifted. Klaus showered the disciplined marauders with high-pitched praise, this time in English. Donned in fatigues, crossbow tight to his chest, I was sitting prey. "Really bad timing, young Weston," he grumbled.

I stammered, "I *thought* this was the agreed upon time."

Klaus lumbered closer. "Maybe, but it's also the same time you chased away my deer and upset my dogs with all your racket."

"Oh. Sorry."

"Alright, Colby Weston. You chased off a month's worth of Bambi vittles. Take your best shot."

"First, can I ask about the violin?"

Klaus rolled his eyes. "It's a viola. It attracts animals and it's a stress reducer."

"How's that working out?"

"Fine," he stared at me gruffly. "Most of the time. Now, why'd you come?"

As I spoke, Klaus half listened, as he showered affection on the bloodthirsty hounds. When I finished the recap of my immediate plight, he said, "Yep, sounds like your daddy ain't adjusting too good. No surprise there . . . we got that in common. Go on."

"And now he wants me gone," I said.

"See? I always knew a wolf was lingering underneath that sweet demeanor."

"All he's interested in, it seems, is drinking and playing the blues. He's kind of shunned everybody else."

"Sounds like a man after my own heart." Klaus yanked on his beard. "My *old* heart . . . I don't get it. You're his pride and joy. Jack talk to the man? They're close."

"He tried, nothin' doing."

"Happened to me at about your age, a little younger. My dad kicked me out." Klaus shook his head. "Man gets tormented enough, that's a cold, tough beast to slay. Wish I could wave a magic wand, boy, but I've never been mistaken for someone in the people business."

"C'mon, Klaus. He won't listen to me. Thinking a heavy boot will do."

"Colby, the other day I did your dad a favor, more than I usually do. Give the man time. My dogs got their hungry, impatient faces going. Anything else?"

I sighed and moved on to the other part of the plan.

"You've heard of custom vans for disabled drivers?"

"Done one or two at the body shop, yeah." He looked away.

"He'll need one." I withdrew a photo from my pocket. "But here's something that might really get A.L. back into the game."

"What game?"

I handed Klaus a picture of a modified dirt bike. He stared at it. "What *is* this?"

"Something I found online. Apparently, he's not the only one to suffer after a fall. This is what they put together for one ex-pro so he could still ride."

Klaus mused over it a couple of seconds. "Looks like something dropped from space. What's A.L.'s take?"

"Haven't showed him. He'd first have to promise I can stay."

"And sober up, from the sound of it."

"Hopefully, that too," I said.

"Look, waving some wish list won't fix what's whacked."

"But the right guide might, Klaus," I insisted.

His steel eyes burned into mine. "Forget it."

"You can take him away into the woods. Get him away from the drink, let nature calm him and do the rest. Might not cure anything on the spot but maybe steer his thinking towards the good."

"What? No, no Colby. I don't see any of this," Klaus said.

"I'll pay you."

"Y'all better have one fat piggy bank, boy. Look, you came, we talked. Maybe I can help with the van mods, later on. I'm sorry you guys aren't seeing eye to eye, but shit like that happens."

"He's going to kick me out of Darin!"

"And I'm afraid I have to ask you to go, too. Sorry kid."

"Guess everything they say is right."

A storm seemed to invade the man where he stood. His foul reaction was enough to stir the wind. "I'm losing it. The dogs are losing it! You need to go. Right now!" Klaus turned crimson and cursed the ground as he paced. His dogs fed off his mood and began snarling. He reached for his crossbow, my cue to get the hell out of there.

"Wait a minute, boy!" The dogs lunged. "Hold it!" Klaus said.

Too late. I threw Silver in gear and bolted. I couldn't outrun the crossbow's arrow that sunk into a pine ahead of me. Full throttle, I may have pulled off some of my finest moves to date. I hit the smooth blacktop but relief was brief. I had outrun Klaus's arrows though not the feeling of total despair; brimmed with grand schemes but had no useful allies to employ them. *How naive.* What was I expecting? Klaus to lighten up and offer himself like a friendly uncle? Guess we were both nuts. I rode a little ways, then pulled Silver over to a ridge that overlooked Darin, whose lights began to twinkle in the late light. Nothing twinkled for me. My life was down to one final exam, a court date and saying adios to a handful of close friends, my animals and dreams.

A.L. sat slumped over a delivery pizza he had half-demolished. He curtly asked where I had been. I didn't say. I waved off the gooey slices when he pushed the box my direction. Mindless legs took to the stairs. "Where do you think you're going?" A.L. murmured.

"Upstairs to study." I paused at the landing. "History final's tomorrow. My last."

Finals done, most of the lingering souls yipped and scooted away for summer's freedom. Ghostlike, I toured the quiet halls for what I believed was my final time. I opened the theater doors and entered a dimly lit, now lifeless room. A thought occurred: I hadn't told Beach; hadn't said goodbye to Benson, Dejon or Coach. My name would become something briefly quipped over at lunch come September.

I popped the front doors a final time and shielded my eyes from the bright sun. Then, through it, a gift! Jillian! The sight of her in the school parking lot sent me into a dead sprint until she hopped into someone's car and was gone before my desperate yelps could reach her. Or maybe they had.

Summer had begun. While Jillian was probably excited for film camp, the only thing for me to look forward to was a day in court.

CHAPTER 38--COURT

"All rise!" The few chairs shrieked across a courtroom floor as old as the town. Voices hushed and all stood in the presence of the Honorable Judge Kant, whose robes ballooned behind him as he entered.

"Be seated," he said.

I simmered on a legal hot seat, squeezed between my ever sweaty but ready Attorney Pierce and A.L. Maybe after the judge's final verdict, A.L. might also reveal his, regarding my living arrangements next year. *What poor bastard was ever sentenced twice in one day?* Win out, playoffs, pro scouts, motocross stardom, were no longer on the tip of anybody's tongue. Worse? I couldn't steer my own fate anymore; it was all down to begging and promises. Once the judge's mallet banged and things began in earnest, I pictured high drama, accusatory exchanges of rage, and thugs being carried off kicking and screaming after their sentencing. But it wasn't TV. Case after trivial case slogged on like bureaucrat water torture.

Attorney Pierce had insisted on no phones or anything that might make me appear disinterested. With time to kill, I took in the details of the court. Above me, Greek frescoed gods pointed and judged from the ceiling, while the other accused, like me, awaited their fates. What was the point of it all? When an audible yawn escaped me and I stretched out one arm on the bench, Attorney Pierce hushed me and hissed, "Hands in lap. Sit up!"

A.L. piled on a snappy stare I pretended not to see. Since I had already entered a guilty plea, the only question left was what kind of mood the judge might be in. The sentence he handed down on the first case didn't buoy my hopes.

"Six months!" The judge's gavel punished the block.

The defendant got upset. "But, Your Honor! I have a child to support!"

"What a coincidence, so does your accuser. Next case!"

And so it went until . . .

"Colby Weston!" the clerk barked. Attorney Pierce stood and motioned with his hand. My cheeks puffed and spewed hopeful air before I slapped on a contrite mask. "Step forward."

"My client is ready, Your Honor," Attorney Pierce said. To my surprise, A.L. did not hang back but rolled to our side at the bench.

The judge sifted through the paperwork as if unfamiliar. Each paper shuffled, each cleared throat, echoed like thunder off the high ceiling where the gods' smirks grew wider. Perhaps the arduous pace would count towards time served? There was that horrible moment when the church giggles almost betrayed me. Thankfully, it passed without incident. My eyes strayed briefly to A.L. He shot back a reassuring nod, a degree of unity and support not shown since Marionville. The judge's eyes bounced between me and the paperwork. He finally spoke. "This says you're a pretty good student."

Attorney Sweatbox jumped in, "Actually, he *has* made honors, Your Honor. Colby is also a gifted athlete, has been involved with his school's drama club and is currently mulling future options."

"Attorney Pierce, do I have the right kid in front of me?"

"Yes, Your Honor. In fact, Colby has caught the eye of pro motorsport scouts."

"Explain?"

"AMA. Moto sports. He races, Your Honor. Dirt bikes."

"Ah, dirt bikes!" the judge said. "Here? At the local track in Darin?"

My eyebrows rose. "Yes sir," I volunteered.

The judge eased back, then shrugged with indifference. "How would these pro scouts react if they knew of your misdeeds?"

I opted for silence.

"Young man, will you please explain why you would jeopardize such a bright future by throwing a cinder block through a storefront window?"

I passed the ball to my attorney with a sideways glance but his stare tossed it back to me. I said, "Your Honor, before all this, I had met with Mr. Carlyle to ask him to stop deliveries to my father after his recent accident."

"Oh, it gets more interesting. Why?" the judge asked.

I glanced towards A.L. "It's stalled my dad's recovery."

"And what was Mr. Carlyle's response?" the judge asked.

"He got all like, *it's not my business*."

The judge's eyes darted to A.L. then back to me. "Technically, Mr. Carlyle was correct. And so?"

"So, one night I was driving home. I was already upset over something else and let my anger get the best of me, I guess."

"Your guess is correct. You know, yesterday, I got so mad at somebody in chambers I wanted to wing a paperweight at him. Did I?"

"You're still up there, sir."

"Right. But you acted impulsively young man. Do you understand?"

"Yes, sir."

"I also factor your age and this frustrating transition, but tell me, did your actions help resolve the issue or persuade Mr. Carlyle to change his mind? Did your dad ultimately benefit?"

"No, to both, Your Honor."

He tapped his temple. "Stay with this young man. Don't throw your dreams away on ephemeral impulses. Any repeat offenses of this nature will jeopardize any and all lofty goals you seek, if they haven't already. Do you understand?"

"Fully, sir."

"And it sounds, in your case, that might be a bit of a shame."

A.L. surprised me when his voice quietly weighed in. "If I may, Your Honor?"

The judge beckoned him to speak. "Please."

"My son and I have always enjoyed a close relationship. Following my divorce, I have leaned on Colby to fill the void. During my recovery, I've had to rely on Colby even more. I know I haven't been myself, and I've got some things to work out . . . what you've seen here isn't Colby, sir. I'm in contact with his mother and we're considering some possible changes to assure he'll find his right path again. That's all I have to say, Your Honor."

"Duly noted, Mr. Weston."

A heartening pitch from A.L., but my immediate fate sat with the guy in black robes. The judge set down the papers in hand and leaned forward. "Young man, you've reached a bit of a crossroads. This morning you've gotten a glimpse of what happens to repeat offenders. Well?"

"Sir, I'm just trying to get life back to where it was. That's what this is—*was* all about. I'll stay cool and make things right with Southside."

"Indeed you will." Judge Kant cleared his throat and delivered his verdict in rapid fire. "Colby Weston, you have pleaded guilty to vandalism of a privately-owned business. This court fines you reparation fees and forty hours of local community service. I won't be so lenient next time." He whacked his gavel. "You are free to leave this court on your own accord. Good luck to you both."

Once outside, A.L. and I shook Attorney Pierce's hand and thanked him before he ambled off. My wheels began spinning again. The judge may have put the ball back in my court when he explicitly said, *local* community service. That would buy me a little more time. I helped A.L. into the truck and parked his folded chair in the bed. Inside, I allowed myself a moment for a blank stare through the windshield.

"Glad that's over," said A.L.

"Appreciate you sticking up for me in there, A.L."

Nothing.

I brought the truck to life. Hunger pangs hit me. "Hey, A.L., let's celebrate freedom. How about lunch at Spanks? On me," I said.

"Any money you have, you'd better save. It'll be hard enough finding a job around here to pay off the debt." A.L. rubbed his face with his hands. "Lord, that was no fun. Don't do anything like that again."

"No, sir, I have dabbled with crime and have seen the light. In the coming weeks I plan to fulfill the court orders and get myself ready for the Regional at Middle Run."

"Either way, it looks like any departure from Darin will have to be postponed. Find that job and some community service thing fast so you can knock down those forty hours. Playing games, dragging your feet won't help your chances with me none, either."

"All good, but I beg to bargain. If I go ahead and qualify for the national championship at Loretta Lynn's, putting me top forty in the nation, I do my senior year here. Agreed?"

His glance stayed locked out the window. He spoke softly. "I'm not in a bargaining mood now."

"Hate to see you rush your decision," I said and slumped as glumness returned.

A.L. then unveiled the Daisy Cutter of all bombs. "You get down to what you need to do. Myself, I'm heading out for a while, starting this coming weekend."

Wait. A.L. was actually going somewhere? Sweet for both of us but I was confused. "Where, A.L.? Did you score time with Miss Triffle?"

He stared straight ahead. "No. You won't believe it."

CHAPTER 39—JILLIAN'S FAREWELL

I couldn't stand the silent treatment any longer so I rode over and after a couple of deep breaths, braved the doorbell. Mr. Carter yanked the door so hard I was almost sucked inside. His, *what, you?* expression stayed for a beat, then eased.

"What's up, Colby?" he said.

"Hey, Mr. C. You're home early."

"Uh huh. Better than too late." He shot me a look.

"Makes total sense to me. Wow, feels like midsummer, don't it?" I rubbed the back of my neck.

"What are you selling, son?"

"It ain't rail passes Mr. C." *Why had I said that?* "Just kidding. Is the princess in?"

Cautious words left him. "She's pretty busy now, Colby, packing for camp." A taunting smile found him. "Two weeks she'll be away."

Bastard. "Packing, huh? Won't take much of her time. Swung by to wish her bon voyage."

"Okay, then." He turned and wailed, "Jillian! You've got company!"

"Send them up, Dad." She sounded cheerful about *them*. Wondered how she'd feel about *me*? Mr. C. waved me past, eyeing the small bag I held.

I paused before Jillian's open door. The piles of clothes that covered the floor could have outfitted six J-Girls. I arrived unnoticed. Jillian sat at her desk, back to me, staring at her laptop and madly photo editing. Finally, I broke the silence, "Any masterpieces?"

She swiveled around quickly. "Oh my god, Colby, you scared me!"

"Stop looking at me like I made the Ten Most Wanted, J-Girl."

Her initial horror slipped to cold. "Sorry, I was expecting a couple of friends from the photo club, that's all."

"Like who?"

"Just friends." Jillian talked to the screen. "You caught me in the middle of some editing."

"That's odd."

"Right . . . Always hard knowing which to weed and which are worth keeping."

"Easy. Stay with the winners," I said.

She saved her work and spun back to me. She sat low, like she had partially melted there. Long, delicious, summer legs spilled from her yellow shorts. The chair released an easy groan when she pulled her knees to her chin.

"How'd court go?" Had she meant the words to come off snide?

I shrugged. "I preferred our runaway train trip, but one can't always choose their spots, huh?"

"True, but one can try harder not getting into them."

"Sometimes they ambush you, J-Girl, but I'll keep the advice in mind. Court worked out better than hoped. All doable. And you? Everything good? Excited for camp?"

"Yeah, but my brain's running a thousand miles an hour. Lots to do before I go."

"Me, too . . . Lots to get done, holed up in thrilling Darin."

"Don't pine, pal-o-mine. You're still a free man, right? If you ain't got thrills, you should be planning for them."

A smile came. "Oh, I'm doing plenty of planning these days. Planning and scrambling."

She tapped her lips in thought, then rolled her chair away from the desk. "Look at all these piles. Where to begin?"

"I'd just light a fire, but uh . . ."

Her eyes dropped and a slight smile sold her out. "Whutch ya got there?"

"Oh this?" I lifted the bag. "A small going away treat, nothing big." I brought it to her.

From the mini bag she removed the small, white box, then the gold ribbon around it. She held the ribbon to her hair and made a silly face. "Hey, I can use this."

A reminder of why I missed her so much.

"There's also something inside the box, J-Girl," I said.

"Really?" She opened it. "Ooooh. Fudge? You shouldn't have." She sampled one. "Oh my god, Colby." She soft-tossed the box for later.

She sprung up from her chair, but hopes for a thank you hug were dashed. Arms waving, she said, "Thanks . . . Ugh! How am I going to deal with all this?"

"Start," I said.

"I started on editing, that's the problem."

"It's crack, J-Girl."

"I know, once you begin . . . Hey, can I show you one thing, quick?"

"If you've got money, honey, I've got the time," I said, quoting an ancient, A.L. favorite.

She pulled up a picture. "What do you think of this one?"

I drew closer. "It's really out of focus . . ."

"It's supposed to be, go on," she said.

"Wait. Is that Cindy Rowe? Now I get the out of focus part."

"You're bad."

"I like your black and white stuff. Grainy. Moody."

"Cool, thanks. I was thinking I might shoot my first short film in black and white at camp."

"And out of focus?"

"That's another idea. Maybe I'll try that in a scene or two. You're a natural born director."

"I can yell, CUT a lot."

She smirked at least.

"What's your movie going to be about?"

"Thinking horror. Woods, idyllic lake, city dudes getting bumped off . . ."

"Why pack for some distant camp? Hang back here and follow me around for a day or two with your camera. I'll show you horror."

"You'll survive, C-Boy. No, this girl's down for the getaway."

As in, get away from me? "Can't wait to see what you come up with when you're back."

She sighed heavy. "Yeah, well." She closed the laptop and eyed a pile of clothes. She went over, picked up two blouses and studied them at arm's length while I studied her.

I said, "Take the red one. I've always liked that on you."

Her first genuine smile. "C-Boy, my new fashion advisor. Red it is." She flung it on the keeper pile.

"Also, don't forget your zoom lens. Probably want that to keep the zombies at a distance."

"Check! Already packed."

"Really? What's that long, black thing poking out of the pile on your desk?"

She grabbed it, then lightly tapped the lens on her forehead. "Thank yoooou. I'm no good at organizing, C-Boy."

"Doesn't show. Then again, I tend to only see the good stuff," I said.

"A charmer to the end, Weston, but that can get you in trouble sometimes. Hey, want to help?" she said.

"Name it."

"You pack while I take Blue for a ride. I hate making decisions."

I blurted, "Then don't make a bad one." I felt the silence. "Maybe you and I might peel off a ride before you go."

"Wish we could. Time's tight, C."

"You'll be missing the next race coming up at Jack's," I said.

"I know. Bummer, dude. Can't do everything, I guess. Good luck with that."

"I've been riding Silver again. Game's coming back."

"Yeah? That lame paw of yours healed?"

"Getting there," I said.

"How's A.L. doing?"

"Doing . . . You know, after Jack's I'm headed to Middle Run for regionals. Ever been?"

"I don't even know what state it's in," she said, holding up a top.

"Ours. Join me. Bring your camera. Should be cool."

"I don't know, C-Boy. Let's see what happens. Either way, good luck, or should I say, *Break a leg?* That's what all you theater people say before you get started, isn't it?"

Dagger! Every aggressive scritch, scritch, scritch of the closet hangers screamed DANA! About the time I expected to be tossed, Jillian's mood turned back to agreeable. She grabbed her laptop again, plopped it on her unmade bed and patted the space next to her. "Sit down, get comfy for a sec."

She didn't have to ask twice. The bed yawed as I settled in close. Blue light bathed her excited eyes as she pulled up the camp website. "Look." She nudged closer, close enough for our legs to barely touch. She tilted the screen towards me. "So here's where I'm headed." She scrolled through the mission statement, the activities and a page of old photos. Some showed dudes shooting movies with large, Hollywood-type cameras. Others were of campers hiking and splashing each other in the lake. Why did all the male campers appear older and sophisticated, like Grant from my play? As Jillian exuberantly pointed things out, my eyes shifted from the site to her. Then something brought me back to the screen. Jillian's profile shot was totally glam. Stunning. Jealousy soup boiled over.

"Wow, Jillian, pretty hot shot of you, kid. Not too campy. This yells J-Snacks are served."

"Never crossed my mind," she said.

"And look at these personal notes to you on the message board. *Jillian, Hope you'll be in my movie. I'll be auditioning in the Wilderness Cabin.* Uh, do not enter the Wilderness Cabin without mace, J-Girl. This soulless dude is ready to venture into *your* wilderness, is what."

"Colby!"

"Just saying."

"Yeah. This from the scented candle master of seduction himself." She rose and took a few steps away from me. "I don't know what you're so worried about." She turned, picked up her yellow bikini and whispered to it. "I'm sure everything will be closely supervised."

"Shoot me, J-Girl. A dead dog lies with no regrets."

"Aw, C-Boy," she said playfully as she opened her fingers and dropped the thread-thin bikini on the keeper pile.

I wanted to flop with her on Clothes Mountain; feel her closeness again. Like a wounded child, I got up and wrapped my arms around her sculpted middle. She didn't slap, scold, hiss or even recoil, but gently peeled me off like something clammy and wet. She walked over and withdrew a piece of the fudge, crammed it in her mouth and began rapidly chewing. "Mmmm. Good!"

I sulked. "I'm sorry about my comments, J-Girl. I was just being a little—"

"*Possessive*?" She sucked three of her chocolate glazed fingers loudly.

"Sorry, I've been missing you. Look, I want you to have a blast there . . . Of course, I can't wait for the frequent updates, progress on your film. Just no selfies from the Wilderness Cabin, please." I forced a fake laugh.

She went all business. "About that, C-Boy, texts I mean. I might fire off a few but I'll be very busy with shoots and—"

"Having fun. I get it."

"What about you? Anything happening besides the ride?"

"Basically, a summer in the salt mines for me."

Jillian came over and put a hand on my shoulder. More big sister than lover, yeah, but I couldn't be choosy. I drank in the whiff of the same sweet perfume I had once gifted her. She pulled me in. I took it as a message of hope. Her hand brushed my cheek. Wait. Maybe something wonderful was about to happen. No. "Gotta let you go now. Don't you pine for me, C-Boy." But I already did. I breathed her in, one last time. "You have something that needs finishing. Push your ride over the top. Forget everything else. Show the world your stuff, Colby Weston. It's waiting."

I pulled away, half surprised to see her eyes, like mine, glossed over with tears.

CHAPTER 40—JOB HUNT

The sight of A.L. boarding a vehicle with Klaus Ketty for some fishing trip was alien even if I had arranged it. I may have sent A.L. to his doom, based on Klaus' last cold, hard stare before shushing his hounds who were flashing their teeth at me.

I ruled El Relaxo once more, cool, but there was still much to figure out. In this weird storm of efficiency, the driveway dust hadn't settled before my nose found its way into the Help Wanted section of the paper, then online. If I could knock down a job or community service by A.L.'s return, that might tilt things back in my favor. Unfortunately, there were no MX jobs I could do from Silver. Most took actual skills I didn't possess. Coming up empty, I conceded to balling up on the couch and binge-watching. An idea hit me.

I braved a call to Pastor Paul. When I finally stopped babbling, he began to rattle off a few community service options. The mere utterance of soup kitchen piqued my interest. Ever since Aunt Demi's unannounced visit, I had taken to the escape of El Relaxo's kitchen. Flooded with culinary visions of tall, white hats and plumes of fire from shaken pans, I cut Pastor Paul off right there, thanked him, and dialed up the number.

The skeptical, lifeless voice of the church secretary didn't exactly build my confidence but at the end of the call I had earned myself an interview, a shot. Charged, I celebrated my good luck with a leg over Silver and a few laps around Jack's track. My hand still throbbed a bit but even the normally laconic Jack commented on how en fuego my ride appeared.

I descended through a twisty labyrinth of halls and stairs that seemed to be leading me into a cathedral's catacombs. When I finally reached the kitchen, a thin, exhausted-looking guy with stringy blond hair, wearing a baseball cap and a badly stained apron, was consumed with browning meat on a massive gas stove. He shook the big skillet in an almost-violent way. I stood unnoticed for some time while the second hand of an old electric clock took several laps around its face. All the while I checked out his technique and thought, I can do that.

Minutes dripped by and my patience zeroed out. Maybe this cramped, gloomy space with its greasy, chicken fat yellow walls was not my place. About the time I was ready to pull the plug, the cook killed the burner. He shuffled to the sink, scrubbed his hands and towel dried them at a silent, tedious pace. Done, he leaned back into the counter and ran his palms down his face and bloodshot eyes. "Who are you?" he said.

I stepped his way, hand thrust forward and introduced myself. He took it with a dead man's grip. He growled out a few typical questions, *Why are you here? Any experience?* I tried to sell my kitchen technique before I was informed that my responsibilities wouldn't even involve any cooking. They would consist of serving up meals and cleaning up afterwards a few days a week. No thrills, but it was a gig that would log hours and fulfill the community service obligation. One down! Surely A.L. would be impressed at my quick action when he returned. If he returned.

Now the hard part—how to earn a fast, seven hundred bucks for Southside's damage. After a couple of days of trying and coming up empty, I threw my frustrations out on Jack's track. This part wasn't about meeting the judge's or A.L.'s demands, but my own. I had unfinished business, and slowly my ride was working its way back. After one run, I sought Jack's opinion but found him in a foul mood. Thinking avoidance might be the best play, I jumped back on Silver. Jack yelled, "Wait!" He shared that Hugo, his long-time assistant, had just quit on him to be closer to his grandkids in Arkansas. For Jack, the timing couldn't be worse because we had a moto event coming up. "What am I going to do?" he said more to the sky. "There's a ton of work to be done before the weekend."

I looked at him a hard second and said, "At your service."

Turns out, Jack could create longer to-do lists than Aunt Demi, but here I was getting paid. I flung myself into everything from touch-up painting, to small repairs, to contacting vendors. Whatever he dreamed up, I did. Sometimes he'd even get into the business of things and I was surprised how much I took to that part. This might not be the summer of riding in the Baja with Jillian, but what had gone to plan? All my efforts might be enough to swing A.L. back to his senses and rethink ejecting me. Maybe even win back Jillian.

Dawn, Saturday. Funny, my first thought was not on that day's race, rather the fact that there'd been no word from the

A.L. or Klaus, the latter who was scheduled to ride in the event. Strange, for all Klaus' faults, missing events wasn't one of them. From the porch rocker, I stared out as I sipped coffee and chowed down breakfast. I relived the old days when A.L. and I would be totally focused on the event and Jillian committed to getting it all on film.

I was greeted with an arm-length list of tasks the moment I reached the track. Venders, who had set up shop the night before, needed assistance. Jack stalked around taut as barbed wire. My walkie-talkie squawked with unceasing commands. I felt rushed but important, too. At least I got to whirl around on his golf cart. He seemed to have forgotten and grumbled at my request for a short break—to compete! No surprise, Jack had moved my group to the earliest slot following the morning rider's meeting. This way, regardless of outcome, I could immediately swap my racing suit for Carhartts. All good, but still missing was Klaus and A.L. A little concern? Yeah, but they were grown men, sort of.

I felt totally ready. The gates dropped and wouldn't you know, a minor slip at the start dropped me back to the lower third of the pack. I treated this like a last hurrah, I wouldn't be denied. I hunted down one rider at a time until in the last lap I took the lead. The call from the PA was the highlight of a productive week.

"And it's... Colllllllllllby Weston at the finish, ladies and gentlemen!" But no silly monkey rolls for me this time. Jack leaned out of the window from his elevated booth and hollered, "Well done, boy! Now park your bike, peel off that suit and check with the girl at the entrance to see if she has enough change."

As I checked in with her, a leather-clad, bearded man entering the place like a fiend led a billowing dust cloud. *Late to the dance, are we, Mr. Ketty?* I shouted at him as he passed,

"Hey Klaus, how did everything . . ." VROOM! His dust settled on me ". . . go with A.L?"

The girl leaned out from her tiny booth, hands on her hips. "Hey! Doesn't he have to pay, Colby?"

"Nah, I said, "He already did."

CHAPTER 41--SWAN SONG

"Colby!" *Hi, Commander.* I entered El Relaxo more nervous than excited at A.L.'s return. Klaus hadn't offered too much in the way of retelling in our short hook-up at the track. "A.L.?" I said softly into the still air. He was prone and passed out on the porch swing. I had expected more of a wild man look but A.L. was cleaned up, a bit closer to his old self. I placed my plaque next to his glass of iced tea now pooling on the table. I left him to snooze while I rummaged for leftovers in the fridge.

After a few moments, A.L. wheeled in, groggy and sunburned. I raised the milk carton in salute after a long chug. "We have glasses," he said.

"Forgot about that, thanks."

"I see things went well at the event," A.L. said.

"Closer to the old self," I said.

"Don't get too confident. You weren't battling the top riders." *Was it always necessary to slam me back in place?* "Did Klaus make his start? Traffic tied us up on the way back."

"Yeah, he made it. Barely. Some new rider I hadn't seen dominated the field, robbed him at the end."

A.L. clicked his cheek. "There's always someone new. What else? Any progress with the rest?"

I shrugged. "You might say that." I disappeared outside.

Over the spaghetti and meatball dinner I fixed, A.L. lightened up and told me tales from his trip. I fought off soda blasting from my nose after hearing how Klaus tried to force this god-awful root concoction on my dad. Then, when A.L. refused, rolling him off the dock, wheelchair and all! Of course, this just netted more work for Klaus who had to extract his drowning mate and later his heavy wheelchair. For the first time since the accident, El Relaxo heard collective laughter. Would A.L. ever do something with Klaus again? A.L. became introspective, shrugged and said, "The man may be a bit insane and unpredictable, but why not? We've always enjoyed the same things."

This small thaw in A.L.'s attitude was hopeful. Maybe there was an opening of concession in him. It was only a chance but I seized it. I informed him of the rest of my weeks' conquests while he had been away. Based on his focus and nods of approval, maybe he'd reconsider my banishment. Yet there sat, a proud, principled man, fidgeting with my fate in his hands. It grew quiet. I cleaned up and grabbed my jacket. A.L. asked where I was headed in such a hurry. I told him I needed some air. Bubbles and B.K. followed me outside.

Next order of business. I had given Jillian some breathing room after her camp. I braved a call, hoping my recent success might net a little bump in her rankings. She hemmed and hawed over the phone, but finally agreed to meet at Harriet Pond.

Jillian arrived with a demeanor lower in the mix than hoped. I was eager to share how things had turned around for me, hoping it might pique her interest. When she didn't respond I asked her about camp. She provided few details. I thought a few Frisbee throws might lighten the mood. It worked for a little while, but the sharp flair of her Frisbee throws ultimately sagged and became as errant as us. The game ceased. She wandered over to water's edge and skipped a flat stone over the pond. "I sold Blue."

"What? You sold Blue?"

"Yeah, I was on her at a stop light when this older guy yelled over 'How much?' So I gave him the finger. Then he said, 'No, the bike.' And I thought right then, wow, this could pay for that new lens I'd been looking at. So I took his number and he swung by and cut me a check. Then Blue was gone."

"How could you just sell Blue . . . to a complete stranger?"

"C-Boy, most sales are between complete strangers."

"No. I meant, at all. Think of the times you and I have shared on Blue." I searched for the nearest flat rock then winged it. It kept going and going until Jillian said, "Uh Oh." Before I could say anything else, a terrible squawk emitted from Old Tom Swan. She said we should go and I thought why not, because things between us felt finished.

I headed for my truck and she hers then she cried name, "Hey, C-Boy."

"What?"

"You can have my helmet cam . . . fifty bucks."

I finally accepted that all our crazy, wonderful times would live in the past.

CHAPTER 42—BACK IN THE SADDLE

I sat glued to the campfire at Middle Run only lifting my head to get a read on A.L. Since court and his getaway with Klaus, A.L. had showed signs of finding a better path towards his recovery—mental and physical. He resumed many of his work responsibilities from home. His drunks declined and long runs in his chair over our rural road helped to restore his strength. Despite the small sample of time, I stayed hopeful. What still remained a mystery was my fate. I still didn't know whether I was coming or going. All I knew was J-Girl or not, I wanted to finish senior year in Darin—and finish strong here.

I escaped into my phone to study the course for the next day's run. A.L. finally spoke. "Put that damn thing away. You're missing out on the stars."

"They'll be there for a while." I tucked the phone in my coat. "But that's about the only thing I'm certain of these days."

A.L. didn't bite. "I think you'll like the track's well-groomed, thick soil. Tires grab it well. You'll see tomorrow during the practice run. You can get more aggressive, especially on the hairpin turns."

"I got it, A.L."

"Yeah? What's up with the low gear? The Jillian thing still nipping at you? "

I snapped. "Damn it, A.L. You've got something more important that needs saying. Why are you torturing me like this?"

A.L.'s stern glance softened with a sigh. "I'm not torturing you, man. I thought we were getting along fine. Don't be so sensitive."

I underhanded a large log onto the fire that unintentionally sprayed him with cinders before making their way skyward. "Whoops . . . It's just that I met every condition of yours and the court's, in record time, and I'm looking for my just reward."

"Reward before the race? What sense does that make?"

"Like how I finish might influence it? Dude, that's—"

The sound of footsteps spun our heads.

"Weston boys!" The night shielded Klaus, but his gravelly voice was unmistakable. "What's happening? What did I miss?" He plopped down.

A.L. glared. "Perfect timing, Klaus." All I could do was shake my head and smirk.

Klaus rubbed his hand together and squeezed next to me on the log. "A bit chilly, huh? Now, what'd I miss? I heard y'all three sites away. I was hoping for more of a brawl than pansy bickering."

A.L. flashed annoyance at Klaus. "Your timing is a little off as usual, my friend."

I said, "What? I thought Klaus' timing was the best since he sprung me from juvie. You see, my dad is still trying to figure out which bed he'd like me to sleep in next year."

A.L. shook his head.

Klaus glared like his Dobermans. "What? Still haven't decided, A.L.? I get the accident left you fuzzy and all, but that's just hogshit, brother."

A.L. snapped back, "Funny, don't remember you being invited to the conversation, nor being asked to referee it."

Klaus stared a beat. "I can wonder off and walk some circles under the stars." He stood and addressed the sky, "Should've let the bastard drown in the lake."

"Guys, can you save the trash talk?" I suggested.

Klaus said, "See, A.L. You're upsetting the boy before his big race."

A.L. grumbled to his boots. "Alright, I don't care; you can stay if that's what you want."

"Actually, I had no intention of leaving," Klaus said.

"I wasn't talking about *you*, Ketty," A.L. said. "I was talking about Colby, *my son*."

I had half-floated away but quickly reeled back reality. "A.L, wait . . . what are you saying?"

A.L. shrugged. "Long as you play by the rules and the cop visits taper."

Klaus spit tobacco to his side. "Phew. Thank god that's behind us." His foot began to pump. "Now we can get on with the matters of winning championships. Boy, did I mention Middle Run's got this hill riders refer to as The Bomber? Tall and bumpy, a sort of weed-out hill for the lesser riders. Now my approach would be just this . . ." Klaus's tutorial rolled over me as relief kicked in. A.L. and I locked eyes but this time for swapped quick grins.

Once the group before us roared away, we descended to the pit gates at a leisurely pace. My first moto at Middle Run had been a good one. A.L. showed he hadn't lost his gift for fine tuning; he fussed with Silver until she had a sharper edge. I was one good run away from the national championship. I felt confident. I knew I belonged. I had something to prove, not to the world or A.L. or Jillian, but to myself.

Don't keep the world waiting, Colby Weston. Jillian's words echoed as I started her helmet cam. Throttles snapped to three quarters and our line belted a shrill scream. Green light. Clutches popped and the broad line of hopefuls began to chew up the soft loam and spray it behind them. *Was this my old friend charging at my side?* I veered and cut off Tooley. *Sorry, bro, this spot's taken.* Of course he stayed right on me, waiting, waiting for me to mess up and somehow get by me. I steadily lost position and confidence sagged a little. Motivation is no further than the guy in front of you. In my case it was Tooley and his middle finger. I stayed right on him and joined the leading clump of six.

I took my final ascent up The Bomber and got good air. Silver wobbled on the landing but I got her under control. We were whittled down to five after one rider's stumble. A quick glance back. He was getting up, good. With half a lap left, I saw another opening and slipped into third. My next pass brought me within spitting distance of Tooley. We hit rut territory and it caused my rival to lose his footing. He now fell back a couple of lengths. This was Marionville all over again! I swear I picked up Klaus's boisterous yip from afar.

Tooley wouldn't concede. He angled right back like it was nothing. I figured my combined event time was good, but I went for great in the final straightaway. As a tribute to A.L., I indulged myself and the spectators with a mudslinger above the bump. Smooth landing. I had won and was moving on! Commence Colby chimp roll!

Tooley Cumberland brushed by, totally pissed off at himself. But this time he didn't repeatedly slap his own face. He turned to me and said, "You got me again, Weston." A slight smirk followed his shaking head. "We'll settle this at the championship, asshole." He stunned me when he reached and gave me a dead man's handshake, but a shake all the same!

Incredible! After years of fantasies I was actually going to Loretta Lynn's for the AMA Amateur National Championship. As Silver and I parted the crowd, back pats and well wishes came from riders and total strangers. But the most animated one came from the madman with the gold tooth. Klaus bowled through the crowd in a dead run for me. "Oh baby!" Klaus yelled. He nearly broke my wrist with his high five.

I yipped. "How about you, Klaus? You want some?" Klaus looked out, snarled to the track like his dogs, and I already felt sorry for the senior class. I took off my helmet but didn't remove Jillian's cam until I cried, "I did it, Jillian!" and kissed the lens.

A.L. and his chair were obscured by Mark Beck who embraced him. When Beck pulled away the old pride and joy returned to A.L. eyes. *Finally*. Maybe hope and conviction would follow. I drank in the moment and fixated on what I had pulled off.

Klaus's miserable first couple of laps kind of killed the good vibe. Seemed the only way he was going to pick off the number of riders in front of him was if he had packed his crossbow. Somehow he rallied and one by one passed himself back into contention. He battled back, but two laps from the finish, any chance of moving on fell victim to a hairpin turn he couldn't make. That took the sugar out of his cotton candy.

Chapter 43 — THE BIG SHOW

It finally sunk in. I was racing in the AMA National Motocross Amateur Championship. A.L. and Klaus joined Beach and me at this cradle for future pros. The week before the big event, Beach and I had made the drive over to test out Loretta Lynn's legendary track. The venue then was relatively sleepy compared to the motohead carnival of riders, fans and vendors that was unfolding.

    I was touched by the number of riders who took the time to check in with A.L. Many had heard of his accident—some had witnessed it. Had it been a couple of months before, fresh off his ordeal, A.L. would have shied away from any spotlight; now he enthusiastically engaged with people and asked about their lives. Jaws dropped when shared he had returned to riding. That was true. Klaus and I had basically succumbed to illogic and transformed Gremlin into something my dad could scoot around on our property. Klaus welded on protective aluminum bars so A.L. wouldn't be crushed in the event he went down. I even volunteered to act as stunt driver and test-ditch it a couple of times. I was jolted but unharmed. In the end Gremlin was reborn along with A.L.'s passion—he had wings again!

I rolled Silver through rowdy crowds to my gate for the first of three motos. Stomach in knots, this felt like my first stage entrance on opening night. To be real, there were probably thirty-eight others who felt the same—well maybe not old pal, Tooley Cumberland, whose cockiness was due to the ice running through his veins. Klaus, my designated mechanic, fussed with Silver and made last minute adjustments. A girl emerged in short shorts with a 2 card; reason enough to throttle up the crowd and the riders. Klaus said, "Alright boy, time to tuck those dreams to bed and chase 'em down for real!" The 1 card sparked the scream of engines down the line. The gates dropped; the party began. Then everything kind of went to shit. A mediocre start boxed out early hopes of joining the lead pack. It was tough going, trying to make up for the poor start. Once I passed the laggards, open ground provided running space. Round after round I closed but there were too many to pick off, too late. I finished seventh, disappointed and wanting to forget it as soon as I crossed the finish.

A.L. stayed quiet. Beach threw an arm around me and said, "You're with me." He dragged me along to check out vendors and people-watch. What ultimately scattered my defeatism was taking in the scene from the stands: the din of motors, some bold new stunts, the joy of being a part of all this. I wasn't long watching before the only thing I craved was back in.

I arrived to my second moto armed with an imperative: Be heard not part of the herd. Confidence settled in early after I shot out of the gate. In no time, Tooley pulled even and greeted me with a chin jut—before a kick to Silver's side that escaped the eyes of the officials. For a time, I glued my front wheel on his ass until I fell off a bit. I would finish third, an improvement over the first moto.

The better result lifted us enough to enjoy the surroundings before my final moto. Beach and I decided to hit the road and explore downtown Nashville. He even got inspired enough to try on some cowboy boots but ultimately shit-canned the look. The night before the race, I found pensive faces at our campsite. A.L. stared blankly into the fire while Klaus whittled down a piece of wood with his hunting knife, no words between them. "What up gentlemen?" I said. Ketty stared briefly before the witling continued. Turns out, they'd done something I hadn't—checked the forecast. Heavy weather threatened to pound the field that night before my final race. I shrugged off the concern. "Well boys, looks like we'll have to slap on a more aggressive tread. I brought along Silver's trusty rain boots."

Ketty finally spoke, "What about a life jacket?"

As promised, Mother Nature doused the serene fire and chased us into the Boler. Side by side, our quartet wedged ourselves into the horseshoe-shaped couch. The steady, hard rain did nothing to cool the collective body heat from the four close men. A weak lamp and a candle's warm glow eased the mood. A jar of peanuts and a deck of cards helped pass the time. Klaus, part shark, part cheater, dominated the rounds of penny poker. Eventually, the older men couldn't resist spewing advice which dripped as useless as the Boler's leaky vent hatch.

"Now remember Colby, tomorrow, keep your feet glued to the pegs much as possible in the muddy conditions," A.L. said.

I replied, "A.L., apparently you have forgotten the couple times you locked me out of El Relaxo in a steady rain until I proved my worth on our wet hills."

"Okay, but answer me this," A.L. retorted, "Did you learn how to better negotiate the muck?"

I replied, "That and a better understanding of how serial killers are made. Whose deal?"

Ketty trumped in, "Listen to your damn father. I've heard stories of single boots found after races, imbedded in the mud."

Beach perked up. "With feet still inside?"

"Could be, Beach." Klaus slapped down his cards. "Three kings!" He laughed.

A.L. rolled his eyes and began fidgeting with his beard. "Don't forget your goggle tear-offs. Mud'll be flying tomorrow."

"Got it, A.L." I dealt the next hand.

"No one has said the most important thing," Beach weighed in. "Always wave and smile at the judges as you pass by."

Ketty chuckled, "Good one Beach. Now on a more technical note, figure the higher lip of the track to be drier than the lower."

I went for sincere. "Yeah, but only when gravity's in play, ya think?"

A.L. ignored me. "You're right Klaus, and who braves the outside option? No one."

"Until now!" Beach assaulted the table with four queens.

Next morning, the sun broke through as the last of jeweled drips dropped from the pines. I arrived back to camp after scouting the track's condition. When A.L. asked about it, I explained it was something better suited for mud wrestling than moto. I headed to my bike with two old rain tires.

Klaus spat tobacco juice to the side and rummaged a while in the bed of his pickup. "Ditch those, Colby. Try these." He unearthed a pair of knobby tires that looked deserving of the Mars Rover.

A.L. and I swapped surprised looks. "Those Starcrosses?" I said.

Klaus yipped and accurately bowled one over. "These little babies love to play in the mud."

I thanked Klaus profusely but I hadn't tested them. Once on, at least Silver *looked* badass and ready to boast.

I couldn't wait for my race to begin. Was I anxious for my third and final run? A little, but not overly worked up about it. Maybe that had something to do with the tumultuous half-year from hell I had survived. This race also felt like a celebration of sorts for both A.L. and me. Sometimes you just had to take the mud as it splattered. If only I could muster a final great ride.

My thoughts emptied as I stared at that U-gate. A last look down the line revealed Tooley's goggles staring my direction. Through the battles our fates had been connected for so few words swapped. My eyes drifted back to the track's mudslinging in progress. Some riders coped with the conditions; others let the mud swallow them. The girl in shorts appeared. Klaus, scrambled to finish a last minute change. "National spotlight Colby, chase 'em down! I love you, man!" I briefly looked back at him then reached up and clicked on Jillian's old helmet cam.

The 1 card cued the line's full throat shriek and my competitive spirit flamed up. Gates dropped, the throttle was snapped forward and Silver took charge. Yeah, these tires loved this muck. I wove around several potential blockers with relative ease to claim the holeshot prize. I was exhilarated: the lack of backs, the clear views; not having to tear off goggle sheets. A check behind almost birthed sympathy for my closest competitor; when he tried to pass, he slipped and was swallowed by the mud. I kept up the pace while a small wave of hungry rivals closed within earshot. I wanted that checkered flag. I lowered my head and punched the throttle to full. My Tallahassee rival couldn't catch me this time. A win!

An airborne leap with pumped fist followed. Freeze the look of A.L.'s unabashed pride. We were joined by Klaus and Beach as they hooted and gyrated around us in yipped circles.

We eventually migrated to the results board to see what this did to my final standing.   Third. Third in the nation. Considering the hurdles, that begged for a little celebration. Hey, there was always next year.

Chapter 44—ON WITH BUSINESS

Sprawled on the living room couch, the sound of a vehicle steered my attention from the motocross article I was reading. A.L.'s unassisted entry through the kitchen was old hat by now. He'd turned into a bit of a health nut, too. Nightly pyramid building with consumed six packs had been swapped for a new hobby. He had invested in a sleek, hand-propelled bike to stay fit. Evening and weekend rides down long country roads had become his newest thing. Of course, when he needed a taste of the old thrills, there was always Gremlin II to chase Bubbles around our hills. Now, from the kitchen, A.L ripped open the day's mail as ritual called. When he entered the living room a single, unopened letter on his lap hardly escaped my notice.

I tossed *Motocross Action* to the floor. "How's the new van working, old boy?"

"Loving it. Loaded on Gremlin today and did some laps at Jack's."

"Oh yeah? How'd that feel?"

"Really good. In fact, Jack and I talked about getting me back into some races."

"*Races?* Like compete?"

"Why not? The game's back and I think I could whoop up on some of my old rivals."

I involuntarily snapped up to argue, but as fast, fell back. "What the hell, chase it A.L. One of us has to do something. Fucking rip off."

A.L. stared at my cast.

It happened on our property, a hill I had scaled a thousand times. This time, only days away from trying to qualify for a second chance at a national championship, I had put my foot down a little too aggressively. Hello microfracture.

A.L.'s response came bland. "Everything happens for a reason, so I've been told . . . What else?"

BK hopped up and I began to stroke him. "You tell me. I'm a little curious about that piece of mail that's sitting in your lap."

A.L. played coy. "What? I almost forgot." He pinched the envelope with his fingers and thrust it closer for me to see.

I leaned in with narrow eyes. "That from the University of Tennessee?"

He feigned a need to recheck. "Seems so . . . Admissions Department? Hmm."

I sprang to sitting position. "Well c'mon, toss it here, man."

A.L. frisbeed the piece into my chest and I hurriedly opened it.

"Well? In or out?" A.L. said.

Stoked with a long-term escape plan from Darin, the high school halls felt waxed for a clean getaway. I hadn't talked much with Jillian, but when I spied her in the hallway I greeted her with a shoulder a tap.

She half-startled like I'd broken her train of thought. "Oh hey, gimpy."

"Didn't mean to sneak up on you, but I just got a little news I needed to share."

"And you picked me? Awe. What's up? Riding the Regional next week with a cast?"

"Don't even joke about it," I said.

"At least you got to show 'em your stuff last year. Did I ever mention I tried to organize a parade after that, but . . ."

"Do you miss Blue at all?"

"The good times are filed away, C-Boy, but I'm getting some great shots from my new wide angle. Snagged first place at the county fair."

"Yeah, I saw it. It was just a pile of leaves, but it drew me in."

Jillian said, "Thanks. I included it in the portfolio I sent to Savannah. And oh by the way, I got accepted!"

"Awesome, but I never had any doubt, did you?"

She shrugged. "So what's your news?"

"Well, the University of Tennessee sent me some love?"

Her mouth gapped and her eyes grew large. "What? Congrats. Are you going?"

"Yeah, I've been thinking maybe I'd give sports management a try."

"That works. You can schmooze . . . Well I guess we're still slaves to tardy bells, but not for too much longer. I should go. Congrats, C-Boy!"

My eyes tethered to her as she ambled off. After a few steps she turned. "Hey C-Boy!"

I fought to hold a neutral face. "What?"

Jillian paused. "Eh, nothing."

EPILOGUE

Circumstances recently returned me to Darin after a long time away. Jack had since passed and the track had swapped hands a few times. I'd even been contacted to see if I'd have any interest in running it. My job as an agent at a Los Angeles sports agency had scuttled that idea. Eventually, some condo developer put a stake in the heart of the place and proved again that nothing goes unchanged. So I had driven the distance back to pay a last homage with a four hundred CC dirt bike in tow. As I reentered this once sacred ground I tried to ignore the ominous power shovels and bulldozers, idle for now but poised to flatten the place soon. I took to the track and rode with abandon past Jack's old viewing stands; down the rutted stretches until Devil's Back appeared like a familiar, challenging friend. A high war shriek of an approaching bike echoed from times when Jillian might show to hunt me down. I resisted the look back at first. I knew the sound of that engine. It wasn't Jillian, but A.L. tearing after me on Gremlin II. Side by side we opened up our throttles; vaulted up and over that hill like we'd done a thousand times. We would become suspended above the mundane, if only for a second, to take in long views that beckoned the greater possibilities of life.

ACKNOWLEDGEMENTS

Besides the gallon of tears and toil, writing a novel takes teamwork. I'm deeply indebted to the following contributors for their inspiration, technical insight and expertise: Three-time AMA national champion, Doug Henry and the American Motocross Association; Editors, Susan Schrader, Renee Hammer and Patti Martin; My readers, Jordon's Twelve, William Terrance; Kit Karcher and Georgeann Sabia.

ABOUT THE AUTHOR

Upshot is Eric Hammer's debut novel. He lives in Northwest Connecticut where he's a steadfast advocate for the arts. Eric's photographs have hung in galleries, and he enjoys long walks in the Berkshires.

Visit www.eric-hammer.com

Made in the USA
Middletown, DE
09 June 2021